Wrong Direction

This book is for my friends and family. It would never have come about without the example, support, practical help and occasional incredulity of my lovely wife Heather. I thank her for her constructive editorial eye – and for bothering with it at all.

I acknowledge the debt I owe to the antique dealers who wittingly – or more often unwittingly – taught me everything I know about the strange ways of the trade. I acknowledge the care and professionalism of prison staff who protect the rest of us from some of the most dangerous people in our society. I am grateful for the wisdom and friendship of fellow members of the IMB.

Wrong Direction

Ivan Harrison

Prologue

Baron Henning Ferdinand Busson von Sonnenberg am der Ruhr was annoyed. His wife was leaving him after discovering him, not quite *in flagrante*, with his mistress. In itself that was an inconvenience but not the source of his irritation. His newest painting, by a hitherto neglected Old Master, had been obtained only after protracted negotiations with the previous owner. He had been reluctant to sell; he had claimed the work had been in the possession of his family since it was bought from the artist himself. The baron, however, would not take no for an answer; the price offered increased, the owner's resistance flagged. At last a deal had been struck. The baron was satisfied. He had seen very early that the artist was an up-and-coming name among cognoscenti like himself. He believed that despite the doubts of his acquaintances this was a sound investment.

Lady Louisa had always enjoyed the run of his immense wealth. She had always enjoyed its privileges; she was the titled daughter of a titled Englishman, the confidante of princesses. She flitted around fashionable European resorts; Vienna, Monte Carlo, Paris, London, Rome – spending as much of his fortune as she liked on clothing, jewellery and cards. That was not the reason for his pique either. The money did not matter. His factories, railways and coal-mines were still churning out money as the world was heading again towards War. What mattered was that she wanted his newest acquisition as part of her already generous divorce settlement of the house on the lake that she liked and the very substantial allowance he had conferred on her.

The baron pondered. She wanted to spite him. It was a little act of vengeance for the humiliation she no doubt felt over his little affair. He would see about that. He sniffed at his cognac; he nibbled the end of his corona. He rang the bell.

'I want to write a letter.'

The attendant brought him his writing box and set it up on the little table at the baron's side. The baron wrote a few lines, sealed the envelope and waved the attendant away.

Four months later, in March 1938 the painting was packed and despatched to England. The Nazis marched into Austria that same week.

One

The young police officer had a tight grip on the young man she had been following down Sheep Street as he dodged through the shoppers and tourists.

'You're nicked!'

'What for?'

'Those theatre tickets you were flogging just now. Where did you get them?'

'You can't arrest me for that.'

'I saw money changing hands. What are you doing with tickets for 'Twelfth Night'?'

I was given them. I passed them on. So what?'

Tim Stack lived on his wits. He was a clever lad and observant. He made money working the tourists in his home town of Stratford-upon-Avon. He helped visitors find accommodation, accepting tips from them and little commissions from bed and breakfast landladies. He recommended restaurants in return for the gratitude of the chef-proprietors, cash or sometimes a good meal in the kitchen. When money was tight, which was often, he would work in the kitchens for cash and a good supper. It was enough to get by on and pay for a tiny bedsit on the outskirts of town.

His best thing was selling unwanted tickets to performances at the Royal Shakespeare Theatre. He could sometimes get his hands on unwanted tickets from the many tour coaches that brought foreign visitors in. He would meet coaches from London. He would let it be known that he would buy unwanted tickets. Several drivers knew him and would discreetly mention him to passengers. Tour operators bought in bulk and handed tickets out as part of the deal. A few of the tourists did not know the value of the tickets but many did not care. Sometimes they simply gave them away. He would sell the tickets on; there were always people trying to buy tickets for the famous venue, especially when some well-known actor was playing. He had to shift them quickly as they were always for a specific performance, often for the following day or – trickier – the evening of their arrival. He was surprised at first that anybody would part with them, but enough did, tired out by the unremitting parade of cultural 'must sees' or sometimes just not much caring to go to a play that night.

He would loiter outside Shakespeare's Birthplace, where there were always knots of people standing about. A polite offer to take a group photo was enough of an introduction for him to offer his 'spares' for the official price or occasionally quite a bit more, no questions asked.

He quickly found out that it was risky for a street boy like himself to carry money. There is a certain type in every town who are on the lookout for easy money, though Stack never considered himself in that category. He was once mugged by a pair of druggies desperate enough for him to take their threats of violence seriously. The druggies made their way to their dealer immediately. Tim followed. He saw his money and a little package change hands. The addicts simply hid behind the bushes and took out their gear. Tim did not have to wait long before the two were senselessly unresisting. He went through their pockets, but the money was gone.

'I heard about those kids who robbed you.' It was a rough sleeper in a doorway. He was taking down the little tent he slept in.

'How do you know about that?'

'Word gets round. I hear things.'

'I am keeping an eye out now.'

'Let me hide it for you. I'm pretty much invisible. Nobody pays me any attention.'

'So that you can nip off to your dealer as soon as I've gone? I don't think so.'

11

'I sleep in doorways. I accept the kindness of strangers. I am not a thief. All I ask is a can and a sandwich. Think of me as a safety deposit box.'

In Tim's experience rough sleepers' conversation was limited the usual 'spare change' routine. Everybody knew that all junkies were liars.

'I'll think about it,' Tim said. He was determined that he would not be mugged by druggies again.

He bought a cloth bag with a drawstring opening and put folded newspaper inside. He tied the neck of the bag and placed a tiny fragment of paper within the knot. If the knot was pulled the paper would be dislodged and Tim would know Jez had opened it. To Tim's surprise the trial worked. Jez had not interfered with the bag.

'I don't want your money,' he had said, handing over the bag. 'Maybe one day I will. I'll let you know.'

It was an arrangement. Tim brought sandwiches. Jez hid his money.

PC Honour Webster kept her grip on Tim's arm.

'What money? This?' He pulled out two creased ten-pound notes from his trouser pocket. She knew this was not enough for the transaction she thought she had witnessed. She must have missed something as she followed him through the crowds. She was new on the job, not that much older than Stack. She thought about the reception she would get at the station if she brought this lad in and found nothing. As a rookie constable, still a girl in the eyes of the station sergeant, and as a graduate on the accelerated promotion programme, she was acutely aware of the potential for mirth in the scenario.

'Have you got a street trader's licence?'

'I'm a registered pedlar. I can produce my licence within fourteen days at a local police station.'

It was true, he had one – in his jacket pocket as it happened – but it was not in his name and it had expired. With any luck this would put off this young officer in her nice new uniform. He gambled that she would not know that he was legally required to produce it on demand. The money was already safely tucked away in Jez's sleeping bag, or somewhere worse.

Keen as she was to get a collar she was concerned about making a fool of herself in front of her new colleagues. A caution would have to do. Ticket touts were notoriously difficult to deal with. The law was unclear about re-sale.

'What's your name?'

'Tim Stack.'

'Listen, Tim Stack, I know you now. Watch how you go.'

He slipped through a phalanx of uniformed grammar school kids and vanished into the throng.

Twenty minutes later Tim stood over the bundle of rags and cardboard with an M&S sandwich and a can of cider.

'Tea is served. When you are ready to get clean there is always money to be made.'

Stack looked down on the young man. He supposed he was another derelict from the broken care system, like so many. He could trust this boy with his money and that itself was a puzzle. At first he had expected that Jez, as he was known on the street, would try to keep some back or clear off to the park where the junkies hung around.

'I'm clean now,' Jez grinned. 'Well, I am dirty, but you know, I am finished with smack and all that stuff. It's just the odd spliff these days. In fact I'll probably swap the cider for something healthier later on.'

'Yeah, right. I'll be seeing you.'

Three months later Stack was surprised to see that his drop box in Sheep Street was gone. The grimy belongings were gone too. The pavement gleamed where it had been stained and grubby. The waitress at '*Le Bistro*' was at the door, looking over.

Are you looking for Jez? He's gone. Last week. He just suddenly stood up, gave his sleeping bag a kick, and that was it. Somebody took his tent thing. Nobody wanted the sleeping bag."

'If you see him, say Tim has work for him.'

Tim and Jez – or Jerome as he now insisted on – became a team. For Tim it was straightforwardly for the money. He lived day to day. He could keep the wolf from the door and that was enough. For Jerome it was more complicated. He was from a good family. 'There's money in the background,' as he liked to say on those occasions when Tim tried to draw him out. Jerome hated his father. Jerome would not conform to his father's expectation or

13

follow in his footsteps in the family business. He had dropped out of university. The journey through drugs and bad company had led to the Stratford pavement. He had eked out an existence from begging from passers-by – or as he put it, accepting the kindness of strangers. He stayed in a hostel from time to time but soon chafed at the restrictions and returned to the street.

Then he changed.

'I got bored,' was his only explanation when Stack asked the inevitable question. He had turned up in front of Shakespeare's Birthplace just as Stack had sold two tickets for the evening performance of 'King Lear' to a Chinese couple.

'Tim, I've come for that job.'

Together they bought and sold theatre tickets. It was steady work in its way. Jerome had a disarming manner with tourists and became expert at wrangling tips out of them. The Sheep Street restaurateurs and hotels offering more up-market experiences to tourists were often grateful for the customers he sent their way. Between them they made enough to feed and clothe themselves without too much effort. After a year they were doing well enough to move into a dowdy apartment above a travel agency in town. It had a discreet entrance in the corner of a service area behind Sheep Street which allowed them to come and go unnoticed. They pooled the theatre tickets as they obtained them and worked together to sell them. Their partnership developed into a firm friendship, two bright lads on the edge of the law.

PC Webster kept her word. A sort of bantering relationship grew between the two and PC Webster. Despite her annoyance at never actually catching them doing anything illegal she found them likeable, two roguishly charming young men. She was not stupid and she quickly understood Tim's part in Jerome's rehabilitation. She thought Jerome was rather sweet, in fact. Tim's banter could make her laugh out loud. 'Even so,' she thought, 'they had better keep their noses clean on my beat.'

Often she turned up just as the tour buses pulled into the coach station. Tourists were less keen to sell their tickets under her watchful eye.

'I'm thinking of going to the big city, Jerome. PC Honour Bright is killing us. All she has to do is turn up. She just needs to be there and the punters—'

14

'—stop punting. Where should we go? Honour Bright?'

'PC Honour Webster. She turns up like a shiny penny just at the right moment.'

'Oh, very good, Tim. Call her that to her face. I want to see that.'

'Oh, I have. I think she was pleased. That other cop – the one that looks younger than you – the one that is sometimes on the beat with her? He actually sniggered. It will be all round the nick by now.'

'Oh, very good, Tim.'

'I thought London. Do you fancy it?'

'It's complicated. When I came off the street there was a reason. My sister came looking for me. She told me some family stuff. We keep in touch now. If I go to London we'll still keep in touch, I suppose.'

'You could stay here and carry on with the tickets and the restaurants. There would be enough in the tickets for one and you could keep the flat on. That waitress at *'Le Bistro'* fancies you, I think.'

'I missed Kate when I was away with the fairies, but I am a bit fed up here. The tickets racket is over really. It is getting harder. I could manage, I suppose, but it doesn't really appeal. The waitress doesn't fancy me, she mothers me. She has a thing going with the chef. What were you thinking about in That London, then?'

'Adventure. Streets paved with gold, that sort of thing. Bigger fish in a bigger pond.'

'Don't mix your metaphors, Tim.'

'Oh, college boy!'

'We cannot just go to London, just like that. We need a plan.'

'I'm thinking about it.'

Two

Jerome's big sister Kate was consulted, the flat sorted out. Kate agreed to keep it tenanted and the rent paid, just in case London did not work out.

'We can start by selling tickets outside Wembley and such. It shouldn't be that hard. There will be lots of people hanging about hoping for spares. If we can get hold of some we should be OK,' said Tim.

'We can give it a try.'

London was full of venues and people wanting to go to theatres, shows and sporting events. Famous bands played to huge audiences. There were always fans trying to see their idols and many of them were prepared to pay well over the proper price for the chance. It seemed like a perfect opportunity for Tim and Jerome.

They watched outside venues hoping to see how it worked in the big city. Immediately they saw that there was competition. They had had a monopoly in Stratford but here it was big business. Many of the touts operated as a group. They did not care for outsiders treading on their patch. There were plenty of punters who paid twice the ticket price or even more. The trick, they quickly realised, was having the tickets in the first place. There were lots of buyers, but the few who had spare or unwanted tickets nearly always traded them with the established touts, especially around the Wembley Stadium and Arena. They would walk directly up to touts who seemed to expect them, totally ignoring Tim and Jerome. Their Stratford methods, simple buying and selling on, did not work here. They could not buy tickets because the sellers were unwilling to trade with them. They should admit defeat and cut their losses. They could easily return to their old stamping ground.

They were outside Wembley Arena before a concert. Despite the crowds milling about they had done no business. Not a single spare ticket had come their way. They were about to give up for the evening when they noticed a man squatting on the steps leading onto the long avenue. He looked tired and ill, resting his back against a bollard.

Jerome was first to react.

'Are you all right, there? Tim, get a cup of tea from somewhere. We passed a kiosk a minute ago. That way.' Tim hurried off.

'I am just tired. I get tired.'

'My friend is getting you a cup of tea.'

'Lovely! Just need a bit of a rest. Too old for this lark!'

'What? Are you going to the concert?'

'Nah, I do the tickets. I've had to stop. I haven't felt right all day.'

'We've been trying, but we aren't doing very well. We just can't get them.'

'I've still got a handful for tonight – good'uns. I would pass them on to the regular touts that are always around, but they have just buggered off and left me. I'd rather keep them in my pocket!'

'It's a bit late. Most of the fans have gone in. You won't sell any more tonight.'

'No? I suppose not. What time is it? Has it started? What's wrong with me tonight?' He seemed to be talking to himself, not Jerome.

Tim returned with a steaming paper cup. The man took a gulp, then another. He brightened.

'Thank you. Where did you get that? Tommy's stall, I bet. Tommy is the only one still using paper cups. It's still good tea. He still gets proper tea, not the rubbish you get nowadays. Sweepings-up, I reckon.'

Tim and Jerome helped the man to a seat nearby. He still seemed frail and weak, but already his colour was returning. By the time he had finished the tea he looked a lot better.

'Will you be all right? I am a bit worried about you. We shouldn't leave you until you are OK.'

'It has happened before. I should see a doctor, I dare say.'

'Where do you live? Is it far?'

'Don't you worry. I'll take a taxi.' He waved a wad of bank notes, tens and twenties with the odd few Euros mixed in. They could see that there was a lot of money in his hand. He got to his feet.

'I've been selling tickets here since – oh, since – since—' the man swayed. Jerome caught him by the arm and held him till he was steadier.

'Take it easy!' said Jerome. 'We'll call that taxi.'

Tim and Jerome were discouraged. Their encounter with the old man had given them a glimpse of the future and they did not care for it.

'We don't want to end up like that,' muttered Tim.

'Let's give it one last go.'

'We can sell all the tickets we get. We hardly get any, that's the problem. We need contacts.'

'We don't know anybody. We had it more or less taped in Stratford, and when it was slow we could always hustle a few tips from restaurants for bringing customers in.'

'Where do these guys get their tickets? You see the odd punter selling but the touts have tickets when they arrive. You see them waving them in the punters' faces. That bloke must have sold a load tonight. You saw that wedge of money.'

'One last go, and then we'll think again.'

Outside Wembley Arena the two watched as the happy fans streamed past. It appeared they all had their tickets and they all wanted to go to the concert. There were none of the signs, loiterers on the lookout for anybody who might buy their tickets. Even the usual groups of touts were doing hardly any trade.

'This is no good, Tim. I'm cold. I'm fed up. This is not why we came here to London. Where's the adventure? Where are those bigger fish?'

'I hate giving up, but you're right.'

As they turned to leave they saw the old man again. He still looked ill, but he was steadier on his feet.

'Thank you for what you did last night. I was feeling really groggy. I don't like the cold these days. It seems to sink into my bones! It's Alfie. Everybody knows me here.'

Tim and Jerome introduced themselves.

'Are you feeling better, Alfie? You looked bloody awful last night.'

18

'A bit, yes. I think I should see a doctor, probably. Maybe I should think of giving all this up. You are new to the game aren't you? I've seen you. You've done no business at all tonight. You can't get the goods, is that it? It's all about contacts. You haven't any by the looks of it.'

'You're right. Maybe we are in the wrong game. We were just talking about packing it in.'

'Let me make you a little proposition. Next Friday I'll have a big bunch of tickets for the concert here. More than I can manage, probably. It happens, sometimes. I could pass some on to that bunch over there. That is what I would normally do, but you know what? They've annoyed me. They're – shall I say – *unfriendly*. They're too greedy these days. One time we looked out for each other, but that lot – cut your throat for a quid, they would. I'll let you have a few tickets for tomorrow's show at the Arena, see how you get on.'

'Why would you do that? It was just tea in a paper cup.'

'It was still a kindness, and like I said, there isn't much of that round these parts any more. What you did last night was more like the old days, when we stuck together. Anyway, I'm not giving them away! You'll have to buy them. I'll give you a good discount and you keep what you make.'

Tim was suspicious.

'What do you think, Jerome?'

'Alfie, this is a bit unusual, isn't it? Why are you doing this? What's the catch?'

'There isn't one. Let's say I feel grateful. Or, you know, just good business. Shall we say two hundred quid up front, and then if you do all right we'll take it from there? Two hundred quid's worth of tickets should earn you four or five if you are any good. I'll not be far away. See me for another two hundred quid's worth when they are gone – if I still have them.'

Tim and Jerome exchanged whispers.

'What's to lose?'

'Apart from the £200, you mean? The question is – what's to gain?'

'Let's do it!'

The following Friday Tim and Jerome met Alfie. He sold them tickets and pretty soon the two had sold them on. It was easy. Within half an hour they were back for more.

'Nice work!' said Alfie. 'Another round?'

'Oh, yes!'

By the time the fans were all inside and loud noises were coming from the venue from the support band Tim and Jerome were happily in the money.

'Thanks for this, Alfie,' said Tim. 'We have done really well. We have been living on our fat since we came to London.'

'You were enjoying it, weren't you? There's nothing like honest toil!'

'Not very honest,' replied Tim.

'Not really toil,' said Jerome.

'What laws have you broken? None. And it is useful work, you know,' Alfie replied. 'Think of all those fans who are in there, head-banging away, having the time of their lives. Where would they be without the likes of us, eh? I'll tell you. They'd be out here, looking miserable, that's where!'

'Could we do this again, Alfie? If you have spares, that is.'

'When, you mean. I get plenty of tickets most of the time but it is unpredictable. Just now and again I get a big bundle. I have contacts, people who get free tickets – roadies, agents, you'd be surprised. It isn't like a regular supply, though. Sometimes I get no concert tickets for a bit and then it's off to the football. Chelsea always sells out. You get away fans trying all sorts of tricks but they are segregated, so they don't really want tickets for the home stands.'

'Who sends you Chelsea tickets?'

'Players – not so much the big stars, of course. Sometimes their agents off-load spares on to me. They are usually good tickets, grandstand seats. Ground staff sometimes, but not so much. They are generally cheapies. They all sell, though. It's connections, see. And I've got 'em.'

'Do people offer their tickets on the street? We haven't seen much of that. That is what we thought we could do. We used to sell theatre tickets that way.'

'You'll never get far that way here. Tell you what. You are a couple of likely lads, tryers. I might have some tickets for the big game next week – Chelsea versus Manchester United. I know a couple of United players from years ago. I still get the odd batch from them so I should have a few extras. Be outside the Shed at 12 o'clock. I'll let you have a batch.'

'The Shed?'

'Stamford Bridge. Chelsea Football Club.'

Again, Alfie supplied them and the two sold them on. It became an arrangement. Alfie was reliable. More often than not he had spare tickets and they were doing pretty well. There seemed no reason why they should not continue indefinitely.

One evening outside the Wembley Stadium Alfie turned up later than usual. He looked upset and worried.

'You'd better scarper, lads. There is a bloke looking for you. He has been threatening blokes on the tickets for a cut. It's a plain old protection racket. For a cut in your night's take he will not break your legs. He tried it a couple of years ago. He went down for ABH and things settled down. He's out again and up to his old game.'

'What does he look like, Alfie?'

'Dougie. You'll know Dougie if you see him. Built like a brick shithouse and just about as clever. But don't mess with him. Clear off now. I should.'

'What about you?'

'He leaves me alone. I know his Mum. I've known him since he was a littl'un. He used to call me Uncle Alfie. Go away. Now.' With that Alfie melted into the crowd of concert goers.

Tim and Jerome, shrugged. They had no tickets to flog, and no prospect of having any. They turned to move off.

Suddenly a huge man stood in front of them.

'Oy! Pay your dues. You've been on my patch for weeks. Now you owe me.'

'What?'

'This is how it works, Sonny. This is my patch and everybody who flogs tickets, souvenirs and whatnot pays me. So let's say a hundred. Each week. Then you can work here and nobody will hurt you.'

'What are you on about?'

'Touting, that's what. Don't mess me about.' He glared at the two. He seemed to expand as they watched.

'We haven't sold any tickets. We haven't got any, even.'

'You owe me a hundred and you aren't going anywhere till I've got it, see.' He raised his huge fist.

The two looked at one another. Then they ran.

For a month they kept their heads down. At last they decided to risk returning to Wembley Stadium for the big concert due to take place that night and risk an encounter with the big fellow, Dougie. Alfie was in his usual position. They watched from a distance as he doled out tickets to knots of people and pocketed cash. He was doing well, as always. The crowds had entered the stadium, leaving just disconsolate fans with neither tickets or money to buy them. Tim and Jerome approached Alfie.

'Alfie. How are you doing?'

'I heard about Dougie. You ran off! Very funny, that.'

He didn't really chase us,' said Tim. 'I stopped to get my breath back and I could see him, scratching that head of his. He is not very quick, is he? I think he just expected us to cough up. We took him by surprise.'

'He was never the sharpest knife in the box. But he won't have forgotten you. He will believe he has lost face and will want to show everybody they can't get away with not coughing up. Beneath the swagger and bluster I still see the frightened little boy he was. His old man used him badly, I heard. He has changed since he came out of prison – Maidstone, it was. He is angrier, more aggressive – and the little boy in him makes him lash out. I've spoken to his mum. She is worried sick. She says he met that Reggie Kray while he was inside. Dougie's mum knew a bit about the Kray twins because her dad, Dougie's grandfather, went to school with them. He knew them after the War. He used to tell stories about them. Dougie was interested. She thinks Dougie wants to be like them, to be another Kray.'

'Reggie Kray? That's a throwback. I had forgotten all that gangland stuff. I thought those gangster days were over long ago,' said Jerome.

'They are, really. The protection racket isn't what it was. It's all drugs these days. Dougie just doesn't know that. Dougie has delusions, I reckon. The Krays were villains, really nasty – psychopaths. Dougie is just an idiot. Goodness knows what Reggie has taught him, if he even bothered to speak to him. I dare say Dougie mentioned his grandfather.'

From that moment they were always on the lookout for Dougie. It was only a matter of time, they thought. Their business suffered.

'What do we do, Tim? This isn't really working. It's not what we were expecting when we left Stratford. The thought of Dougie's looming presence never goes away. Where is the fun in that?'

'It would almost be worth paying him.'

'We aren't going to?'

'No.'

They had found two tiny rooms over a gay pub in Greenwich. It was a huge terracotta-faced Victorian pub with several rooms on two floors, Minton tiles and stained mahogany everywhere. The landlord, who went by the name of Gloria, was a semi-retired drag artist who liked to mother them, not minding at all they were not gay themselves and happy for them to make the little snug at the rear their headquarters during quiet afternoons. Gloria sometimes invited them to the shows in the big room upstairs when he did his popular 'Uniforms' song and dance act. So far they had not taken up his invitation.

It was perfect for them, a safe haven. The attic flat was comfortable. They had access with a key at the back door in the side-alley and via the stairs through a door marked Private behind the saloon bar.

They were sitting in the snug.

'We are not thieves,' Tim said. 'Look, in Stratford we bought theatre tickets from people who didn't want them and sold them to people who did. That's recycling! It is not much different here, is it?'

'When I was on my cardboard box in a doorway in Sheep Street I never actually begged, you know, but there were people who slipped me a tenner now and again as well as those who dropped their loose change into my tin. And I always said thank you.'

'You were brought up to be polite, I know. I wouldn't mind taking that bully down a peg or two. We were doing well until he turned up. It rankles.'

'We have managed to avoid him.'

'We have. But we make less now. It would be almost worth paying the protection money.'

'Something tells me that is not what you're leading up to.'

'You are right. We need a plan to get rid of him, or put a stop to him, or something. I reckon he is still on parole. He could go back inside if the police got wind of his protection racket.'

'You mean we should inform on him? I'm not sure we want to get too close to the cops. I don't think they will pay much attention to us anyway.'

'No, I suppose they wouldn't. And they might start asking awkward questions. Let me think it over.'

Days later, Tim announced that he had an idea. 'We just need to offer him something. Something he wants.'

'Money? No!'

'He is just the sort we need. Somebody with cash who can't complain to the police because they are on the wrong side of the law – and Dougie wouldn't go to the police anyway. It hardly fits the image.'

'No, he's more likely to come after us with knives and knuckledusters,' said Jerome.

'He will only come after us if he knows he has been conned.'

'That would be a good trick. People like that may not be educated. They might not be exactly clever. But they aren't completely stupid.'

'I reckon Dougie is. I feel like putting it to the test.'

'What have you got in mind?'

'Dunno. I'm still thinking.'

Tim and Jerome stood outside the famous grandstand, the Shed. It was a London Derby game and huge crowds were thronging outside the ground. They looked out for Alfie with his promised spare tickets. He was not in his usual spot.

'I hope he's OK, Tim. He never looks well, does he?'

'We'll stay here for a bit. He's reliable. He'll turn up.'

They waited for an hour but there was no sign of Alfie. Most of the crowds of fans had gone in with just a few wandering about disconsolately, hopeful of finding spare tickets. These were often the ones who would pay the most, and several asked Tim and Jerome.

A man approached them, a tout they recognised but had never spoken to.

'Are you Alfie's friends? Are you looking for him? He won't be here for a while.'

'Is he ill?'

'He's in hospital. That thug who has been trying to play the protection racket with us put him there.'

'Dougie?'

'That's his name. He has been taking money off the souvenir and programme sellers and the traders that work the crowds and queues round Wembley. He has come down here to Stanford Bridge a few times. He tried it with some of us but we called his bluff. There were six of us together and we told him to get lost. Alfie was on his own. So that Dougie gave him a hiding. He dragged him up the ally there.'

'When was this?'

'Just this morning. I reckon Dougie was waiting for him.'

'Where is he now? Alfie, I mean.'

'Somebody called an ambulance. He'll have gone to A and E.'

'Do you know where they took him?'

'I expect it was the Chelsea and Westminster, just down the Fulham Road.'

The hospital was not far away. Eventually they found the department where Alfie had been admitted. They glimpsed him through the glass panel with wires attached to a machine with flashing lights.

'Are you a relative?' A nurse came out of the room, looking sternly at the two young men. 'You can't talk to him anyway. He is unconscious. Only family allowed to see him.'

'We are work colleagues,' said Jerome. 'We've just heard. How bad is he?'

'He is poorly. He has been beaten very badly. His X-rays show some fractures. He is going down to orthopaedics shortly.'

'When can we see him?'

'When he is well enough. And if he wants to see you.' They followed her down the corridor.

'The exit is that way. Follow the green line to the stairs and the door is straight on from there.' The nurse bustled off.

They exchanged looks and left.

They returned next day. They saw him briefly, conscious but confused and still groggy. His head was bandaged. He had two shocking black eyes. One arm was strapped up. The machinery was gone. A nurse barred their way; he was not yet well enough for visits.

25

They returned the next day and the next. On the fourth day Alfie was sitting up. The head bandaging was reduced, showing a shaved patch and some raw-looking stitches.

'We brought you some grapes, Alfie.'

'Very nice.'

'What happened?'

'Dougie, that's what. I never expected him to do this to me. I've known him since he was a little boy.'

'We know it was Dougie because some of the ticket lads saw him hanging around. They didn't see what happened, but it isn't hard to guess. Have you told the police?'

'Nah, what would be the point? They aren't interested in a squabble between ticket touts.'

'Why did he pick on you? You said he wouldn't touch you.'

'Prison has made him worse, not better. I spoke to his mother. I suppose he wanted to prove a point. He never asked for money. I expect he pinched my takings. There was nothing in my pockets when I looked this morning. I asked the staff nurse if they knew about it. They said not. It was about a grand.'

'We thought it might be because of us.'

'Who knows what was going on in his mind? Maybe it was just a robbery, I don't know. I don't remember him saying anything. He was just punching me. I remember going down and being kicked. It is a bit hazy after that. He must have kicked me in the head. Now I think he was simply angry at everything and everybody and he took it out on me.'

'We've been coming in. We were worried,' said Jerome. 'You do look better now that they've taken all those wires away.'

'Well, that's the thing. While they had me in that room with those pipes and wires, the doctors found something else. I've got heart problems. That is why I have been so under the weather. I just thought I was getting a bit too old to be standing out in all weathers. It has made me think. I'm not going back to peddling my wares on rainy winter evenings.'

'What will you do?'

'Retire to the seaside. It is what I have always promised my missus. She has been on at me for years about it. And I have made my mind up, just this morning. I can afford it. I've earned it. And she loves Bournemouth.'

'I – we – should get even, Alfie, and get him out of the way.'

26

'You shouldn't get involved. He has turned really nasty since he got out of prison. And he wasn't very nice before that, either.'

Just then a plump, homely woman came to the bedside and gave Alfie a big kiss.'

'Betty, meet those two lads I mentioned. They've brought me some grapes, look.'

'I've heard about you two. You were the ones who looked after Alfie that night when he came home in a taxi. I knew something was wrong as soon as I saw him. He never spends money on a taxi, the mean old bugger! Thank you. You should come round for tea when I've got Alfie home.'

'That would be lovely!' said Jerome in his best polite voice.

'When can you get out, Alfie?' asked Tim.

'Tomorrow, if the doctor is happy to discharge me. I have to come back to get the dressings off. He has written to our doctor. I have to go to get my heart sorted out, Betty says.'

'We'll fetch you home – in a taxi. How would that be, Betty?'

'Ooh! I'll bake a cake.'

'And that's more than I would be getting! So come round our house, boys!'

'Cheeky old sod! I make him cake every weekend. And he scoffs the lot.'

'Lemon drizzle, chocolate sponge, mmm.' Alfie grinned – and grimaced. 'Still a bit sore,' he said.

'We'll be off. I meant it about seeing to that Dougie, Alfie. We'll talk about it later.'

'I love lemon drizzle, Betty!' said Jerome.

Betty made a fuss of Alfie when they got him home next day, a little unsteady but happy to be back. They ate the sandwiches and the cake. Jerome declared them to be the best he had eaten since he had come to London. Betty beamed as she picked up cups, saucers and plates and hurried into their kitchen.

'I won't half miss this old place,' she called from the kitchen. 'How long have we lived here, Alfie? Thirty years? But it will be lovely to be beside the seaside!'

'I've told her. I had to tell her everything. Dougie, the heart thing, and wanting to retire.'

'She seems pleased,' said Jerome.

'She'll miss the life here. We were born round here. Betty was born in this very street. But it was her idea. We could always

27

move back, I suppose, if it doesn't work out. But there will always be Dougie, hanging about like a bad smell. I don't want to be reminded of him every time I leave my front door.'

'Alfie, I've been thinking. About Dougie. He can't get away with this. I – we – will take him down a peg or two, somehow. Right, Jerome?'

'Right.'

'How are you going to do that? He's dangerous. You've seen what he did to me. He could have killed me.'

'I've been thinking. He owes you the money he stole. He owes you for putting you in hospital. And you're right, he could have killed you. Oh, hang on! Does he know you are out of hospital?'

'I doubt if he knows I was even in hospital. He hasn't been seen, according to his mother. He used to pop round but he hasn't for a while. Betty spoke to her yesterday. She's worried sick about what he has been getting up to. He's still on parole. He could be recalled if he gets caught.'

'Oh, yes, he could,' murmured Tim.

Three

Tim and Jerome were taking a break from the grind of ticket selling. It was cold, wet February weather, and they were in funds after their spell working with Alfie. Since he was at home they were not getting any of his good quality tickets.

'That Dougie has been on my mind, Jerome. I can't let it lie. We should get him back somehow.'

'I can't help thinking that the tickets game has run its course,' said Jerome. 'With Alfie out of action, I doubt if we could carry on – certainly not in the style we have been. We should be trying something else.'

'We have said it before, Jerome, we aren't thieves. So what are we?'

'We are personable rogues, Tim. That's what!'

'And what are they, if not thieves? It comes down to making money for ourselves, doesn't it?'

'We could do that with a job, Tim. We could always work in the kitchen in *Le Bistro* back in Stratford. I could even go and work in the family business. I could get you a job, too. But that is not what either of us want, is it?'

'Personable rogues, are we?'

'Yes, we are, Tim. We are smart enough to have lived on our wits for all this time. We are not exactly down on our uppers either. We don't much care for the bourgeois life-style and we like being on the edge. What career opportunities do these qualities suggest to you?'

'I've been thinking about how to get our own back on that Dougie. We owe Alfie that, I think. He was good to us.'

'We were quite nice to him.'

'Do you suppose Dougie has money?'

'Certainly. He has got quite a bit of Alfie's for a start. He's been taking money from stallholders, souvenir and programme sellers around Wembley for a while now. Why?'

'I reckon we should get some of it for Alfie as compensation for injuries and loss of earnings – and some for ourselves.'

'You are sounding like a lawyer in the small claims court now, Tim. Natural justice! That is what Dougie needs!'

'Yes, m'lud. Natural justice would be him back in the clink for fracturing Alfie's skull. Taking Dougie's money off him, repaying Alfie and keeping the change for ourselves – sounds pretty fair to me.'

'So, let's just roll up to him and ask him for the money and send him back to his new friend and mentor the master criminal Reginald Kray. Job done!'

'Exactly. That is what we are going to do.'

'How do we do that?'

'He needs to be properly scared. He needs to be convinced that he cannot just punch and kick his way out of it. We have to make him fear us.'

'What would scare him? He doesn't look the scared type to me.'

'What we need is leverage. What *is* he scared of? I'll tell you. Prison. Alfie mentioned that he was a frightened little boy underneath, didn't he?'

'I am frightened of prison, Tim. But just now I'm more frightened of Dougie.'

'All the more reason to get him out of the way. We need a plan. Remember, Alfie said Dougie probably had no idea that he had injured Alfie so badly? What if Alfie had died?'

'Dougie would be facing a murder charge. Even he knows that the police would be after him for that.'

'Yes. That is what we are going to tell him.'

'He would soon find out that it wasn't true.'

'We have to get round that. And we have to help him escape. He has to pay us to help him disappear.'

'We could send him on a long trip on a nice cruise. Oh, hang on! We could do that.'

'A luxury cruise does not seem punishing enough, even in these liberal times, Jerome. And too expensive.'

'That is not what I had in mind, Tim. Something a bit more basic. In fact, a cabin cruiser.'

'And where would we get one of those? They aren't exactly cheap either.'

'Ah, as it happens, I've got one. Well, my father has. He can't sail in it now, he's too ill, but Kate does. In fact she's a very good sailor. She learned to skipper the thing before I went away with the fairies.'

'We could probably get him to pay us for getting him away from London. But there is the little matter of endlessly sailing about. We could hardly drop him off on a desert island with a year's provisions.'

'We could just drop him into the sea, I suppose, and let him sink or swim.'

'Probably not. It is tempting, but no, not that!'

'He's out on remand. That should be something we can use.'

'When is Alfie going off to Bournemouth?'

'Soon, I should think. There is nothing to keep them here.'

'Let's pay Betty and Alfie a visit.'

The move was imminent. Betty had been on a day out to Bournemouth and spent a happy time looking at apartments. She had found one that would do nicely. They were 'upping sticks', as Betty put it, at the end of the month.

'If I'd known you were coming I'd have made one of my lemon drizzle cakes. I know you like them, Jerome.'

'Thanks, Betty. We came to see how you are.'

'And to talk to you both about a plan we are working on,' said Tim. 'First, who knows where you are going?'

'Nobody, really. I haven't got round to saying anything yet to the neighbours. I wanted to wait until everything was settled. Why do you ask?'

'Have you been out at all, Alfie? Have the neighbours seen you?'

'No,' said Betty. 'He won't even go down the pub since he came out of hospital. You haven't been out, have you, Alfie?'

'I just don't feel like it these days.'

'Has that Dougie been back to see his mother?'

'I don't think so,' said Betty. 'She would have said if he had. I saw her last week at the hairdresser's and we had a bit of a natter. She is worried, I can tell.'

'Would it be all right if you kept inside until the move, Alfie? And if you could keep your move quiet for now?'

'I dunno what you are up to, but just be careful. He's a nasty piece of work.'

'He is, Alfie, and we want to be safe. And so do you.'

They found Dougie drinking tea at a stall outside Wembley stadium. When he saw them he swaggered towards them.

'You! I haven't forgotten you. You still owe me a hundred quid. Plus interest for not paying straight away. That's two hundred. Now, or I'll smash your faces in.'

'Calm down. We aren't running away, Dougie. We were looking for you. We have something you need.'

'Yeah, my money!'

'Remember your uncle Alfie, Dougie?' Tim went on.

'He's not my uncle.'

'We visited him in hospital.'

'Nothing to do with me.'

'Ah, but it is. You beat him up outside the Shed at Stamford Bridge.'

'Yes, up that alley. You thought nobody saw you.'

'Wasn't me.'

'It was. You robbed him. You took his money and left him on the pavement.'

'You can't prove it. Who would believe you?'

'We don't need to. Alfie died this morning. It's murder now. There was a big police van outside the Shed today and loads of coppers with clip-boards asking questions. They are speaking to everybody round Stamford Bridge. Everybody knows you. And they aren't exactly friends, are they? Especially not the ones who have been paying you. It won't be long before they pick you up for questioning.'

'They've got nothing on me. I wasn't there.'

'You were seen.'

'But I was—'

'—careful?' Tim asked. What about DNA? Are you sure you didn't leave any at the scene? Did you leave your DNA on the body when you punched him? Sweat? Saliva? Hairs? Fibres from your clothing? That other time, they had you bang to rights with the victim's blood all over you. They'll get you again, easy. They've got your DNA and fingerprints on record.'

'They must be looking for you by now, Dougie,' Jerome said.

'DNA? They put a stick thing in my mouth when they took me to the nick, and then then locked me up. And they took fingerprints.'

'That's your DNA. They never throw anything away, Dougie. You are on file now. They will find something when they do their fingertip search of the area. I bet there is a team down there already. If you touched anything or threw anything away they'll find it. Or if something fell out of your pocket.'

'Just a matter of time, wouldn't you say, Tim?'

'Hours, I should think, Jerome.'

Dougie's bluster had gone. The blood drained from his face. He seemed to shrivel before them.

'Dunno what to do! Me mum – she'll know.' His voice cracked. He was on the verge of tears.

'You can't go there. That is the first place they'll look for you. They are probably there already.'

'Your mother mustn't even know where you are. Then they can't drag it out of her.'

Just then a distant police siren cut through the air. Dougie jerked round, staring wildly.

'It sounds as if they are on to you. Somebody outside the Chelsea ground will have fingered you by now. Lots of people down there know you come here. The cops will have put two and two together by now. They will be asking questions around here before long. They all know you round the Arena, don't they, Dougie?'

'They'll grass on me!'

'Sure to.'

'Oh, God!'

'Praying won't help you – but maybe we can,' said Tim. 'You should disappear.'

'Quick. Today. Now.'

'How?' Dougie whimpered. His hero Reggie Kray was forgotten. 'I should get away. I don't want to go to prison again. It's horrible. What can I do?'

'Maybe we can help'

'For a price.'

'You? How?'

'We can hide you.'

'Make you disappear.'

'Where?'

'Abroad.'

'It will cost you.'

'I'll give you money! Look!' He pulled out a handful of cash in an untidy bundle from his coat pocket. 'I've got more, look.' He delved into another pocket.'

'Give it here.' Tim took the money and calmly counted it. 'That's not enough. It will take ten grand.'

'I can get it!'

'When?'

'Now. Just get me away from them! Give me twenty minutes. I'll come back with it.'

Twenty minutes? You haven't got twenty minutes. Tell you what. Come with us now. We'll take you to your money. You give us the ten grand and we get you out of London.'

'We'll take you somewhere you won't be found.'

'Where?'

'I've said. Abroad. I'll tell you when we've seen the money. Walk round the corner with us. Act natural, and you can get the cash. Then we'll be off.' Dougie obeyed. He was docile now, the blustering swagger utterly gone out of him. His head drooped, his feet dragging.

'Into the car.' Jerome held open the rear door. Dougie climbed in. 'Now tell us where to go.'

In a few minutes Dougie pointed to a block of run-down flats.

'I'll only be a minute. Don't go away. Don't leave!' He set off at a shambling run.

He returned with a grubby shoebox.

'There it is! It's all I've got. Now what are you going to do?'

'What we promised. In four hours you'll be on board a boat. You will be in Spain in three days.'

'Where? Oh, God! What have I done? Oh, Mum!'

'Shut up! There's a patrol car! Get your head down out of sight. If the police stop us you're done for.'

They drove in silence to Weymouth. Dougie crouched in the footwell the whole way.

They drove right onto the dock just as the last of the daylight was fading. Jerome got out of the car, checked to see if there were people about. The marina was quiet. It was off-season. Launches, cabin cruisers and sailing ships from dinghies to tall-masted ocean-going yachts bobbed and clattered their painters against the harbour-side. No-one was about. He walked briskly to the far end of one of the narrow quays to a large cabin cruiser with 'Santa Maria' picked out in gilt lettering on her stern. A Union Jack flapped in the stiffening breeze from a stubby mast over the stern of the vessel. In a moment Jerome had vanished below. He reappeared on deck in conversation with a young woman with a yachting cap set over her long dark hair.

He waved briefly. At the signal Tim got the still cowering Dougie out from the rear of the car and walked him briskly along the quay to the boat. The quay appeared deserted. No light showed in any of the craft they passed.

Jerome spoke quietly to the woman. She burst out laughing. She spoke loudly and rapidly in a foreign language, seemingly to unseen crew members. Tim bundled Dougie on board and hustled him down the steps into the cabin. There he pulled the curtains closed before switching on the dim cabin light.

'You must keep below until you are out of sight of land. After that it is up to the crew. Don't ask them any questions and do as they tell you. You will be at sea for perhaps seventy-two hours. That bucket is for if you are seasick. There is food and water enough for four days, so you should be all right.'

'Where am I going?'

'Near to Santander. You will be put ashore with instructions to meet the men who will hide you. It is being arranged now. The crew speak Spanish – they are Colombian.'

'Are they drug dealers?'

'Don't ask! They have been paid, that's all you need to know.'

'But what if they just take me out to sea and chuck me into the water?'

'Just behave yourself. They know you are a killer. You must act the part. They will get you to Spain. Or you could put your trust in the Met. They must be looking for you by now.' With that Tim turned and left Dougie staring at the bucket, already wondering how long it would be before he was putting it to use. He did not hear the bolt shoot as Tim locked the companionway door behind him.

Jerome hugged the Spanish speaking woman.

'Kate! We are so grateful. You know what to do. Are you sure you can you manage on your own?'

'Yes, little brother, I've been sailing the Santa Maria solo for ages. She is a pretty steady old girl, Jerome. I am going to sail out to the sea-lanes and swan about like any other amateur sailor for three days. Your big man stays below. Once he is totally sea-sick and whimpering with fear I will put him ashore on Worbarrow Beach – in the dark, as near as I can to 20.00hrs on Tuesday evening.'

'That's it, Kate,' said Tim. 'Take the long way home if you like – just make sure you keep the Coast Guard and the Weymouth harbour-master happy.'

'I'll put the fishing lines out. Look out for little brother Jerome for me.'

'Trust me.'

'Hmm.'

'Bon voyage, Kate,' said Tim. 'Come to Greenwich when it is over. We will tell you all about it then. It will be a good story when it is over.'

They strolled across the short gangplank, turned and waved for the benefit of any witnesses and returned to the car. As they turned, the Santa Maria was already under way. Katie waved from the helm and puttered quietly out into the narrow channel, inching past the moored craft, cleared the marina and set off briskly out of the anchorage into open water.

As soon as Dougie felt the swell of the Channel in a stiff breeze he felt his stomach heave. He eyed the bucket. He caught a whiff of diesel. He looked at the stock of food and the plastic bottles of water. Perhaps a drink would settle his stomach. He took a sip. The water was warm. He took another sip. He slumped in a narrow seat running lengthwise along the side of the little cabin. Sitting was worse. He stood up. His head bumped against the cabin roof. He found that sitting on the floor with his back against the cabin door was best.

The journey dragged on. And on.

Suddenly the little boat lurched. It was as if something solid and heavy had smashed into it. Dougie looked out through the little port-hole and could see nothing but the darkness. He tried the other side and there he spotted the enormous outline of a ship. It seemed to be about to crash into the little craft. Then its wake smashed up the side and for a moment obscured the port-hole. Dougie thought his last moment had come.

Then the Santa Maria turned and the ship vanished from his sight. Kate appeared at the doorway.

'*Eso fue algo cercano! Comer! Asentará su estómago!* Then, in English, 'That was close. Eat some food, Englishman. It will help with *enfermo de mar.* There is worse coming. We must cross shipping lanes. Is risky, no?' Then she was gone.

He ate some of the sausage he found. It was peppery – and greasy. He drank more water. He kept both down. He began to feel a little better. He was a fugitive from justice, just like Reggie. When all this was over he would be somebody. He would be respected. He lay along the seat with his head against a thin cushion. The sea seemed to be calmer and he slipped into a fitful sleep.

When he woke the boat was being tossed about again. The bucket was rolling about on the cabin floor. Lucky for him he had not made use of it yet. He set it straight and relieved himself. He tried the companionway door. It was not locked. The woman in the cap was at the helm as the boat chugged into the calmer water behind the wake of another vessel, pitching a little less in the swell.

'*Sobre el costado.*' She gestured. '*Sobre el costado del barco! Sobre el costado del barco! El lado de babor!* Over the side! Port side. That side.'

Dougie at last understood. The wind caught the contents of the bucket and hoisted them away from the boat's side.

'*Bien.*'

'Where are we?'

'Here. Nowhere. Take some air. Two more days *en el mar* and you will be *en Espagne.* And we will be rid of you. *Coño de puta!* Soon it will be storm. *Ve por debajo de la cubierta.* Go. Go below.'

She laughed and turned the boat's heading into the breeze. The bow rose and fell. Dougie went below and almost immediately stuck his head into the smelly bucket. He was sick, sicker than he had ever been. He had only one thought, for this to end. From time to time he sipped at the water. His empty stomach craved food. He nibbled more of the Spanish sausage. He heaved. The water and the sausage ended up in the bucket. He left it there. He tried to lie down and sleep. Lying was worse. He sat up. Better. Then the boat gave another lurch.

At last the woman called to him from the companionway.

'We are here. *Ven a cubierta.* Come.' She beckoned. He stumbled on deck into the dimming evening light. He could see the cliffs off to each side, high and unclimbable. Ahead was a beach in a bay between the cliffs.

'We get you close to land. You jump.'

'I am not a very good swimmer.'

'When the boat - *encallado* - catches the land, jump. You will be good. OK? See ahead. There is path. Go on path to red light. Wait there. Do not make noise. Men will come, *Me entiendes?* Understand?'

She opened the throttle. The bows lifted and the craft lurched forward. The keel crunched into the coarse pebbly beach. Dougie leapt for his life. In a moment he was splashing, arms flailing. Then his feet touched bottom. He struggled ashore and flung himself onto the gravelly beach. He lay still. Then he wept, grateful to be on land. When he felt strong enough he stood and turned back to the sea. The Santa Maria had already lifted off the shingle and was nosing out to sea again. The young woman glanced back. He heard that laughter on the wind and watched as the craft gathered speed.

Dougie was hungry and thirsty – and tired, more tired than he had been in his life. He staggered off over the pile of shingle towards the path in the fading light. The path was steep. His city shoes were useless on the sandy earth. He slipped and slithered his way until he reached a proper track. He followed it uphill, and there it was! A red light, unblinking. That was the sign. He began to feel safe. When he came to the light he noticed a bench. He slumped onto it. The wind was chilly as it caught at his wet clothes. He would do as instructed. He would wait.

He waited. The dark pressed against his eyeballs. He closed them and began to drift into a doze.

A loud crack broke the silence. Dougie jerked awake. It sounded like a gunshot. There was a volley. Then a second and a third. Dougie crept under the bench. Had he stumbled into a gunbattle between rival drug gangs? Would anybody come? His body shook and shivered. He let out a wail of terror and despair.

'Bloody Hell, sarge! Look what I've found.'

'Cease fire! Cease fire!'

Dougie whimpered. 'Don't kill me! Don't kill me!'

'What are you doin' here? Didn't you see the warnin'? I know it was showin'. I checked the bleedin' thing meself. What a bloody mess you are! Have you been bathing – in this weather? Corporal, get this man to the transports. Give him a cup of tea and a sandwich. And call the Redcaps.' He turned to the wretched Dougie. 'We'll get you nice and cosy. You need a nice cup of tea inside you.'

Dougie just shook his head. There was some mistake. This was not Spain. These were British soldiers.

In half an hour Dougie had warm dry clothes and a hot, sweet cup of tea. In two hours he was tucking into bacon, eggs and beans on toast. Then the military police arrived. They began by asking what he was doing on the range. Didn't he know that the red light indicated night firing? The red light was there for a good reason. Hadn't he read the signs? He was lucky he had not wandered into the dead ground in front of the target zone.

'I – I – was put ashore here. Something's gone wrong. I thought I was in Spain.'

'You thought you were in Spain? Who are you, laddie? Wet through, half-starved by the looks of it.'

'Dougie. They took my money and promised to take me to Spain.'

'And who would they be, Dougie?'

'They were smugglers, I think. I only saw one of them. They tricked me.'

'Never come across anything like this, Sarge. What should we be doing with him?'

'Normally I'd keep him till daylight, give him a decent breakfast and send him on his way.' The sergeant turned to Dougie. 'There's definitely something fishy about you, Sonny. We'll keep you here and hand you over to the local police in the morning.'

Dougie groaned. They would find out who he was soon enough.

He was going to prison.

He talked to the Dorset police officers who arrived to interview him. He even told them his probation officer's name. After a long phone call with her they took Dougie to Guys Marsh Prison to begin what was left of his ABH sentence. Nobody mentioned a murder charge.

Tim and Jerome sat in the snug. They had counted the cash they had received from Dougie. Altogether, counting the money from his pockets, it came to nearly ten thousand pounds.

'That went well,' said Tim. 'Two hundred to Gloria for the loan of his car, a grand for Alfie as compensation and repayment of what Dougie stole. 'What about Kate and the boat?'

'She will have enjoyed herself. She loves sailing. She is the only one who is still interested in Dad's boat. We should offer her something for the fuel, but I think she probably still tops it up on the company account. The firm pays for the boat, I expect. A tax thing, you know.'

'Let's say, three grand each, plus a good bit to put by for contingencies. And a deep sense that justice has been done.'

'OK, Tim. I just fancy a slice of lemon drizzle cake. Let's go to the seaside.'

'We'll take the train this weekend. While we are there we can pay Alfie his compensation money.'

'You know what, Tim? I'm never going to sell tickets again. We need a career move.'

Four

Arthur Golightly was an antique dealer. He was not one of the run of the mill dealer-collector types that stand, or more likely sit, behind a stall full of china at antique fairs, nor the sort offering high priced pieces in carefully lit shops on or just off high streets in any provincial town. He was a runner. He bought and sold entirely within the trade. He trawled through second-hand shops, fairs and markets and bought at auctions. He had a keen eye and was constantly on the lookout for sleepers, unrecognized treasures from the past which he would buy without fuss – and without the slightest sign that he was particularly interested. He might spot a Worcester first period vase or a Vienna bronze for a tenner at the back of a shelf in a junk shop. He was always ready to spend big money on a piece if he could see a profit in it, especially when he knew of some dealer who was hoping to lay hands on such a piece for a customer.

He knew the business better than most and he kept his knowledge to himself. Dealers looked forward to his usually unexpected visits because he always seemed to have something they wanted, what customers were seeking. The little piece he put on the counter would as likely as not be something a regular had enquired about recently so that the dealer knew he only needed to make a phone call.

There would be no negotiation with him. He had his price, told it and expected it to be accepted. The price always allowed for a good profit. Despite his blunt manner and evident ill-humour he was a welcome visitor in antique shops around the Midlands and Cotswolds. He was a goldmine.

He could detect a rarity in a moment, after the first glance or touch. It was a knack, his special gift. It sometimes seemed to him that he knew before seeing it when he had found an undiscovered treasure among the bric-a-brac of some second-hand shop. In these moments he felt a buzzing sensation. Sometimes he thought he felt the tingle before he saw the thing.

He was a regular at auction houses throughout the Midlands. Nobody would ever pick him out of a crowd or guess that somewhere within the greasy overcoat he carried more cash than many people had ever seen in one place. He was a nondescript, indeterminate sort of fellow, the sort that lingers by the door or against the back wall at sales. You might never see him bid. A twitch of the hand, a slight nod or a wink got the auctioneer's attention. The auctioneers all knew him by sight so he could usually bid without needing a word said or a number card raised. He was careful not to let his competitors know what he bought or how much he paid. That way he kept a certain edge when it came to the resale which would follow within days, sometimes hours. He always paid cash at the office and took his prizes away immediately. This way he kept his profile low. Salerooms did not usually mind so long as the money was right.

It was at an auction in Birmingham that he heard a rumour which set him thinking. He was waiting for a lot to come up which he would certainly buy if he could when he heard the word 'Vermeer'. He edged closer to the two men who were chatting quietly at the back of the room.

'I reckon it is one of those 'after the artist' pieces, said one. 'Whatever, it will never come up for sale.'

'It would be out of your league if it did.'

'Yeah, I know. And yours, I reckon.'

'We can dream, I suppose. Where is it?'

'Not far off – Warwickshire. In one of those stately homes. Binton Chadlow.'

'Never heard of it.'

'My missus goes round those places with her sister. She saw it. "Once attributed to Vermeer" – that's what she said was on the plaque on the wall. She said it was the best thing in the house and it was being completely overlooked. The lady in the room – sort of guide – was only interesting in the porcelain.'

'Your missus? Is she in the business?'

'She's a decorator. She knows a bit about paintings. More than me. Not my sort of thing. Hang on. Lot 229 – I'm having a go at that.'

Golightly had heard enough. A chance conversation overheard at the back of a saleroom! He recognised the feeling, that tingling, faint but there. Stranger things had happened. A country house sleeper! He decided he would have a little look; one day when he was passing he would call in at this Binton Chadlow.

He never visited stately homes. To him they were mausoleums for antiques. That day was an exception. A Vermeer? Fat chance! He would see for himself. He unloaded a pretty Georgian mahogany wine table on a trader outside Coventry. Binton Chadlow was practically round the corner.

He stayed among the paying public. He shuffled along with them from room to room, until they reached the morning room, as the guidebook called it. The room was lined with glass fronted display cases. They contained porcelain, all finest quality pieces. Golightly skimmed them, professional enough to see that they were expensive and rare. 'Meissen,' he thought.

His eye swept past the cabinets to take in the room. He saw the painting instantly. It was hung in a bad light, over a fireplace. Sunlight from the mullioned windows chequered its surface making the colours difficult to make out. He pushed past the tourists who were listening to a lady telling them about the 'very important Meissen collection' the family had put together over several generations. His eye was caught by a vase on a pier table used to screen the fireplace. 'More Meissen,' he thought. 'Not in a cabinet. Cracked, or repro.' He thought the bronze bust beside it was out of place too.

He looked hard at the painting. The palette, the style of interior, the light from an unseen window suggested Dutch all right. A woman sat at a table with her hands to her hair. The face of the young girl in the middle ground was reflected in the mirror she held. She was looking towards the artist, or perhaps the viewer. She was not plain, not pretty. Her expression was quizzical, as if she was sharing a secret. On the back wall was a map. The floor of the room was tiled.

Vermeer? It could be.

He left the room abruptly, got himself out of the house and into his van and away. He could feel that tingle.

43

Five

Jerome went back to Stratford. His sister Kate would tell him about their father's health. They met in a tea room in Sheep Street. They laughed over 'that horrible man's' voyage.

'I thought the Spanish crew was a terrific idea. Did he find out that it was just you and himself?'

'Of course not. He was too busy being sea-sick to think anything through. I made sure we hit a few big waves every now and again. I just kept out of view of the shore. I dropped anchor on the big shoal off Portland Bill for the nights. It was pretty foggy. And choppy! I don't think anybody would take much notice even if they had seen me. I cast a line and caught some sea bass and a lemon sole. I ate the sole and gave the harbour master the sea bass. I think he has an arrangement with one of the restaurants. He is a sweetie. What about him, that fellow? Do tell all!'

'He is a bully – well worse than a bully, really.' Jerome filled Kate in with the essentials of how Dougie had robbed and hurt one of their business acquaintances and how Dougie had come to believe he was wanted for murder and paid Tim and Jerome to get him away.

'You should have seen him when he jumped into the sea at Worbarrow Beach,' Kate laughed. 'I never thought to ask him if he could swim. It was touch and go for a moment. I thought about throwing him a line but he found his feet. He was only yards from the beach. You can get right into shore, the shingle is so steep. I got away as fast as I could. Why Worbarrow Beach? I can think of easier places to land somebody.'

'Because there is night firing on Tuesdays on the military range just a mile from shore. You told him to wait at the red light? Did you hang around to wait for the gunfire?'

Kate laughed again. 'That must have brought him up short.'

We thought that the army would find him sooner or later and hand him over to the civilian police. He was on licence, so he would be whisked back to prison straight away for leaving London without informing his probation officer. Breach of parole, you see.'

'Can they do that? Shouldn't there be a trial or something?'

'No. Let's change the subject. How is the Old Devil?'

'Father's heart is worse. It is to be expected with his history. There are treatments but all they do is prolong his life. He will not get better. Mother is not coping well. She misses you, Jerome. She does not understand why you dropped out of university. She reads those letters on that college notepaper over and over. You were doing so well, Jerome!'

I painted a rosy picture, Kate. But you know about that.'

'The business is holding up for now but it needs leadership and some fresh drive. Father hasn't got it now.'

'Why not you, Kate? Would he consider you in the business? You seem to be doing well these days.'

'I am happy where I am, Jerome. My boss deals with some high profile people, handling investments for them. I think he trusts me. He treats me as a colleague. He is giving me a lot of responsibility, almost a free hand advising some major clients about investing their money. I love the work. Father would never treat me like that. He is a Neanderthal when it comes to women in business. One reason why he never gave me a hard time was that he had no expectations of me. I was just a girl.'

'I suppose so. I just thought you were his favourite.'

'Come home, Jerome, please. I worry that Father—if you two are to settle your differences, please do not dither. We both know it will be difficult because you are both total mules over it. Tell him you will go back to your studies, you will follow him into the business, anything.'

'Kate, not after what was said. He wants me to be another version of himself and I will not, I cannot be like him. I might come back home eventually. I'm just not ready yet.'

'You would rather have Mother sick with worry about you? Come home to see her. You need not see *him*. He hardly leaves his bedroom these days.'

Jerome sat silent for a long moment.

'I will see Mother,' he said at last. 'I am not coming home to stay, though, Kate. I was wondering about the flat.'

'That's good. It takes a weight off me, too. I worry about you nearly as much as Mum – and I see you now and again. I was going to mention the flat. It has been empty for three weeks. You could move in today if you won't come home. I thought maybe I could move in myself.'

'We could share. It is big enough, though maybe a bit Spartan for a sophisticate like you.'

'Oh, Jerome, remember calling me that – Sophisti-Kate?'

'When you turned up looking like a Sloane Ranger? Oh, yes.'

'You were so funny! Wherever did you pick that up?'

'At school, I suppose. I was being sophisticated too.' Kate's laughter filled the tea-room.

'It is lovely to see you, Tim. I think it would be lovely to share with you. We have some catching up to do, starting with what you were up to in London. The last tenant was a bit slobbish, so it could do with a bit of a clean and tidy. I will soon smarten it up. When can you come to see Mum?'

'I should smarten *myself* up a bit first.'

'At least the beard and that smelly kaftan has gone!'

'Long since. Tim and I have made a bit of money in London. I might tell you about it some time. I think I'll get some new togs and a bottle of after-shave to cheer the old girl up.'

'I'll pick you up from the flat tomorrow. Mother will be thrilled. There will be tears for the Prodigal Son's return!'

'And a fatted calf?'

'Probably scones and ginger cake in the garden room. The terrace will be too chilly for her.'

The meeting with Jerome's mother began awkwardly. She was sensible enough not to ask too many questions and avoided any mention of his homeless time. They skirted round his dropping out of Oxford. Jerome spoke a little about London, saying only that he and a friend had made some money running 'an agency'. He asked after her health, the garden and even her friends from the Bridge Club. She told him she was relieved to see him looking well. They avoided the issue of Father's failing health. There was no mention of the icy silence between him and Jerome.

They relaxed a bit over the scones. Kate made her joke about putting the cream before the jam, just as she had in happier times.

'Jerome, dear, I have missed you so much. I cannot tell you what a thrill it is just to see you. Please come a little more often. I understand that you are a grown man and won't ever come home to live.' A tear hovered on her eyelid. 'I am just a silly old woman, I know.' She slumped in her chair. She suddenly looked frail.

Kate went to her. 'No, you are not, Mum! Jerome should—'

'—what?' Jerome barked at Kate. 'Sorry, Mother. I don't want to quarrel.'

Mother looked miserably up. 'Let's not, then.'

'Sorry, Mother. You are right. I am a grown man and I should know better than to upset you.'

He bent to kiss her cheek. She struggled to sit up. At last she regained her composure.

'Have some ginger-cake, Jerome. Kate, would you, please?'

Jerome helped his sister move into the flat. Working together was a little like the old days when they had lived in the house. He had always adored her, his glamorous big sister who was protective when his father was sarcastic about his achievements at school, on the sports field or in the classroom.

'This is nice, Kate. I will have to sort stuff out back in London. Tim and I – I owe him a lot.'

'Yes, there is a regular train service. You can be a commuter.'

'I will come to stay here now and then. I will visit Mother when I come. She is a bit – well – fragile, isn't she?'

'How long is it since you have seen her, Jerome?'

'Four years?'

'More like six. And you weren't around much then, were you?'

'I'll come and visit, I promise. I still have stuff to do in London. I owe Tim a lot.'

Tim was taking it easy. They were flush with cash. While Jerome was away Tim set about discovering London's tourist places. He strolled in the famous streets, did a bit of window-shopping in the West End. Just reading the street names was exciting, like revisiting the Monopoly board of his childhood, before his mother had left and things had begun to go wrong. He loved gazing at the jewellery in New Bond Street shop windows. 'As good as Howard's in Wood Street,' he decided.

He wandered about Whitehall and Trafalgar Square, Leicester Square and Piccadilly. He found the National Gallery. He discovered the British Museum and the British Library.

'Everything you could possibly want to know is here,' he thought.

He saw the Guards at Buckingham Palace, strolled in the Royal Parks, drank beer with his pie in Victorian pubs.

Tim discovered the Portobello Road Market. The market held a fascination for him – the bustle, the quick exchanges, the rolls of cash, the sheer exuberance of so many of the traders. He spent a happy hour or two browsing and drinking the very good coffee at one of the cafes, Mabel's, along the street. He sometimes chatted to stallholders when they sat outside the cafe over their coffees, one eye on the stall and ready to jump up when a customer picked up something. They were a mixed bunch. Many were just happy to sell anything to make a living, while others were enthusiastic specialists who loved their stock. On the whole they struck Tim as hard-working, honest traders.

Maggie was one of the enthusiastic sort. She sold vintage clothing; she wore vintage clothing. She sometimes had a sit down and cup of coffee in the cafe, in a spot where she could keep a sharp eye on the stall. An elderly man who specialised in timepieces ran a stall a few places down from the clothing stall. The two evidently knew each other and occasionally sat together chatting over their drinks. Tim sat quiet, observant. He liked to see their friendship, based, he guessed, on their shared enthusiasm for the life of the market. He realised that since Jerome had left on his family business he had barely spoken to anybody. The girl was nice, he thought. She was pretty. Her reddish hair was always tied back in a business-like way. He imagined it loose. 'She never notices me at all,' he thought.

The old fellow, on the other hand, chatted to anybody nearby. He was evidently a man who had been places, seen things. He spoke to Tim one morning when they were the only customers in the cafe.

48

'I've seen you a few times here, but you aren't a dealer, are you?' He spoke with an accent Tim could not place.

'I just love it here. It is like nowhere I've ever been.'

'Hmm.' The man smiled, lopsidedly. 'Maggie's very pretty.'

Tim found himself blushing. He knew her name now.

'Customer! Excuse me.' The man drank up and bustled back to his stall.

The cafe began to fill. Casual customers were sitting outside in the sun and a few were inside. The girl with the reddish hair, Maggie, was working hard. Tim saw her flitting from customer to customer, holding up items from the stall and sorting the dresses on her racks. Business seemed brisk.

After a while, when the market throng began to thin out she slipped into the seat opposite Tim. Mabel the waitress and proprietor brought her coffee. Her face was inscrutable when Maggie caught her eye.

'You two,' Mabel said. 'You should talk to each other.'

'Mabel! Stop it! Behave yourself!'

'Chef and me – we are taking bets.'

After that it was impossible not to fall into some polite conversation.

'That Mabel! Said Maggie. 'She's really embarrassing sometimes.'

'You know each other?'

'Yes, we often have a bit of a banter. She can be a tease, but she's all right. She is like that with lots of the regulars.'

They discovered that both were from Stratford-upon-Avon. They even knew some of the same people, though they had not gone to the same school.

'Oh, look out! Somebody wants something I've got!' Her abrupt departure ended their conversation.

They nodded to each other the following Saturday morning when Tim saw her at the same table sipping coffee and alert for customers. He slipped into a seat at the table.

'Morning, again!' Tim smiled awkwardly. Maggie briefly returned the smile and relapsed into her thoughts.

'How's business today? As busy as last week?'

Maggie looked up. 'To tell you the truth, I am a bit pissed off. I've just been conned.'

'No kidding! What happened?'

'A bloke tricked me into buying a load of tat. He showed me a suitcase full of quality frocks – good labels, pukka stuff.'

'How did he trick you?'

'Not sure, but I think he must have somehow swapped the case with another one that looked the same. I never even checked. I shoved it under the stall to deal with a customer just after I had paid him. By the time I had finished with her he was gone. It was quieter after the early rush so I thought I would sort through it and see what I could mend and what needed a wash and press. It was total rubbish, not what I had seen when he opened the case.'

'London is full of thieves!'

'Yeah, I know. I am angry with myself. I should've known better. He's got my morning's takings plus the cash I always have handy for moments when somebody brings stuff to me.'

'Are you broke?'

'Just about. I'll get over it. It is just so bloody maddening!'

'What was this bloke like?'

'I didn't pay much attention to him. I was more interested in the clothes in the case. He was tallish. Shabby. Scowling all the time. There was a woman there who was rummaging through my stock – making a mess of it. I had to deal with her in the middle of the business with the clothing. Ugh! I remember her painted fingernails tugging my silk stuff about. I remember thinking how badly her nails were painted. Then I just took the case and paid.'

Suddenly she jumped up. 'A customer! I've got work to do.'

'OK, be seeing you.'

Tim felt himself hating the man who had upset this girl, Maggie. He hardly knew her yet he wanted to put things right, somehow. He and Jerome had put matters right once before. Why not again? He tried to dismiss the thought but it returned, along with the memory of her reddish hair held back with the ribbon.

The following Saturday morning Tim was back at the market in the seat by the window, watching the bustle of customers. He saw Maggie working hard to sell a vintage handbag to a young lady. He smiled as the handbag and the money changed hands. Maggie was back on form.

Maggie glanced up, caught his eye and gave a little wave.

In a moment she had spoken to the stall-holder neighbour and darted across the pavement into the cafe. She sat at Tim's table.

Hi, Maggie! Have a coffee on me this morning. Have you got over being robbed yet? I watched you sell that old handbag just now. From here it didn't look anything special, but that girl paid up and went off happy enough.'

'It was a good bag. She got a bargain. I'm getting over it. I have had a really good day so far. It's been really busy. I have even sold some of the rubbishy stuff that geezer fobbed me off with. I had to mend some of it and go over some of the seams. It is cheap and I have to sell it for what it is and I'll never get my money back. But what else can I do, except just carry on and be a bit cleverer in future?'

'I have been thinking. I might have a plan to get even with your man if ever we find him.'

'Fat chance of that. He's long gone.'

'How much did you give for that suitcase?'

'I paid him five hundred! I can still hardly believe that I paid him all that! I keep telling myself I was stupid, but it was a fair price for what he showed me. A light wash and iron – and maybe a bit of stitching and I would have doubled my money.'

'Maybe I could find him.'

'What good would that do? He's hardly going to give it back just because you ask him nicely, is he?'

'You never know. Stranger things, and all that. I might have an idea about it. Can I ask you a bit about your business?

'Why?'

'Let's just say I'm interested. I'm fascinated by this market. There's nothing like this in Stratford, is there?'

'There's nothing quite like it anywhere. Is this something to do with your idea?"

'Maybe! Tell me a bit about how you get your stock.'

'OK. I'll just see to that woman looking at my frocks.' She jumped up.

Tim watched as she held up the frock and held it in front of herself first and then the customer. She took the fabric between her fingers. Soon the customer did the same. Tim watched the dumb show, imagining the patter. The woman nodded, Maggie put it into a bag and held it as the woman took out her purse. When it was all done Maggie shot a triumphant glance towards Tim.

In a moment she was back.

'Oh, I love selling! She's happy, I'm happy.'

'As we were saying,' said Tim.

She sipped the last of her coffee. It was cold.

'Mabel, can we have two more of these, please?' she called. Mabel made no comment. She merely rolled her eyes as she set them down. Maggie ignored her.

'OK. Mainly I buy from people I know. I give a good price for the right quality. Quite a few ladies bring me stuff they have found in charity shops and nearly new shops. One or two will bring me bags of unsorted clothing. I always go through them and there is often some vintage labelled fashion item. They are usually pleased with what I pay them. I always buy what they bring me to keep them warm. Sometimes people come to me here on the off chance with vintage stuff. I thought that bloke was doing that.'

'What counts as vintage? Is it like Victorian furniture?'

'Anything that has gone out of fashion counts as far as I'm concerned! You'd be surprised how good quality clothing is chucked out just because the celebs have stopped being seen in that style.'

'Do you do repairs? Do you sometimes run short of stock? Can you make your own?'

'Well, yes, as a matter of fact. I am a trained seamstress and I knock out the odd replica dress from photographs. I love doing that. They sell well. Sometimes I am sorry to see them go. I wonder how they look on the buyer, but I never see them again, of course. They do very well, but it takes too long to do them properly without a proper tailor's bench. I would actually like to make a living that way. And I might if I get a bit of money to set myself up. Anyway, enough about me. What about you? Between jobs, you said. Sounds like unemployed to me.'

'Can we stay with "between jobs" for now? Or maybe, "seeking new opportunities"?'

'It still sounds like unemployed.' She darted out of the cafe. Tim could not see any customer at the stall.

Six

Ben was a pickpocket. Mergim Sharki had bought him from an Albanian trafficker who had bought him from his parents in Albania when Ben was six years old. His journey to the streets of London was a dark memory of night travel, the pervading smell of onions and the stench of human beings crowded together. Sharki quickly put Ben to work in his team of child pickpockets. The children's job was to distract the mark, receive the wallet or other small item from the dip and pass it to another child. Ben had learned his craft well as one of those, so well that Sharki trained him to become an expert dip. He became as good as Sharki himself. When he was sixteen he was allowed to be the dip with a gang of his own but was still forced to give Sharki everything. He decided that he could escape from Sharki and work alone – and keep all the proceeds for himself.

Ben *belonged* to Mergim Sharki. If Ben wanted to be free he must repay all the money Sharki had paid this man. If he did not pay, Sharki would report him to the police as an illegal immigrant. He would be arrested and sent back to Albania. His family would be 'hurt by people' back home in Albania. He must continue to work for Sharki.

Ben had other ideas. He had heard a rumour of murder and disappearance spreading among the others in the house where he was kept. Ben asked around the shadowy network of beggars, street pickpockets and shoplifters he had met in his own line of street-work. He pieced together the story of two ticket sellers who had made a protection racketeer 'disappear'. The story emerged of a man who had been throwing his weight about outside concert venues, football grounds and the big arenas. He had been demanding a cut from the earnings of the traders, programme sellers, souvenir pedlars and ticket touts. He had been tricked and had somehow disappeared. One of the touts – a well-known figure among the regulars outside sporting venues – had been beaten up by the racketeer. Nobody could tell him the details, but two ticket sellers had abruptly gone missing shortly after. Some thought that the two men had stage-managed the whole thing.

What if Sharki could be tricked somehow? What if he could be made to vanish? Ben would be free of him at last.

He set about finding the men who might be able to work the miracle of releasing him from his bondage. Nobody knew them, but the touts all knew Alfie, the one who had been beaten up. With Alfie his only lead, Ben set about his task methodically and painstakingly, starting with Alfie's beating. He tried the local A&E centre. From there he found his way to the East End. Then he went to Bournemouth.

Ben found Tim one Saturday drinking coffee in the Portobello Road café, in his usual place. Ben had worked the market occasionally, attracted by the sight of the money as well as the crowds of tourists and shoppers out for a bargain.

Ben slipped into the seat opposite Tim. 'Mr. Tim, isn't it?' he said quietly.

Tim was startled. He had not noticed Ben until the moment he spoke.

'My name is Ben and you have never seen me before. I have been looking for you since I heard about that man who beat up the man called Alfie.'

Tim glanced up sharply.

'What do you know about that?'

'Only what the guys that hang around Wembley have told me. They say that you made somebody vanish.'

'Yeah, I'm a magician. What do you want?

'If I buy you a coffee will you listen to me while you drink it?'

'OK. And you can tell me how you found me while you are at it.'

'That might need another cup. It wasn't easy.'

Ben launched into his story; how he wanted to free himself from Sharki and fend for himself. He talked quietly for an hour. He left out nothing; the journey to London, his life as a pickpocket, his perpetual servitude. He ended with his desperate need to get out of Sharki's control. Tim ordered a plate of the sandwiches always to be had wherever market traders were to be found. Tim paid for them, ignoring Ben's offers.

'That is quite a tale. I think I get it. You want this Mergim Sharki fellow to disappear – and you think I'm your man.'

'Yes. That is what I hope,' said Ben simply. He sat still in the seat, his eyes suddenly filling with tears. He brushed them away with his sleeve.

The young man who had sat down uninvited dissolved into a little boy. If Tim had had any doubts had about Ben's tale he dismissed them in that moment.

'The man who disappeared. What do you think happened to him?'

'He's in prison, some say.'

'Do you think I put him there?'

'I don't know.'

Tim spoke gently. 'I am not a policeman, Ben.'

'I don't know how you did it. Just do it to Mergim!'

'I can see why you want Sharki to disappear. Tell me all you know about him. I'm interested.'

'I will be always in your debt, Mr. Tim!'

'No. If I get you out of debt to Sharki it will not be to put you into debt with me. I need to consult my, er, colleague. I will only agree if he agrees. We are a team.'

'How will I know when you have decided? How will I get in touch?'

'You have managed pretty well up to now. You'll find me here next Saturday.'

Ben's face lit up. 'I'll be here.'

Then he stood up, left the cafe and disappeared into the throng. He seemed to leave no trace of himself.

Just then Maggie walked into the cafe and ordered her sandwich. Everything else slipped from Tim's mind.

Next Saturday Ben met Tim as arranged.

'I got some funny looks this morning,' he said. 'That is a bad sign. A dip must go unnoticed. And I wasn't even working.'

'Is that what brings you to the market here? There's always cash changing hands here. The dealers are forever flashing it about.'

'It's the work of boys. I want to live as a man now. Have you thought about what to do with Mergim? Something that gets him away from me and makes me safe?'

'I have thought a great deal. Tell me, what does Sharki do with all the money he makes? How does he spend it? Where does he keep it?'

'I think he sends some of it home to Albania. I have watched him when I could. He puts the money from the children into a bag and I have seen him take it into a little Eastern grocery shop. When he comes out there is no bag. He never seems to buy anything. I think he has an arrangement.'

'So, sending it abroad, maybe. Or transferring it into a legitimate account, something like that. Does he never spend money – on anything?'

'I have seen him go into those betting places. Maybe he likes to gamble. He has an expensive car. I have seen him go to it. He keeps it in a lock-up garage not far from our—the place where the children stay. He does not live there. He comes very often – twice a week, sometimes three times – to collect the money. He must have a big house somewhere.'

'He's rich. He would be. Rich is good, but I need something to work with.'

'He collects watches.'

'Watches?'

'Expensive ones. I think he keeps them just to gloat over. Watches are difficult to steal so the boys don't get many. Once a team brought in a watch. Mergim put it straight onto his wrist. It is the only time we saw him smile, I think.'

'Then we must sell him a watch.'

'I want to work with you, Mr. Tim. I am a good dip, one of the best. I can work alone. Most dips need at least one or two to work with. But I am tired of dipping. It is only a matter of time before I am rumbled. Those funny looks when I was looking for you. I cannot work here again.'

'You are a smart lad, Ben. Do you want a go at something a bit more ambitious? We – me and my partner – hit on a plan for Dougie and we can dream something up for Mergim. It will take a bit of nerve, but no more than picking pockets. First there is another job I am lining up. You can cut your teeth on that before we tackle Sharki. Think of it as a career move, a step up the ladder. And you won't have the cops after you because you won't have broken the law. At least that is how I want it to work.'

'Yes, please, Mr. Tim!'

'Good.' He slipped Ben a folded sheet of paper. 'Meet me here at six o'clock tonight. I'll be in the back room. Don't be put off by the folk in the bar.'

Ben slipped away. He had a way of disappearing, Tim thought.

Suddenly Maggie was sitting in Ben's seat, flushed with anger. 'I saw you with that lad. I'm pretty sure he's up to no good. He must be a thief. I've seen him sliding around the stalls. I've never caught him but I reckon he filches stuff under our noses. Is that what you are, a thief? You can tell people by the company they keep.'

'Oh, you are keeping an eye open for me! Should I be flattered?'

Maggie's face reddened even more. Tim noticed how her blushing emphasised the sprinkle of freckles across her nose. He had not noticed them before. How pretty Maggie was! Her hair was pulled to the nape of her neck with ribbon – a bit retro, as always, but still very nice.

'That was Ben. You are nearly right about him, he is – or was – a pickpocket. I am hoping that is all behind him and he comes to work for me.'

'You *are* just a common thief! I thought better of you!' She stood up to go. Tim touched her arm, gently, calmly.

'Please give me a moment. Please sit down for a second. I am not a thief. I have just offered him a job. He will not be doing anything illegal if he takes it. He is clever, with – I hope – skills I can put to good use and keep him out of trouble too.'

'What sort of job? What *do* you do for a living?'

'If Ben works for me he won't be breaking the law.'

'What are you, Tim? You seem so nice – and yet you tell me nothing. You said you would tell me. Are you a dealer? I see lots of them round here but they never ever waste their time chatting the girls up—'

'—is that what this is, Maggie?'

'I'm confused by you. You keep turning up, but—'

'—but what?'

'Nothing. Forget it.' She turned and left. Tim did not see the tears suddenly welling up.

Ben came to Greenwich that evening. He carried himself differently, more erect, less sliding in his carriage.

'Here I am, Mr. Tim.'

'Tim. Just Tim. Are you hungry? I think you should try one of Gloria's famous pies.'

In a moment Gloria appeared carrying a steaming pie with chips and gravy. He put it on the table before Ben.

'We can talk as you eat. First, how did you find me? London is a big place.'

'It is big, but not so big as it seems to somebody like you. You don't know it like I do. It was not too hard to find you.'

'How did you do it?'

'I have been on the streets since I was little. Lots of people know me. I asked about the disappearing man – Dougie? Eventually word came to me. And there you were, sitting opposite that pretty girl's stall in the Portobello Road.'

'That easy? I think there was a bit more to it than that.'

'Yes, I found Alfie.'

'You've been to Bournemouth?'

'And Hackney. And Greenwich today. I followed you here.'

'And I never saw you.'

'Nobody sees me if I don't want them to.' He put the piece of paper with the pub name on it on the table. 'I did not really need this.' He looked sheepishly at Tim.

'You have a talent, Ben. Before we tackle the problem of the disappearing Sharki there is another job I am working on.' He outlined the trick that had been played on Maggie.

'That is Maggie? The lady you look at?'

Tim passed on hastily. 'We need to find the man who took Maggie in. He is unlikely to try the same trick in the same place twice. Maybe he goes from market to market. I could never find him just by looking. He could be anywhere. I don't even know what he looks like. I think it's a job for you, Ben!'

Gloria was perfectly happy about Ben moving in upstairs. Tim was careful to explain that this was not a 'relationship'. The drag queen landlord understood. Maybe his pub was not ideal, but Ben brought out what he thought of as his 'mothering instinct'. He

58

would protect Ben. The flat was not much and he was pleased to keep it let. Tim and Jerome, when he was there, were good tenants who paid promptly, made very little noise and occasionally spent money downstairs. Gloria decided that Tim would look out for the boy – and if Tim didn't he would.

Tim briefed Ben. 'You are a clean skin here. The locals don't know you. The regulars take a bit of getting used to, but this pad is just the place for us, except for the noise in the upstairs room on Friday nights. The one who brought you the pie is the landlord. He likes to be called Gloria and the noise comes from his drag queen act. Nobody pays any attention to the upstairs tenants. Not many people even know the place exists. I think Gloria keeps discreet about it so that there is no tax to pay on the rent. There is a spare room for you. You can come and go through the back gate or down the stairs into the saloon bar. Don't be tempted to lift any wallets.'

'I want to be finished with that. Anyway, dipping needs a crowd, especially for a soloist like me.'

'When we finish this job I'm planning we will tackle Mergim Sharki, I promise.'

Ben started his search for the man by discreetly asking street kids he knew about a dodgy character who worked a switch at the markets. When asked, he indicated that a friend had a score to settle. His friends knew not to ask any more. He drew a complete blank south of the river.

He went up West and repeated the process among lads he had worked with. Some asked about why he had given up on the dipping. Some had concluded that he had been lifted by the police or been scared off by one of the minders that plagued them. He told them that he was no longer interested in dipping. He had run away from Mergim. He would never belong to Mergim again. He had a new boss and a new home.

One of a little gang of shoplifters came to him with a possible lead. He said that he had heard about something like the Portobello Road switch happening at the Camden Lock market. It had been the talk of the traders there for a few days. A man with a mixture of costume jewellery with some diamond rings amongst it had sold it at a fair price – except that the diamonds were no longer there afterwards. 'That sounds like the one I'm looking for,' he thought.

Ben decided to follow it up. He strolled through Camden Lock Market, looking at stalls which could be possibilities for a switch. One or two were selling jewellery, antiques, some clothing, but most seemed to sell craft goods they had produced themselves. He approached one or two stallholders who brushed him off saying nobody here would fall for anything like that.

He sat down to watch, eating a hot dog from a kiosk. An elderly man sat down on the bench beside him.

'I heard you asking about a switch scam. I used to do vintage stuff on the Portobello Road till I got chucked off my stall after a disagreement with the Management. Tell me a bit more about the bloke you are looking for.'

Ben outlined the scam that had been pulled on Maggie.

'That old dodge! I know who that could be. Charlie. That is just the sort of thing he used to get up to. He worked the markets years ago. Old clothes, you say?'

'Proper vintage stuff in the case when he showed it. Old rubbish after he'd gone.'

'If it is who I think it is he is called Charlie Parsons, or sometimes Charlie Pearson, or Perkins. He usually works with a woman. I think she might be the brainy one, not old Charlie. You might find him in the Bermondsey Market but I don't know what he is doing now. That's the last I heard. He could be in the nick – or dead for all I know. Why do you want to find him?'

'A friend of a friend has a score to settle, I think. Thanks. If anything comes of it I'll look you up. There could be a something in it for you.'

'They tried it on a mate of mine once, but he saw through them and sent them on their way. I hope you do find him.'

Seven

Tim was pleased with Ben's initiative. Ben stood a little taller. He was not used to praise.

'Shall I go to Bermondsey next Friday to see if I can spot him? I could ask around like at Camden Lock. Maybe somebody there remembers him.'

'Have you heard of the Kansas City Shuffle?'

'What is it, a card trick? I'm not doing Find the Lady if that's what you are talking about. It is too much bother. You spend half your day running away. And everybody is onto it these days.'

'No. It is selling something. What is on offer is shady – and the buyer knows this. The buyer – let us say, Charlie Parsons or Perkins or whatever – is offered something for sale. He knows he is dealing with a crook so he expects that the goods are stolen. He thinks he is smarter than the seller. Only he is sort of guided by the seller—'

'—In the wrong direction.'

'Yes, he goes right when we go left.'

'With his money! Oh, yeah, sounds simple enough. "Here, mate, give us your money. OK, how much would you like?" I think I should go back to dipping.'

'I am working on it, Ben. I am going to sell this Charlie something he thinks he can get more for, without any bad consequences for him because he has bought something he knows is stolen. If we have found this Charlie P – the way I see it is that I sell him something and somebody else buys it.'

Selling something I understand. Where does this buying person come it?'

'He doesn't really. He is bait for the trap.'

'Clear as mud, Tim.'

'We're going to sell Charlie P. a frock. I haven't worked out all the details yet. I am still thinking about it.'

On Friday morning, very early, Ben took a bus to Bermondsey. He wandered around aimlessly. He did not really know what he was looking for. It was all antiques that day and not very promising. After a couple of hours he paused for a rest, sitting at a table with a bacon sandwich and a cup of tea, leaning his back against the brickwork of a railway arch. He had a view of a stretch of stalls. Dozens of people sauntered past, paused to look at a stall and continued. 'All very nice but I'm getting nowhere,' he thought.

He saw a young man bump into a middle-aged fellow, mutter an apology as he slipped his hand into a pocket, slip out something – a wallet – and palm it off to a small boy. The two separated and then came together again just in front of him.

'Eddie,' Ben whispered. The young man was instantly alert. He glanced round.

'Ben! What are you doing here? This is miles away from your beat. I thought your lot stayed North of the river. Stay where you are for a second and I'll be back. Work to be done.'

He tapped the small boy on the shoulder. The boy strolled off. Eddie walked a few yards in the opposite direction stood quiet and still for a minute. When he was sure all was well he returned and sat down next to Ben.

'I heard you were on your own now. What about that minder, the—'

'—Mergim. He's not here, is he? He never crosses the river.' Ben glanced to each side, suddenly anxious.

'Easy, Ben, I haven't seen him. How is it going?'

'Fine. I'm doing other work now. I'm finished with dipping.'

'Somebody told me you were on the lookout for somebody. Is that what you are up to, Ben?'

'Yes. I know a bit more now. I think he may work on the market here. He goes by the name of Charlie Parsons. He has other names.'

'Do you mean Charlie Pearson?'

'Could be that.'

'I know about him. He is not a regular stall-holder.'

'What do you know about him? There'll be something in it for you.'

'He knows his way about. Buys and sells stuff. He's not down here so much these days since the market has gone all touristy.

He used to work the switch on traders, I heard. With a woman. She acted as decoy.'

'That sounds like him.'

'I hear that's his bread and butter work these days. He can't work the switch here. The market people know him. He fences stolen stuff to sell on to rich folk who don't care too much about where it came from.'

'What sort of things?'

'I dunno. Nothing that comes my way. This is Bermondsey. There are still people trading here from the market overt days. They still hanker after selling stolen gear in the dark. That is why this place is buzzing at four in the morning. You used to be able to sell stolen goods before dawn and the police couldn't touch you. Some of this lot still do, sometimes. What I do know is that the woman supplies collectors with specialities, rare things, no questions asked.'

'I think this sounds like the man. How do you know all this?"

'You know how it is when you are dipping.'

'Yes. You see things and you hear things.'

'Yeah, always on the alert. Particular, she is, supplying stuff to order. I think she's a trader here doing vintage clothing. People buy that stuff, dunno why.'

'This is good, but I still don't know where Charlie is, do I?'

'Try the pub on the corner, The Shepherd's Inn. Somebody there is bound to know him. Careful how you ask, though. It's not your average pub. They say you can buy anything in there, and given how free and easy the market is—'

'—I'm a big boy now, Eddie. I'll take care.'

'I'll just pop in with you and buy pies for me and my little helper. If he's there I'll give you the sign.'

The pub was dark and broody, one of those Victorian city pubs, with alcoves and corners filled with huddled men talking quietly. At the bar Ben could survey the room. He glanced about cautiously.

'That's him!' Eddie murmured. He brushed by Ben, marched towards a small group sitting at a table in an alcove. As he passed he did a quick movement of his hand only another dip would understand. He slipped out of a side door and was gone without a backward glance.

Ben stood at the bar, wondering what to do, when the man stood up and made for the door. Ben slipped out before him and stepped back against the wall. Charlie Parsons walked straight past him without a glance. Ben stepped out onto the pavement and watched him. He followed him onto the tube and all the way to a house in Kilburn.

Tim was impressed. 'That was pretty smart, Ben. Now we have to do a little bit of research on the sorts of things he looks for, what he has picked up in the past. We know he is sometimes in the – what was it, the something Inn?'

'The Shepherd's Inn, yeah.'

'Go there. Listen to the talk. You are young, they won't take much notice of you.'

'Nobody ever sees me. What then?'

'Nothing. Listen and learn.'

The next day it was quiet round Bermondsey Square, just a few wanderers and regular shoppers, a few kiosks and stalls open, doing little trade. The bar of The Shepherd's Inn was almost empty; a barman polished glasses and stared at nothing. A few regulars clustered at the bar. Ben took up station on a bench with the window behind him with an orange juice and a newspaper and a clear view of the drinking men. They spoke about the days of the market overt and the weird and wonderful characters who haunted the market in those days when the ownership of goods sold between sunset and dawn could not be challenged. Stolen goods were often sold this way – legally and without consequences. They all had a story to tell of those far-off times. Ben sat still, unheeded, taking it all in.

A young, well-dressed man entered and strode up to the group at the bar.

'I say, have you seen a man called Charlie, any of you?'

'Charlie? There's a fair few Charlies come in here, mister.' The others laughed.

'Who's asking?' One of the men looked sourly at the new arrival.

'I have a little bit of business for him. If you see him, perhaps you would kindly let him know I am looking for something he might be able to get his hands on.' He looked about the bar-room as if he was expecting the man he was seeking to materialise.

Ben thought. 'He hasn't ordered anything. He's not staying.' He quietly folded his paper, let it slip onto the bench and stood up. He was at the door before the man, held the door open and followed him out, getting a good look at him. The man stepped into a waiting car. It pulled smoothly away. Ben had time to see a peaked cap at the wheel of the car and the silver 'B' set in a pair of wings as it turned the corner.

He thought for a moment. 'Now, why would a bloke with a Bentley want to see Charlie P?'

Another thing to find out. He would have to take a chance with the gaggle of men in the bar. He would have a pie and try to get into conversation with them.

He returned to the bar, ordered a pie and another glass of juice, this time remaining standing near the group.

'Charlie is in business again!' said one. 'He used to be a regular in the market. He was always up to something.'

'Always on the hunt for stuff. It was usually the rag trade but he has bought good quality jewellery from me—'

'—when you had any! When was the last time you had anything worth more than a fiver?'

They barneyed back and forth for a while, old friends from the market's glory days.

'Last time it was frocks! He bought an old dress off a stall and went off happy as Larry.'

'Excuse me. Can you make money from old clothing?' asked Ben. 'Like antiques?'

'They *are* antiques!' cried one of the men. 'I used to sell old porcelain here at one time, till the bottom fell out of the trade. Never did frocks, though. Each to his own, I suppose.'

'Till the bottom fell out of your teapot, more like.'

'That Charlie – he's the one to talk to about vintage clothes, if he'll spare you the time, son.'

'Fat chance! He's as tight as a fish's arsehole! He plays his cards close, does Charlie. Don't bother.' He turned back to his cronies.

'He used to do the switch around the markets. Tell you what, though. I heard he's done some really big deals. I heard he tricked some pretty big fish up West with that.'

'I heard he finds stuff for collectors – the sort who aren't too bothered about provenance.'

'Like the good old days!'

The men resumed their conversation as if Ben had never spoken. Ben slipped outside. Nobody noticed him go.

He reported back to Tim.

Now they had a way to get to Parsons the way was clear for Tim's plan.

'Parsons is some kind of finder. He buys to order with specific customers in mind,' said Tim as they sat in the snug.

'Yes, that makes sense, Tim. The worst that could happen is that he doesn't want what we offer him. What will we offer him?'

'Let me explain about the Kansas City Shuffle again, Ben. I sell Parsons something, let us say a dress – a really good one, something collectable and rare – and a total fake.'

'OK, so far. That is just a con. And it is definitely a crime.'

'True. Parsons will have to believe it is much more valuable than my asking price. Let's say he finds a buyer and offers it to him for much more.'

'Like the toff in the Bentley.'

'Ah, yes, the toff in the Bentley. He's the surprise, the ace card.'

'I'm lost.'

'Let's say I offer Charlie P a really exclusive vintage dress. And the toff in the Bentley wants it—'

'—You know nothing about clothes, vintage or any other. Me neither.'

'Ah, but I do. I've been busy too. Look at this.' He pointed to one of the pictures in a magazine lying open on the table.

'It's a woman.'

'In a dress, a very famous one. That is Wallis Simpson on her wedding day.'

'Who's she?'

Didn't they teach you anything at school?'

'I didn't go to school.'

Tim gave Ben the gist of the story of how the King abdicated and married Wallis Simpson and how it caused a bit of a stir back then.

'The dress is famous. It is by a famous maker and it is in a museum in New York. This is well known among the people who are interested in such things. There is a rumour that Mainbocher, the fashion house that made the dress, made two, identical except for the colour. The bride decided on a different colour when she saw it on her. We are selling the first dress, long lost and forgotten about. The first step is getting him interested. Remember the toff in the Bentley.'

'Yeah, but how do we get hold of it? You aren't going to just find it.'

'No, we are going to make it, of course.'

'We? Should we enroll at night school? I think this is going to take some time.'

'We aren't, but I know somebody who might.'

Gloria knew a bit about fashion. When Tim next saw him he chatted a while about this and that before slipping in the name Mainbocher. Gloria knew the name.

'How could I get hold of one from the thirties, Gloria?'

'They would cost more than you can afford, Pet! They are pretty rare. They are in collections. You could probably get hold of one in poor condition. Collectors like them minty fresh and clean – or with the faint odour of their film star owner! These people can be a bit queer.' He sniggered.

'That would do. I don't want to wear it.'

'No comment, Tim. I'm a bit wrong for them myself. They are far too classy for the act, and I'd never get into one. Look at me. They were made for sylphs!'

'Where do you get your drag costumes from? Are there shops?'

'Yes, but they won't help you. You need to talk to somebody I know. In fact he comes in here sometimes. Would you like to meet him? He's quite safe, for an old queen!'

Gloria knocked on the apartment door three days later.

'He's in the snug, the bloke I mentioned. I talked to him about your Mainbocher. I think he'll help you. He is a little bit eccentric, even for this place. His name is Walter.'

'Thanks, Gloria. I'll be straight down.'

Walter wore a slightly ambiguous overcoat which hung open to reveal rather too tight trousers stretched over plump thighs and what Tim thought was a blouse. And mascara.

'Tim, is it? Gloria said you were interested in Mainbocher. A little drink, dear?' He waved his glass.'

Tim took it to the hatch. Gloria already had another ready along with Tim's usual pint. He arched one eyebrow but said nothing.

'Cheers. Yes, nothing valuable, anything really as long as it is pre-war.'

'I have nothing of his pre-war – I wish I had, dear. Lovely! The material he got for his dresses in those days! He couldn't be so particular after the war, what with the shortages and his European suppliers going out of business. Must it be pre-war, dear?'

I want it to look the part, especially the label.'

Oh, if that's your worry, you needn't concern yourself. His labels didn't change – ever. They stayed the same for forty years. It is a lovely Deco style, like cinema lettering if you know what I mean.'

'Have you got a sketch or something?'

'Here you are, dear. Look at this. This is a late model.' He tugged at a carrier bag under the seat and took out a neatly folded garment. 'Have a feel of that, dear! He was never into miniskirts – too vulgar! This one came just above the knee. Unfortunately, it has had an accident and it is a bit dog-eared.'

He unfolded it to reveal a nasty tear with some crude attempts to tidy it up.

'It came to me in this condition with another one which is much nicer. I had to buy them both but I really only wanted the other one. You can have this thing – for a song. And you know how much we all like a song here, especially upstairs!'

Tim thought he heard Gloria's snigger through the hatch. 'He's listening,' he thought.

Walter turned the skirt's waistband to expose the label, intact and undamaged. The Deco style was clear. 'Bingo!' Tim thought.

'I see what you mean about the lettering.'

'Mmm.' Walter seemed to be entirely at ease, chatting. He was savouring the moment, prolonging it. Tim thought that was a simper on his fleshy lips. There was something intelligent in his eyes. Tim thought, 'He knows what I'm up to. And he is amused.'

'OK. How much – here, downstairs, in the snug?'

'Should we say two hundred, dear?' That look was still there.

Tim did not want to appear too eager. 'Should we say one hundred?'

'One eighty.'

'One forty?'

'One sixty, dear boy, and it is yours.'

Tim counted eight twenty-pound notes, put them on the table, and that was that.

'Good luck with it, dear!'

Walter's face still had that knowing, amused simpering smile. He gave a cheery wave of his glass as Tim tucked the skirt under his arm, and leaving his own drink on the table, got up to leave.

He glanced towards the hatch, but Gloria was serving at the bar.

Maggie was in her usual place. She came over to Tim when he waved from his usual seat. The anger over Ben was forgotten. She chatted happily about the morning's business. Life had resumed its course for her. Tim liked that about her.

'I know a bit about the bloke who scammed you. I know his name. I know where he lives and where he drinks. And I've got a plan to get your money back and maybe a little bit more as compensation.'

'How will you do that? You have still not told me what you do for a living.'

Tim ignored this. 'I will need your help. You said you can make dresses.'

'Yes, I am a trained dressmaker.'

'I want you to make a special frock for me. It has to look the part. It has to convince Charlie P.'

'I can make anything! What is it you want? Is that his name, Charlie P?'

Parsons, Pearson, or Perkins. Some other names too, probably. Have a look at this.' He slid an envelope across the table. She took out a photograph torn from an old Picture Post.

'It's that Wallis Simpson, isn't it?'

'Yes. Look at her dress. Could you make it?'

'Of course I could – if I could get suitable material. It is not as if I could just pop into any shop and buy some off a roll. That will be top quality. This photo must be from the 1930s.'

'1937 as a matter of fact. It is her wedding dress. It was made by Mainbocher. Have you heard of him?'

'Of course. As a matter of fact I have sold a dress made by him. It did very well. It was so well made! The fabrics he used were exclusive to his house. He had them specially woven to his specifications sometimes. He used to insist on a very fine stitch count for his special customers. He dressed film stars. They are worth a lot of money.'

'You know a lot about him.'

'Yes, of course. One of my college tutors worked for him when she was an apprentice, in Paris.'

'Do you think you could make it, or one like it?'

'Of course I could. It looks like silk from the way it hangs. What is the colour?'

'It was famously blue, what she called Wallis Blue. To match her eyes, they say. But I want one in a different colour – pale coral.'

'Off-white, to match her morals? Or your! You are up to something, aren't you?'

'Oh yes! You will need the very best quality silk dress material. Here is some money for it.' He took out an envelope. 'Spend as much as you need. If you over-spend I'll make up the difference. I'll check with you next week. Just one more thing. I've got a Mainbocher here.'

'Let me see.'

He took out Walter's skirt. She gave it a quick look.

'That's a nasty tear. I could mend it but it would never hang properly. What a shame! I can just see some Smart Set girl in this. I bet she just chucked it out when it tore like that.'

'I don't want you to repair it. The skirt is not important. It is the label. I want you to sew it into the dress you are going to make.'

'That would be a forgery! I can't do that. It's against the law. What are you up to?'

'That's why I want you to put in another label. This.'

He held open the envelope. She peered inside.

'Oh, I see.'

'How can I reach you?'

'Mondays are my day off.' There was that blush again, he noticed. He wondered how she spent Mondays, but said nothing.

I'm here Tuesdays to Saturday.' Then she jumped up to serve a customer holding a mini-dress to herself.

Eight

Tim sat in the corner of the Shepherd's Inn in Bermondsey. It was a Friday morning and bustling as traders slipped in and out for the Shepherd's pies, popular with the traders. He was hopeful that he would spot Parsons sooner or later. If he did not appear that day there would be other ways to encounter him, even if he had to stand outside his front door until he came out. After an hour he saw a man he thought had to be him.

Parsons came from the bar with his drink and sat in the corner, not far from Tim.

'Charlie?' Tim spoke quietly.

'Who are you? I don't know you. What do you want? I'm busy.'

'I'm looking for somebody interested in a very nice frock. I thought you might be my man. If you are not, just say. I'll take it to somebody who is.'

'A dress, you say. Why do you think I would be interested?'

'I took it to somebody who mentioned you. He knows you. I know him. Let's leave it at that.'

Parsons sighed. 'I suppose I might be interested enough to have a look.'

'I've got it here.' Tim moved to the corner and sat opposite the man. 'I don't know much about frocks and such but I can tell this is a bit special.'

He pulled out a small suitcase from beneath the seat and put it on the table between them. Parsons turned the case to face him, obscuring it from Tim's view. Tim sat back, unconcerned. Parsons rummaged for a moment. Tim guessed he was looking for a house label. He would find one.

'It's silk. Feel the quality!' said Tim. 'Take it out of the case. Hold it up. Have a proper look.'

He held the dress up to the light. Nobody in the bar paid much attention. It was not unusual for deals to be done there.

'What's so special about it? I'm not falling for a pig in a poke, sonny. I wasn't born yesterday.'

'So, you are interested.'

'Might be. For the right price. What do you think you've got there, son?'

'I've seen the label. Mainbocher. He dressed Hollywood stars in his day. I reckon that it is pre-war.'

'Chuck in the case and I'll give you twenty quid for it. It is just an old frock.'

'No. Tell you what. I'll leave it for now. I might show it to somebody else. Or I'll look you up again.'

Tim took the dress and stuffed it carelessly into the case, noticing the wince on Parson's face at the treatment. He left through the side door into the alley, out onto the square and into the crowded market. Ben was leaning against the wall of the Shepherd's Inn. Tim slipped the case into a large striped carrier bag. Ben turned and was gone. In a minute he was on a bus heading back to Greenwich. He knew a little about switches himself, the way of pickpockets everywhere. If Tim was being targeted, he did not have the dress.

They need not have worried. Tim vanished into the busy market and turned to look out for Parsons. He saw him edging through between stalls. He stopped at one where a woman was trying, not very hard, to sell cheap clothing. As they talked they grew excited. Tim got nearer by pretending to examine the bric-a-brac on the stall across the aisle. He had his back to Parsons but the woman was facing him. If he was spotted now!

'I need to be sure. Three-quarter sleeves. Shoulder pads? Gathered bodice, buttons to the waist. Covered in the same silk? Tailored to the hips and flowing loosely to the floor, covering the shoes? Coral?'

'I only saw it for a moment. It had the label. I'm sure that was right. I have only seen it in photos.'

'Whatever it is it will be worth a shot at it. Let's find out what that bloke thinks it is worth.'

A voice grated in Tim's ear. 'Are you going to buy that or not?' the stallholder asked Tim. 'It's five pounds, take it or leave it.'

Tim edged away and vanished into the throng.

Ben and Tim were in the market the following Friday watching the door of the Shepherd's Inn. Tim had decided on the plan. Tim had the suitcase. He was lounging close by at a cafe table at the edge of the market where he could see the door to the bar of the pub. They did not have to wait long. Parsons turned up with the woman. They let them simmer for a while before Tim sauntered into the bar. He made his way across to Parsons.

'You!' growled Parsons.

'And good morning to you too.'

'Where is it? My, er, friend here needs to examine it—'

'—Look at this.' He held out the Picture Post photo with its ragged, torn edges. The caption was still there. It read '3rd June 1937'.

The two glanced at each other. They were doing their best to be nonchalant.

'It's an old frock,' growled Parsons. '

'Mainbocher only sold to the rich and famous. I reckon the couple in the picture were rich and famous if they were in The Picture Post.'

'I need to see the dress.' She was eager now, leaning forward on her seat.

Tim knew he had convinced the woman. She was the one with the knowledge. She had recognised Wallis Simpson, posing after her wedding. She must know the story of the second dress.

'Fair enough. Wait. I'll be back in an hour.'

Outside, he caught Ben's eye. They walked away keeping apart till they were lost in the crowds among the market stalls.

'The woman was there. She's hooked. She could hardly sit still when she saw the photo. She swallowed it completely. They are waiting for me to show her the dress. I said I'd be back in hour. Let's give it a bit longer. That'll make them keen. Keep watch. I'll disappear for a bit.'

Twenty minutes passed. Thirty. A chauffeur-driven Bentley drew up outside the Shepherd's Inn. A well-dressed young man got out and entered the inn. Ten minutes later he returned and the car sped off.

After an hour and few extra minutes Tim returned. Ben tilted his head in the direction of the Shepherd's Inn. Tim stepped through the door.

'You took your time,' Parsons muttered. The woman said nothing. Her eyes were on the suitcase. He laid the case on the table. He let the woman open it. She pulled out the dress carefully, letting the silk slide into her lap. She peered closely at the bodice. She took out a jeweller's loupe and examined the stitching. She found the maker's label sown into the side-seam of the bodice.

'Yes!' was all she said.

'Twenty pounds, then? With the case.'

'Oh, very good. Twenty thousand, more like. That is Wallis Simpson in the photo. The Duchess of Windsor.'

'Ten,' said the woman. Ten thousand.'

Charlie Parsons gawped.

'Eighteen.'

'Twelve.'

'Sixteen. In cash. That's the last word.' He turned to Parsons. 'I'll throw in the case.'

She paused. 'All right. You are sharp, I'll give you that. I will have sixteen grand by Monday. Bring the dress here and I'll pay you then. Eleven o'clock. No funny business. Make sure it is the same dress. No switching! I know you stole the dress.'

'Not me. You don't need to worry about where it came from. You've seen it. You want it. You know what it is. You did a thread count just then. You'll know if it's not the same, won't you?'

'Yes. I won't be tricked. I know this game.'

'You think you do,' thought Tim. He smiled to himself. Jerome would enjoy that.

'We are all set to go on Monday,' said Tim. This seemed easy, too easy. What if the marks were not there? Or if they had planned to simply seize the dress without paying? If there was muscle involved he would just have to make a run for it. Then the whole thing would be ruined.

'Let's change the plan, Ben. I could be walking into a trap. We need to change the venue. Make it a home fixture instead of away.'

'Not here, surely?'

'No. I know the very place, The Black Horse, off Oxford Street. We could take Parsons to the Black Horse on Monday morning. He wouldn't have time to arrange for a switch – or a simple bit of strong-arming.'

'They haven't seen me. I could let them know. I could drive them straight there.'

'That would work. You can get a car?'

'Borrow one, you mean, just for an hour? Easy, so long as I don't have to ask permission first.'

'You are a man of parts, Ben.'

'When I was fourteen twoccing was pretty much my Saturday night entertainment.'

Tim looked blank.

'Taking Without Consent. Joyriding, Tim. I can get a motor, dead easy.'

'Me too,' thought Tim. 'Right,' he said aloud. You drive up to the Shepherd's, dash in and persuade them to get into the car and drive them to the Black Horse.'

'It'll work, easy!' If they don't come with me what have we lost? Time, that's all.'

'They really want the dress, I know that.'

On Monday morning Ben drove up to the door of The Shepherd's Inn. He could not be sure Parsons and the woman would be there. If they weren't, he could simply walk away from the pub and the shiny black car. It would be a set-back, but not a disaster. He strode in, glancing around until he saw them in one of the booths. They looked tense, their eyes fixed on the door. He walked straight up to them.

'Mainbocher mean anything to you?'

Parsons nodded.

'Slight change of plan. I've got a car outside. If you want the goods come now. It's not far.'

The couple hesitated. Parsons looked at the woman. 'It is her decision,' thought Ben. 'Greed is written all over her face. She wants that dress!'

Parsons got up and went to the bar. He spoke quietly to a very large man. The man stared across at Ben.

'If this is a trick—'

'—No trick! Call off your big dog. I'm just the messenger here.' He turned to the woman. 'Get in the car or the deal is off. If there is some cheating going on it is you. He said there might be trouble and he was right. You thought you could have the goods and not the bother of parting with your money. That is what the muscle is for! If you want to do the deal, get in the bloody car!'

And she did. She stood up, gave Parsons a very hard look and strode out of the pub, a weekend hold-all clutched to her side. In fifteen minutes they were outside the Black Horse. Ben was sure they had not been followed. The element of surprise meant that unless Parsons had a car close by he had no chance of following.

The woman entered the pub. Tim held up the little suitcase. She sat opposite him. In a moment she had the dress out. She looked at it methodically. She was in no hurry. Ben took up his place in the side alley, as Tim had instructed. He had striped carrier bag at the ready.

Inside, the woman finished her detailed examination. Her face was flushed. Her voice was tight.

'Sixteen grand in here. She held out the hold-all.

'Open it, please. Let me see inside.'

Just then a policewoman burst into the bar. She made her way directly towards the woman.

'Is that your car, Madam? I saw you get out of it just now.'

The woman turned to the officer. Tim took the hold-all. He thrust the little suitcase towards her. She grabbed it. He slid out of the seat and out through the door marked 'toilets' and into the side alley.

Ben was there. The hold-all went into the plastic bag and Ben slipped away.

Tim saw the policewoman holding the arm of the woman.

'Are you sure?' the officer asked. 'It has been reported missing.'

'Yes, I had a lift from somebody – a friend – just now.'

Tim did not wait to see how Gloria would make his big finale. He could go on for some time, playing to the audience in his head.

He stepped into a Bentley which purred away into Oxford Street and disappeared into the traffic.

When Ben got back to the Greenwich pub there was a large car outside. As he approached he saw the wings of the Bentley logo. He walked into the snug. Tim was already there. Beside him was a young, well-dressed man in a suit.

'Ben, meet my old friend Jerome.'

'I've seen you! You were at Bermondsey Market. You were in the Shepherd's Inn.'

'And me.' Tim put a peaked cap onto his head.

'The chauffeur!'

'Yep. Wear a cap, Ben. It is better than a disguise. Now, the hold-all, as soon as you like.'

They counted the money. It was all there.

'Jerome here is our frock collector,' said Tim. 'He offered a hundred grand for our dress if it was genuine.'

'I still don't get it.'

'I'm the customer from Heaven. They are going to sell me the frock. I told them I would buy the dress if they got their hands on it. As Tim said, a hundred grand. I told them the tale. I said that there were two dresses made for Simpson. The original one was pale coral silk as she had specified. She just changed her mind and ordered the second dress, in pale blue – Wallis Blue as she modestly referred to it. Mainbocher had to make it, of course. He was left with the original which was impossible to sell without offending the Duchess. It emerged after her death in 1986 and promptly disappeared – into an American multimillionaire's collection where it remained until a month ago. Then there was a burglary, you see? Parsons and his friend knew that Tim couldn't have come by the dress honestly. They thought – or guessed – or hoped – he wouldn't know its value and they could convince him into selling way too cheap.'

'That's brilliant! Tim, you didn't tell me that part.'

'I wanted it to be a surprise.'

'Hello, boys! That was fun!' Gloria was posed, framed in the door to the snug, truncheon in hand, cap slightly askew.

Ben stared in alarm in his corner.

'Gloria! It is you,' he said after a moment. 'I thought we had been caught.'

'Made any arrests lately?' asked Jerome.

'I was just about to slip the cuffs on when I saw those gorgeous nails, so I let her off. No, really, I had a radio call to an emergency. I just turned round and walked off towards Piccadilly, leaving her scratching her head.'

'A radio call? Gloria, you aren't really a policeman – woman – whatever!'

'You should see my act, Pet!'

There was a squawk of static, then a harsh incoherent voice filled the snug.

'There you are. There's a little button I can press.' Gloria raised one eyebrow, waggled the truncheon and swept off. He gave a little jiggle of his broad hips as he went.

Tim and Jerome applauded. Ben laughed out loud.

'I would love to have seen her face.'

'Well, come with me tomorrow and you can,' said Jerome. I have to give her the hundred grand, remember. A deal is a deal.' His face bore a look of earnest sincerity.

'You can borrow my cap,' said Tim. Be Jerome's bag man and carry the money.'

Tim handed Ben a black document case. 'Peep inside. Just open it a crack.'

Ben saw a neat row of bundles of fifty-pound notes.

'We aren't actually paying for the dress. What's going on?'

Ben looked at Jerome, then at Tim. They looked entirely serious.

'Yeah, you will enjoy driving the Bentley, Ben. I can tell you about the power steering and everything as we go. It's got electric windows.'

'Where? What's going on? I don't understand.'

'You will.'

The Bentley drew into the car park of the Blue Water Shopping Centre, parked casually across two bays as Bentley drivers are entitled to. The spot was well chosen, quiet and lit by the low morning sun.

'Stand just over there, Ben. Keep the cap pulled down a bit. The light will be behind you so they will not really see your face. Step forward with the case, open it when I say – just a crack, as you did yesterday. Let them see it then close it, OK? Here they come.'

The woman bustled into view, carrying the little suitcase like a trophy. Parsons was close behind her. Jerome opened the rear door and she slid into the car. Ben stepped forward on cue, opened the case a crack. The pinkish red of fifty-pound notes caught the sun for an instant before he snapped it shut. Parsons nodded.

The woman flung open the suitcase triumphantly.

'Here it is. Feel that material! Here is the Mainbocher label. It is a pleasure, Mister. Let's do it again.'

Jerome unfolded the dress in silence. He took his time examining it. He took a glass to one of the seams. He looked at the Mainbocher label, nodded. He continued painstakingly.

'I must be sure, he said. 'You will understand.'

'Yes, yes. But don't take all day.'

He turned the neck. He paused. He frowned. A fine thread was loose. Jerome gave it a tug. The seam parted beneath his hand to reveal another, tiny, label.

'What's that?' He pointed to the label printed with the words 'Deluxe Retro. Made in China.' There was a printed bar-code.

'Get out.' He gave her a shove. 'Take your frock with you. Evans. Drive. Now.'

Ben stepped smartly forward. The Bentley swept out of the car park.

'Oh, I get it!' said Ben. 'We have let them know that they have been conned.'

'Maybe. They can't be sure. It is plausibly deniable, as they say. Maybe Tim was tricked. Maybe the American multimillionaire was tricked. Maybe there never was a version of that dress in pale coral. Who knows?'

Tim had his moment with Maggie when he next saw her.

'I owe you an explanation, I know,' he said over their customary coffee. 'First, your money. I said I would get it back.'

'Was it got honestly, Tim? I would really like to know who you are. I won't take the money if it was stolen.'

'Tim, from dear old Stratford, of course! And it wasn't stolen.'

'That is who you used to be. That Tim didn't go about with loads of money to throw around. I like you, Tim. I want to know who you are if—'

'—if what, Maggie? I like you too, you must know that. I am still the Stratford lad inside. I suppose I have changed a bit. Let me tell you about Jerome and me. Then I'll tell you about the money. Maybe you will be able to work out who I am these days.'

Tim talked about his and Jerome's beginnings, selling theatre tickets to tourists and taking commissions from restaurants for bringing in custom. He left out the part about Jerome's life on the street. He left out the part about his own hurried departure from his bullying father. He explained how they tried to sell match tickets and concert tickets round Wembley, how they were on the point of giving up and how they encountered Alfie the veteran ticket tout; how they helped him when he was ill; and how they had avenged him for the beating he received from Dougie.

He told her that they had found the thieving couple who had worked the dodge on Maggie; how they had done it to others. He told her how much they had received for the replica frock from the woman with the painted nails who had rummaged through her stock – the man's partner in crime.

'So here is the money you paid for the suitcase of clothing. We could not have done it without you!' He handed over a brown envelope.

'It still does not seem very honest. You still as good as stole it from—'

'—from a crook who stole it from you – and who knows how many honest traders he has swindled over the years? And don't forget the woman. Young Ben realised that she was the brains, not Charlie, when she had your dress in her hands and took over the deal from Charlie. It was Charlie who did the switch while she distracted you with all that rummaging through your stock. She took the original case and Charlie handed over the rubbish. Take the money, Maggie. It's yours. You earned it by honest business. They stole it from you – and we got it back.'

'We? You mean you and that shifty character I saw you with? Ben, you said.'

'Yes, Ben. You were right about him. He *was* a pickpocket. He was trafficked into the country in the back of a lorry full of Albanian onions by a very dodgy guy – Albanian, probably. He helped us, but he never broke the law. I told you – and him – he wouldn't have to.' Tim didn't mention the detail about the 'twoccing' – taking the car without consent – at the crucial moment. 'And Jerome, of course.'

'The fact remains, Tim. You and this Jerome conned these people out of their money. That's what you are – confidence tricksters!'

'We are not thieves, Maggie. We did not steal the money. It was handed over for goods received. I will admit that the item was something of a disappointment for the buyer. Take the money, Maggie. Put it towards that business you want to set up.'

'I really do want to make top quality clothing. I suppose it is mine. I *was* robbed and now, by a wonder, I've got all my money back.'

She took the envelope, pushed it into her apron pocket, stood up, walked calmly round the table. Tim stood, awkwardly scraping his chair back.

She kissed him.

Mabel the waitress called out to everyone in the place.

'Thank Gawd for that! That's been a long time coming!'

Maggie blushed, swept out of the cafe leaving Tim in front of the applauding customers.

The snug was unusually full. Tim and Jerome sat in their usual corner. Kate sat opposite Jerome, sophisticated as always. Her new job was paying well. She had splashed out a bit. Maggie perched on a stool, dressed in a sixties outfit originally from Biba and tailored to her own figure.

Gloria popped his head through the hatch occasionally. Their glasses were refilled without them asking. Gloria was in a fine, generous mood, still a little puffed up over his stint as the 'police officer with the walkie-talkie'. They were celebrating their success with the 'Mainbocher' dress, and all were in fine fettle.

Ben, as always, was on the periphery. It was a deeply ingrained habit which he never seemed to shake off. He was 'an illegal' and being invisible was a way of life, his safety. Here he felt more secure than he could remember. The shadow of Sharki had receded – for now. He never crossed the river. He would not find him here.

Tim and Jerome decided to have a few days away from London. Jerome would return to Stratford to see his mother. Tim fancied a weekend in Paris with Maggie. Maggie agreed to get a pal to run the stall for a couple of days.

'What about me? I cannot go anywhere.' Ben hunched into the corner. 'I have felt safe here for the first time ever.'

Kate looked hard at Ben. She had not paid him much attention up to this point. Now she saw the fear that lurked in his restless eyes. She noticed how he seemed to be in perpetual shadow. She decided he was just a boy who needed his mother.

'You need a holiday too, Ben,' she said. 'Come with Jerome and me to Warwickshire for a few days.' She turned to Jerome. 'Couldn't he stay in the flat with you? I should probably stay with Mum and Daddy for a couple of days. Mum gets horribly lonely these days.'

'Ben, would you like that? You are a free agent now, you know. It is up to you.'

'Warwickshire? Where's that?'

'Not far away from here.'

'Far away from Mergim?'

'Oh, yes, far enough!'

So it was agreed. Ben looked at beautiful Kate adoringly. He had never met anyone like her in his life.

'That brings us to our next business,' said Tim. 'Ben here needs to be done with that Mergim Sharki character. We need to think of a way to make that happen.'

'I know what's coming,' said Jerome. '"I've been thinking..."'

'Funny that. It's just what I was going to say.'

Nine

Tim and Maggie were on the Eurostar on the way back to London when Tim brought up the subject of Ben.

'I meant it when I promised Ben to fix his minder, Maggie.'

'Mm? I'm still dreaming about Paris. I've had a lovely time and I am not ready to think about tomorrow. The women are so stylish. I don't think I saw a single woman who wasn't well-dressed. And the clothes shops – so chic!'

'And the restaurants and those little places with sort of glass fronts right over the pavement. I've never eaten so much good food. Every time we sat down – anywhere we went.'

'Mm. I've never had oysters before. I didn't expect to like them, but I did. I think the champagne helped.'

'I loved that boat trip up the river. You don't get that in London. And the oysters – and champagne. We must go back some time.'

'So, what about Ben? He's a sweet boy. He is like a man in some ways, and yet so boyish sometimes. I think he's sweet on Jerome's sister.'

'Kate? She is a bit old for him. She's older than Jerome. She's nearly as old as me.'

'I didn't think he was exactly fancying her the other night. Didn't you see him? He just sat in his corner and worshipped her. I don't think he has met anybody like her in his entire life. To be fair, I don't think I have either. It is as if she had cast a spell on him.'

'I don't think Ben has had much of a family life. He was only little when he came here. I think his father sold him. That tells you something about what kind of life he had, doesn't it?'

'You want to help him. That's lovely. But what can anybody do?'

'Dunno. We have got him away from his keeper. He's safer with Jerome and me but we can't be there all the time. Have you seen that hunted look in his face?'

'He is like a rabbit. He is always checking sudden noises. If I didn't know anything about him I would call him shifty. I wonder how he is getting on in Stratford.'

'Maybe he will be feeling safer there. Jerome says his family are well off. They've got a factory or something, and a big house in the country.'

'So why does he hang around with you?'

'That is a story for Jerome to tell, not me. I've been thinking. Sharki collects watches. We should sell him one. I don't know anything about watches except that they can be very expensive – Rolexes and that sort of thing."

'Me neither. But I know somebody who does. And so do you. Mr. Goldman.'

'That nice old guy who has a stall just two or three down from you at the market?

'Moshe. Yes, he really knows his stuff. To look at his stock you wouldn't really know, but he deals in really big-ticket timepieces – clocks as well as watches. He showed me an antique clock once. He said it was four hundred years old. Imagine! He is a lovely, gentle old man. I wouldn't want him to be put in any danger because of some wild idea you might have.'

'You helped over Charlie Parsons and you were never in any danger. None of us were, because we built in a little safety device – your 'Deluxe Retro' label, remember? I would never want anybody to take risks.'

'What about Kate? She took some risks in that little boat, didn't she?'

'I suppose so. Are we having a quarrel?'

Maggie squeezed Tim's arm.

'I hope not. Moshe is a sweet old gent. I don't want him involved in anything risky.'

'I promise he won't be. I only want him to explain about watches, not to go anywhere near that man Sharki.'

'He loves to talk about them. They are his passion – those and the proper antique clocks he deals in.' Maggie snuggled in close. 'Let's change the subject. We are still in France.'

Tuesday was a gloomy sort of day. Rain clouds blocked the spring sun. A few souls pottered about the Portobello Road. It was one of those slow days. Tim sat in his usual seat as Maggie did her best to sell to a few loiterers. Nobody's heart seemed to be in it that day.

Mr. Goldman entered the cafe.

'Mabel! My usual tea, please, and another coffee for Romeo.' Goldman sat at Tim's table.

Mabel brought Tim's coffee and set down a little glass in a metal holder.

'On miserable days Mabel puts a shot of slivovitz in it for me. How was Paris?'

'Very Parisian, thank you. Have you been talking to Maggie?'

They chatted for a while. Goldman knew Paris from his youth when he had worked with his uncle, dealing in jewellery and antiquities in the Marais. He talked fondly of his days there, laughing and occasionally pausing to let out a sigh. At last he stopped reminiscing, set down his glass and came abruptly to a point.

'Maggie says you have become very interested in watches.'

'I'll be straight with you Mr. Goldman. You will be doing me a favour—'

'—and that young lad I've seen round the market?'

'Yes. What has Maggie told you?'

'A bit. Why don't you tell me what you are up to?'

Tim explained about Ben, his history, how he was an illegal, a trafficked child and how he wanted to be done with his keeper, Mergim Sharki. Tim had decided to undertake the task.

'Poor child!'

'Ben says Sharki collects watches. Most of his collection is probably stolen. Wristwatches are hard things to steal, but they have come his way through his gang of thieves. That is how Ben knows about them. My idea, such as it is, is that I obtain a watch he wants, offer it to him in exchange for Ben. That is, a condition of sale would be for him to give up his claim on Ben, like part-exchange. I know it is a bit vague so far. I'm still thinking about it.'

'And how do you think I can help?'

'My knowledge of watches and clocks is enough to tell the time, but that is about all.'

86

'You think I can give you an education? I have been in this business for forty years and I am still learning.'

'I really only need to know about one watch – the one that I have for sale.'

'You have a watch to sell?'

'No, not yet.'

'You want to sell a watch to an expert, but you haven't got one and you don't know the first thing about them. I have heard better plans.'

'It is a bit thin, I agree,' said Tim. 'I still need to think it through. I will think of something.'

'Many men who collect expensive watches, like this Sharki, are both buyers and sellers, collectors but also investors. This Sharki perhaps could be tempted to buy if the price is a bit low or if he thinks the value will increase.'

'Mm. I can see that.'

'Get to know him, maybe learn about the watches he already has and which he most desires – find out what his passion is, what he most desires. If we are to catch him out we must get to know his weakness. He will not be interested in just any timepiece if he already has one – unless he also sells.' Moshe stopped. He looked hard at Tim. 'This, I think, is what you do better than me.'

Tim said nothing. 'He sees through me,' he thought.

Moshe resumed. 'If this man bought – or sold – rare watches it is likely I would know of him. After forty years in the business, I know a lot of such people. I don't know him.'

'We? You said, if we are to catch him out.'

'I did. Maggie likes you. I am fond of her. I think you need a hand with this so-called plan of yours. What a thing to happen to a little boy! Where is Ben now?'

'He is tucked away in Warwickshire, away from Sharki and anybody who might lead Sharki to him. Ben is certain that Sharki will want him back, and he is really afraid of him.'

'If you can persuade him, bring Ben to me. I would like to talk to him.'

'I will need to find Sharki before I can do anything, even supposing I come up with something. Ben will know how to find him. I had better get him back to London. When we meet again I hope to have a proper plan, Mr. Goldman.'

'Moshe. Call me Moshe. Maggie's friend is my friend. And I might just have some ideas of my own.'

Jerome brought Ben back to the flat in Greenwich. His clothes were new. His hair was cut. His shoes were polished.

'Kate has taken him in hand. She decided she would take him to meet the family. Mother has been spoiling him with proper breakfasts. I swear he has grown out of his old clothes.'

'He visited your parents? What did they make of him?'

'They both took to him. I could have been quite jealous!'

'Ben! How did you like Warwickshire?'

'I loved it. Jerome's garden is bigger than a park!'

'I have a bit of a plan, Ben. I need to find Sharki. I think you are officially our finder now, after that business with Charlie Parsons and the lady.'

'He is a scary man.' Ben looked almost ready to run off at the mention of the name. 'I can find him easy, Tim. He collects the money and the credit cards regularly from the house. He must not see me. He will want me back if he sees me.

'Trust me, Ben. I will be beside you. He won't get you if I'm there. First we will visit Maggie. She has a friend who might help us – help you. He wants to meet you. Don't worry, he is nothing like Sharki.'

Tim and Ben sat in the cafe on the Portobello Road. Maggie waved and turned back to her customers. It was a busy day. The market was crowded. Mr Goldman slipped into the seat opposite. Mabel brought him his special tea – with the dash of slivovitz in it. He greeted some of the regulars in the place with a smile and a wave. Then he turned to Ben.

'Thank you for coming. I have heard about you from Tim and my friend Maggie. I know you from your game in the market. I hear you want to live in a different way.' His eyes were penetrating. Ben's shiftiness had gone. He returned the gaze steadily.

'Yes, sir, I want to get away from—'

'—Mergim Sharki. He wants you to work for him still, is that right? What are you worth to him?'

'He treats me – treated me – as if I am worth nothing. I belonged to him. I was his best—'

'—dip. Pickpocket.' Moshe said it very quietly. 'I know. I am an old man but my eyes are sharp. I know a dip when I see one. I saw you.' Then he spoke up again. 'Mergim Sharki will not let you just walk away. He will want to keep you. Your skills are valuable to him. He trained you, am I right? You want a better life?' Ben nodded. 'Tim here has offered to help you. I am offering to help Tim. You have been treated cruelly. I don't like that. I know something about cruelty myself.'

He turned to Tim.

'Look at this.' Mr. Goldman took out an envelope from his overcoat pocket. He slipped out a wristwatch and laid it on the table. 'This is for you. Let me tell you about it.'

Tim picked up the watch. It was heavy. He looked casually at the face. He saw that there were three small dials within the main face, and the correct day and month showing in little oblong windows. He turned it about in his hand. The case and the bracelet certainly looked like gold.

'It looks expensive.'

'Yes, it is expensive, but it is not the real thing. Look at the name on the dial.'

'Patek Philippe. I know the name.'

'Yes, it is famous. The most expensive watch ever sold was a Patek Philippe. So it is to be expected that it is the most faked. And that makes such watches the most carefully scrutinised. This one is fake, of course, but it is very good. The weight of it, the look of the dial, the pointers, the numeral markings, everything. Even the back looks right. It will fool most people. It fooled me. I bought this piece forty years ago. I spent almost everything I had, because I was convinced. Now look closely at the name. Read it.'

'Patek Philippe. As I said.'

'Correct. Now look at the day and date apertures. See the size and shape. They are the wrong size. It is a tiny detail. Almost everybody would miss it. This watch, known as 'ref 1518', was brought out in 1941. The name on the front was 'Patek Philippe & Cie'. Those apertures are right for the 1518 which was made throughout the War. After the War the company changed the watch slightly. The '& Cie' was dropped and the day and month apertures were reduced – by less than a millimetre all round.'

'So the apertures are from 1941 and the name is later.'

'Yes, from 1956 at the earliest.'

'Who would be able to spot that?'

'Me, for one. I can see it for what it is now! I only saw what was wrong when I saw another of the post-war models. And they were side by side.'

He sat back, sipping his tea and slivovitz. For a moment he was lost in thought.

'Ah, Elye my friend, where are you now?' He sighed and took another pull at his drink. 'Elye was the friend who set me right over my unsellable watch. He pointed out the difference in the aperture size. He taught me nearly everything I know. He even let me have some of his stock at cost price – well, almost! Now, the question is – would Mergim Sharki spot it? Maybe he would. I had to see the real and the fake together. Very few people can ever do that, because both the real ones and the fakes are so rare. We should put it to the test.'

'I would have to bring him to you. I don't like the idea of putting you in any danger.'

'You won't if you take it to him. You can borrow the watch.'

'I was going to offer to buy it, but something tells me—'

'—it is not for sale? Maybe I would sell it. I am a dealer, after all. Something tells me you couldn't afford it! It is a fake, but even fakes have a value, especially a rare one like this.'

Tim laughed. 'You will lend it to me? I think it means more to you than money.'

'Put it on. Let us see it on you.'

Tim slipped the watch over his hand. It sat snugly, almost inconspicuous, on his wrist.

'It looks all right.'

'If it was the real thing, who knows, maybe £200,000. One sold at Sotheby's in New York for that.'

'And this one?'

'I should not sell it. I have a reputation as an honest man. Maybe I should really destroy it. I keep it as a reminder of the lesson I learned.'

Tim turned to Ben.

'I will need to get to Sharki.'

'I will take you to him, easy,' said Ben. 'I can show you where he will be, at least. He won't see me.'

'Are you not afraid, Ben? asked Moshe.

'Yes. But I will do it.'

'I will do the rest,' said Tim.

'What will you do? asked Moshe.

'I'm still thinking about it.'

'He's there.' Ben pointed to a figure in the distance. He was walking along the street. He was a nondescript figure, easily ignored. There was nothing memorable about him. He was little more than a brown shadow cast by a low sun on the brown pavement.

'He doesn't look very scary,' said Tim. 'Or rich.' He looked down at Ben, who had edged back and was out of sight of the man.

'He is cruel. He has no heart. He used to beat me when I was small. All of us were terrified.'

'I doubt if he would dare to now. Where is he going, do you think?'

'He'll be going to the shop where he never buys anything. Ali's.'

'I am going to get closer. You had better be off. Your job is done here.'

Ben had already turned into an alleyway Tim had not noticed was there. 'He trained me to be difficult to see. I learned well. He will not spot me. Go, Tim. Do not lose sight of him.'

Tim walked briskly in Sharki's direction, passed directly in front of him and entered a grocery store. He hoped this was the right place. There were piles of boxes in front of the windows with tired looking fruit and vegetables displayed on top. The shabby facia was half obscured by the torn awning which hung over it. He could see the letters 'Al' in peeling green paint and hoped he was right.

Sharki walked in behind him, ignoring the woman keeping shop and disappeared behind a plastic curtain. Tim shuffled about, feeling conspicuous. He seemed to be the only customer in the place and he could almost feel the woman staring at his back. He turned to her.

'Have you any milk?' he asked. She pointed to a cabinet immediately behind him. He picked up a large plastic bottle of milk and went to pay. Sharki emerged from the rear of the shop just at that moment and strode outside. Tim fumbled his change in his haste to keep him in view. The woman paid no notice as he called his thanks and darted out of the door. He need not have worried. Sharki was in plain view, his shadowy figure moving purposefully.

Tim followed him to a betting shop on the corner. Tim thought it was risky to go inside. He found a grimy little cafe over the street where he could watch without being seen. He smiled inwardly at the sign over the betting shop – Wallie Crookes. 'You couldn't make it up,' he thought.

Sharki was there for an hour. At last he left and returned the way he had come. Tim caught the expression on his face. He was scowling and muttering to himself. Tim had to decide whether to follow or to see if he could find out about him from inside the betting shop. There was not much point in just trailing along behind him. He was after knowledge which might be useful. On an impulse he crossed the road and stepped inside the betting shop. A listless bunch of men were watching a horse-race on television. Tim had been in betting shops before and knew the drill, though he had never seen the point of that sort of hopeless gambling. Nobody paid him any attention. He found a place in the corner and turned the pages of one of the Sporting Life newspapers lying around. He had no idea of what to do next.

Then he had a stroke of luck. Sharki returned, stood opposite him with his back turned. He watched as Sharki took a bite out of a sandwich, consulted the newspaper and scribbled on a betting slip with one of the scattered little pens.

Two men approached him. One muttered something Tim could not quite catch. Sharki shouted at the men, tore up the betting slip and chucked it on the floor. He stood up, shaking with rage. Tim thought he was about to strike one of them. Sharki seemed to think better of it, gathered himself and pushed past the two men. He made for the door, muttering, his face twisted in his rage.

Tim sat still. If he left to follow Sharki he would draw attention to himself. He might learn more if he stayed put. He buried his face in the Sporting Life. He glanced at the tv screen. A horse race was in progress, watched raptly by the shabby clientele. Nobody paid any attention to him.

One of the men called to the man behind the glass screen.

'Wallie, I'm sick of that Mergim! You should ban him or something. I only asked him the time. There's no need for that. He almost hit me just now.'

The second man broke in. 'I'm sick of him always calling me a loser. I win as often as he does, don't I?'

'Yeah, what's so bloody clever about him? We are as good as him any day, bloody jumped-up bastard!'

Wallie, the man behind the glass looked out calmly.

'I can't bar him just because you don't like him. His money is as good as yours. This is a business, even if you think it is social club for you and your mates. You aren't forced to come here, are you? Anyway, what's he done?'

'I only asked him the time. Why would he get angry about that?'

'You didn't want to know the time, did you? There is a big clock on the wall behind you. You were having a go at him because you think he's a thief, weren't you?'

'It was a joke! He's always showing off some classy watch or other.'

'He is a thief. I've heard the rumours,' the second man said.

'You don't know that,' said Wallie from behind the screen. 'I heard a rumour that you had got a job. I don't pay attention to rumours,' said the man behind the glass.

'Well, I reckon he is dodgy,' said the first man. 'He bets large. He always has money. Where does it come from, all that cash? Eh?'

'Maybe he works for a living. Not like some.'

'He comes in here at all hours. He can't be doing what I call regular work.'

'And what do you call regular work?' said Wallie, safe behind the glass. 'When did you last do regular work?'

'Wallie's got a point, Jimmy,' the second customer said. 'The hardest work you do is signing on.'

The race on the screens ended. Men tossed slips onto the floor and made off. One went to the counter and pushed his betting slip through the aperture. The man called Wallie paid without a word. The talk about Sharki was ended by the transaction. The two men left the shop.

'What was all that about?' asked Tim through the grille.

'Pay no attention. They are jealous because Mergim got a bit of a win the other day.'

'Is he a big player?'

'Nah! Not like on the course. I've taken thousand-pound bets at Ascot, no bother. But he is the biggest of the regulars in here. He never stays long, like some, just a couple of bets and he's gone.'

The last of the gamblers made his way to the door, leaving Tim alone with the man who was clearly the proprietor. That had been the last race of the afternoon. The screens went blank.

'You're too late to put a bet on today's races. If you want odds for tomorrow be quick about it, I'm closing up.'

'I had a tip but I missed the off. Just as well, it did nothing. About that guy, er, Melvin was it? Those two didn't like him, did they?'

'Mergim. Nobody does. He's been coming in on and off for years and never has anything to nice to say to anybody. This place is a bit of a club for some of the punters. A lot of them know each other and there's usually a bit of banter, especially if somebody has a decent win. Mergim never joins in. He wins now and again, but no more often than the rest. Nobody gets on with him. He's more trouble than he is worth.'

'Oh, how do you mean?'

'It's his sour-faced attitude. He gets people's backs up. I couldn't tell you how many people have stormed out over some remark or other he has taken offence to.'

'Strange name, isn't it?'

'I heard he is Albanian. It's no skin off my nose, his money is as good as anybody's. Some of the regulars reckon he is bent, but I don't know. Don't want to. I can't afford to be too choosy about where their money comes from.'

If Tim was to glean anything now was the moment. He took the plunge. 'What, a crook? What sort of thing does he get up to? He has the look of a gangster now you mention it.'

The man stopped checking the till roll and looked hard at Tim. 'You are not from round here, are you? What has Mergim done? Are you checking up on him?'

'Why, what *has* he done?'

'Are you checking up on this place? I run this place and it is straight.'

'No, no, not at all. I was just chatting.' Tim thought he had misjudged the moment. Wallie glanced around as if to check on eavesdroppers. He lowered his voice even though there were just the two of them in the place.

'There are rumours he has some kind of property, houses he lets out to immigrants – illegals. I wouldn't put it past him. He's never short of money, I know that. I see him taking twenties off a big roll.' Wallie stood back and continued in a louder voice. 'I'm locking up now. Look at the mess. I put waste bins out and they just chuck their slips onto the floor. At least they are ones I don't pay out on!'

Tim grunted and turned to the door. The watch thing seemed to be confirmed. Maybe he liked to wear his watches. He would return and make contact.

Tim visited Wallie Crookes' place again and mixed a little with the regulars. He placed small bets entirely without success. Jimmy was the first to comment on his poor bets, and Tim agreed.

'Maybe I should take a few tips from you.'

' I wouldn't if I was you,' replied Jimmy's pal from the other day. 'Jimmy never wins either.'

After several days Sharki made his appearance in the betting shop. Tim observed him over a copy of the Racing Times. He joined him at the hatch just as he was placing a bet.

'Excuse me.' Tim pushed his betting slip towards the counter. His arm poked out of his shirt-sleeve. Moshe's watch was briefly under Sharki's nose.

'What do you fancy?' asked Tim.

Sharki ignored him. Had he noticed the watch in the under-powered strip lights?

They both withdrew, Tim back to his spot near the back wall. After a minute or two Sharki came over to him.

'Nice watch.'

'Oh? It's my dad's. He says it is valuable.' Tim shoved his arm out again for a second. He watched the scowling face. He saw for an instant the flicker of interest.

'Valuable, you say? Lots of fakes about. Probably a fake.' He thrust out his arm. 'This one is real. I show you.' Sharki's face was transformed. A look of earnestness had replaced the scowl. Tim suddenly thought of Moshe saying you could only tell if the two were side by side.

'Here. Look. Patek Philippe. It is good watch, not fake.' He slipped it off his wrist and held it towards Tim's face. 'See the face. Swiss made.' Sharki put the watch into Tim's hand for a second before whipping it away and back onto his wrist.

'I am sure you are right. When I see Dad I'll tell him I've seen a real one. How could I tell if my old man's is a fake?'

'Feel its weight. Fakes are lighter.'

'I see what you mean. Yours felt heavy for something so small. You can see the class.' He took off Moshe's watch. ' Oh, this is quite heavy as well. Feel it.'

Sharki took the watch in his thin fingers. He turned it over and back again. For an instant Tim saw a look of greed pass across Sharki's face, a glitter in his eye under the neon lighting. Then the old scowl returned. The moment had passed.

Tim left it for a week before he returned to Wallie's betting shop. He sat in the cafe across the street until Sharki appeared.

'Now is the moment,' he thought.

Inside the scene was unchanged. 'The same hopeless men chasing the same unlikely dreams,' he thought. He slipped into his usual place and picked up one of the creased racing papers. His lips moved a little as he read through the lists of horses.

'You.' Tim glanced up. Sharki was suddenly standing next to him, just a bit too close.

'Hi, er, er—'

'—Call me Mergim, please.' A ghastly smile appeared on Sharki's face. This was Sharki being nice. Tim thought he was out of practice.

'I wondered if I might bump into you again,' said Tim.

'You still got the watch?'

'I mentioned what you said about the watch. Dad doesn't care about it being a fake. It was his dad's – my grandfather's, that is. He says it has sentimental value 'cos he was given it on his deathbed – my dad, that is. Here is my grandfather in this photo. He was in Germany – Munich, he said – at the end of the War.'

Tim laid the photograph on top of the open Racing Times. It was dog-eared and torn. It showed a man in uniform with an American and a British soldier flanking him.

'That is my grandfather there. The big fellow is the one he got the watch from. He never said who he was.'

'He was given the watch by this man?'

'That's what he told my dad. He said the German bloke committed suicide shortly after. There was a big fuss about it, apparently. He was a German general or something. What do you fancy in the next race? I think I'm going for Gets Her Man. She likes the heavy going.' He looked up from the photo. Sharki was half-way to the door.

'That went well,' thought Tim. He slipped out after him and followed him to a row of lock-up garages behind a block of flats. He emerged in a big black car.

Tim stayed away from Wallie's for two days. The third day he was there as Wallie slid back the locks on the front. Sharki was not far behind him, his habitual scowl grimmer than ever.

'I see your watch again? I am interested. Maybe I buy it from you for a good price?'

'Well, there's the thing, Mergim. It's my father's watch, not mine. At least not yet. He's going a bit, you know, senile. He doesn't always know what day it is, if you see what I mean.'

'Tell your father I give him good price.'

'The way things are with him I don't think he will understand much. He's on his own. He doesn't look after himself. He is going downhill. I thought I'd look after his watch for him, sort of. He doesn't really know I've got it.'

'That photo. Is it real?'

'Of course it's real, what do you think?'

'I'd like to buy the watch. And the picture. I will give one thousand pound.'

'You know, I'm not as green as you think. I reckon it is worth more than that. See you tomorrow.' Tim stood up and was gone before Sharki could speak.

The next day Tim found him again in the betting shop.

'I have been asking around. I reckon the watch is worth a lot more than you offered. So let's put it to the test. One hundred thousand pounds.'

'That is impossible!'

'You want me to steal it from my dying father. You offered me peanuts. I reckon you really want the watch.' He raised his arm to reveal it, shining on his wrist. Sharki stared at it. His face worked as he struggled to look unconcerned.

'How can I get in touch?' said Tim. I won't be coming back to this place again for a bit. I'm sick of it.'

Sharki scribbled a telephone number on a blank betting slip. 'After seven any night. I will answer.'

'He has taken the bait,' thought Tim. He left Wallie Crookes's betting shop for the last time. He had arrangements to make.

They were in the crowded concourse of Euston Station. It was Saturday evening and crowds of commuters, shoppers and day-trippers were heading for their trains. Others were lingering in front of the information boards. A school outing streamed through. Football supporters wearing their team strips were milling around. The police escorts were keeping a close eye on them. A Salvation Army brass band was playing hymns. Unintelligible announcements echoed round the concourse.

'Do you think he will come?' Maggie sat on a bench against one of the giant pillars with a giant shopping bag marked Harrods beside her. Moshe and Jerome flanked her.

'He will come.'

'Will he have the money?'

'He might try to cheat us,' said Maggie.

'He already thinks he has cheated us. We will out-cheat him,' said Tim as calmly as he could. 'Here he comes. That's him in the dark coat. You know what to do. No eye contact. You are strangers waiting for trains.'

Maggie looked nervously at Tim. He smiled back, hoping he looked more confident than he felt.

'Now, Maggie, go.' Maggie stood and picked up her shopping bag. She strode away, leaving a space between Jerome and Moshe. She melted into a crowd of Aston Villa fans under the eyes of the special constables patrolling the concourse.

Sharki hesitated for a moment. He glanced round the concourse in his shifty way.

Tim stepped forward.

'Here, Mergim, sorry to drag you all this way. I just wanted to be sure. Are we all set?'

'Yes. The money is all here. It was hard to get it together in the time.' He took out a cloth bag and opened it enough for Tim to see the wads of fifty-pound notes done up in elastic bands. 'Let me see the watch.'

Tim took an oblong box from his pocket and opened it in front of Sharki. The watch lay on a silk lining, gleaming in the station lighting. Tim lifted it out so that it dangled in front of Sharki. Sharki stared hard at the watch. At last he nodded.

Tim returned the watch into the box. 'How do I know that the money is all there?'

'It is there, all of it. See.' He took out a wad and riffled through it. Tim could see the pinkish red of fifty-pound notes.

'Do that with another bundle.'

Sharki did so.

'The photograph. I must have that!'

'Here.' Tim held out an envelope. Sharki snatched it from him.

Tim took the money-bag and Sharki took the watch in its box. He slipped it into the pocket of his coat.

At that moment a woman in Salvation Army uniform and bonnet took Sharki's arm. Sharki whirled round.

'What do you want?'

'The War Cry,' she said. 'Buy a copy. Every penny goes to help the downtrodden, Pet.' She held on tightly to his arm and waved a copy of the magazine in his face.

'Go to Hell!' Sharki pulled away from the woman. There on the seat before him sat Ben. Sharki stared, amazed.

'You! Why are you here?'

'I should have mentioned. Ben here is part of your payment. He is free of you now,' said Tim calmly.

'That was not part of the deal. Ben, come with me now or else—'

'—or else what?' Jerome stepped between Ben and Sharki.

'What has this got to do with you? Keep out of my business.'

Moshe suddenly called out.

'Help me, please! Call an ambulance! Ooh! Aah! Help me!' He waved his arms about and wailed in agony. Maggie saw Moshe's wave. She pointed him out to a pair of special constables. They turned away from the football fans and strode across the concourse.

'Are you all right, sir?' asked one of the officers. Sharki kept his face turned away from the officers.

'All right. Have the boy,' Sharki snarled. 'I've got the watch.' He patted his pocket. He could feel the bulk of the box inside. 'A hundred thousand?' His eyes blazed, triumphant. 'You fool!'

He slipped into the crowds making their way to their platforms. In a moment he disappeared as another phalanx of football fans barged into the concourse.

The Salvation Army struck up a rousing hymn.

Monday at the Portobello Road market was mainly fruit and vegetables. Mabel was surprised when regulars from the antiques and vintage days turned up in her cafe. They squeezed into a corner table away from the door and the noise of stallholders calling out their wares. Once settled and the pleasantries exchanged, Tim began. 'I have counted the money and it was all there. I hope you noticed my little surprise – it was Ben's idea to have a distraction while he switched boxes. Gloria said it should be the Salvation Army. He spent a happy half-hour practising with Ben.'

'That was Gloria? Of course! She fooled me completely,' said Jerome. 'Gloria strikes again! I didn't know she did a Sally Army lady.'

'We really must watch the show some time. The timing was everything. Ben was brilliant. Who saw him coming? None of you!'

'So, here is an envelope each with your share. I have given Gloria his bonus with the rent for the next three months. I think he wants nothing more than the thrill of doing his act in public. Maggie, you can put your share towards that classy dressmaking business. Moshe, for you – and thank you for your help and inspiration. I expect you would like your watch back.'

'I was not looking for any money. Kindness for kindness. Ben, you are safe. That is what I wanted.'

'That of course – and your watch. Ben, give Moshe his watch.' Ben said nothing. He handed Moshe a crumpled paper bag. Moshe reached into it, pulled out the box and opened it to reveal a watch.

'Ben, this is not my watch.' Maggie, Tim and Jerome looked at it.

'It's mine! Look!' Jerome held out his arm. Where his watch should have been only a pale outline showed on his skin.

'Put your hand in your pocket, Jerome,' said Ben. 'What is there?'

'Oh! A watch!'

'My watch!' cried Moshe.

'That is the last time I will pick a pocket,' said Ben solemnly. 'I just thought I should end with my best work.' He stood up and gave a courteous, elaborate bow.

Moshe spoke. 'Sharki was very insistent about having a photograph, Tim. Are you going to tell us about that?'

'Oh, that. Here is another copy. Tim laid it on the table. Moshe looked closely.

'I know the man in the middle. It is Herman Goering. Oh, very clever, Tim!'

'I don't understand,' said Maggie.

Moshe spoke quietly but there an edge to his voice. 'Herman Goering went on trial at the Munich War Crimes Tribunal. He committed suicide before he could be executed. They say he bribed his guard to bring him cyanide. I have heard the story.'

'That was the clincher for Sharki. He believed he was buying Goering's watch. That is why he called me a fool – for not knowing the true value of the thing.'

'One of his guards fetched Goering the cyanide in return for his watch. The soldier in the photo. A lovely touch, Tim.'

'We are not quite finished,' said Jerome. 'Mergim Sharki has still to be dealt with. It will not have taken him long to realise how he was conned. He will be after us, especially Ben. He must know that Ben did the switch when Gloria grabbed him.'

'I took care of that,' said Tim. 'Tell them, Ben.'

'He will never know the switch happened because within a minute he bumped into a friend of mine. Eddie.'

A young man approached their corner. 'Here is the box, Ben.' He laid it on the table.

'A friend? You retrieved the substitute box?' Moshe was the first to understand.

'Eddie helped me find Charlie Parsons. Now he has helped me again.'

'Let me get this clear,' said Maggie. 'Sharki, the master of pickpockets, had his pocket picked twice in two minutes?'

'He will never know he bought a fake,' said Tim.

101

'Shocking,' said Jerome. 'I bet he is really cross about it.'

'London, eh,' said Tim. 'It's full of thieves.'

Ten

Golightly parked his old van behind the row of shops where he usually did on this errand. He liked to slip unnoticed from place to place. It was his way to be cautious because he always had cash or a decent antique in his pocket. He turned up his coat collar against the drizzle and jammed his old cap down. That afternoon his second last call was Jasper Jameson's drab little shop. There was a reproduction Tiffany table lamp in the window. It cast its inadequate light on an arrangement of antique porcelain set unsystematically on a few small items of furniture. The sign on the door read 'Closed'. There were no lights showing inside. Golightly gave the door a sharp rap with his knuckles and waited in the shadow of the doorway. A door from the back shop opened, casting light on a wooden counter and a line of drab chapel chairs.

A figure appeared from the back, peered at Golightly, switched on a light over the counter and unlocked the door.

'What have you got, Arthur?'

Golightly revealed a miniature portrait on ivory of a pretty Regency girl, all pink cheeked and curled hair, then another. Finally, he withdrew from a pocket another miniature which he put down with a flourish.

'This is Sir Grigsby Shotterie. It isn't signed but it is fine work. It should sell well because of the quality. Nobody will have heard of him, but if they ask don't say that he was a slaver working out of Bristol. The pretty girls here will fly out.'

He glanced around the shop, amused at the idea of actual customers here. He supposed there were customers.

'I want £750 for the three.'

Jameson examined the miniatures. He looked at the painted surfaces, turned them over, jammed a jeweller's loupe into one eye, turned them back and forth in turn. Finally he put his loupe away.

Most transactions between dealers were leisurely, protracted affairs with sighs, sucking in of breath, offer, a counter-offer or two and finally a sale. It was expected, even savoured. These were the moments some dealers lived for. Golightly had a short-cut: take it or leave it. He was well known for his uncompromising attitude. Dealers were used to him and nearly always took it.

Jameson brought out a roll of money held together with an elastic band from somewhere inside his coat. He counted out fifteen £50 notes and placed them beside the miniatures. He did not say a word. Golightly knew his man. He knew not to check the cash. He had counted it already, but he would take on trust that they were genuine, despite knowing that forged notes had been circulating. He palmed the money into his pocket.

He turned to leave.

'Wait a minute, Arthur, I might have something for you.'

Golightly stopped with his hand on the door.

'Come into the back.'

In the rear of the shop it was even darker and unpromising. Golightly made out a figure amongst piled-up furniture and bric-a-brac. It was draped with a blanket but was unmistakably a human form, about half size. There was no sign that the piece was anything out of the ordinary; one of those plaster casts of a Greek statue or perhaps something cast-iron, in which case Golightly would not risk his back lugging it about.

'Before I see this I want to know why you want to sell it to me. I might offer you a fair price for the piece but you will be wanting retail. And you are keeping it in the back here, not out in the shop window. Why isn't this on view?'

'You and I have done business for years, Arthur, and in that time I have never tried to sell you anything. I know how things stand. You are a finder. I don't blame you for being suspicious.'

'Where did you get it?'

'It was a walk-in. A geezer with a Land Rover brought it in. I have never seen him before. He just stopped on the double yellows, cool as you like. I was in the front shop at the time with a customer. He waited in the car till she had gone then heaved this out of the back.'

'Get to the point.'

'He wanted me to take it. He wouldn't say how much he wanted for it. I told him I had never seen anything like it and couldn't give him a price just like that. He offered to leave it with me. He gave me a phone number.'

'That is a funny way to do business. You know I like to deal with people in the trade.'

'He was no dealer, I could tell. Posh, I thought. I decided to let somebody give it the once-over. There was something about his manner that put me off, but if it is not bent I would go for it. Have a look at it at least.'

Jameson pulled the shroud away. Golightly felt the old tingle. At that moment the clouds parted. Sunlight fell from the skylight upon the figure. There, radiant as if illuminated from within, was a marble figure of a woman, not much more than a girl. She stood in a classical pose, with one arm raised, bent towards her hair and the other modestly held before her. She was poised on a naturalistic pedestal. There was some drapery, finely executed, seemingly diaphanous. Her body was slightly turned so that her glance was over her shoulder. Her face was exquisite; her expression tranquil, as if some happy memory had just occurred to her, or in contemplation of a happy meeting or fond parting. Carrara marble for sure; that white smoothness, the luminous sheen; the graceful form; the pose; the delicacy of the drapery; the tranquility of the face; the yearning, aching loveliness! For a moment Golightly was lost in it.

He knew from that first sight it that was the most beautiful object he had ever seen outside a museum.

Jameson was silent too. They stood, awed by her as the sun cast its light on her hair and her face into shadow. Then the clouds passed over and the spell was broken.

'You see? She is almost heart-breaking, she is so lovely. I was going to show it to that bloke with the classy shop in the Cotswolds who drops in from time to time, but he hasn't been here. Condon, his name is. I thought I would maybe get a finder's fee. Then you turned up, as you do. So, there it is.'

'Bloody Hell, Jasper! Bloody Hell!' Golightly's customary reticence had gone. He scratched his head under his cap.

'It is good, isn't it?'

'It's Friday. Don't show it to anybody over the weekend. I'll come back on Monday. I might make an offer for it.'

Arthur Golightly left the shop as he had entered, quietly and unobtrusively, out of habit. He sat in the van oblivious of the Queen Anne chairs in the back. They were to be his last call of the day but they were forgotten as if they were commonplace. His mind was racing now. First, he would get out some of his books. Then, maybe talk to some people.

That weekend was a busy one for Golightly. The statue in the back shop was ever-present in his mind, a phantom glimpsed from the corner of his eye. It had struck him even as he spoke to Jameson that he knew what it was: neo-classical; Italianate, probably Venetian; certainly by a sure eyed, confident master craftsman.

'Canova!' He had almost said it out loud.

Did Canova always sign his work? Who commissioned him? There was a Catalogue Raisonné. Who was the man in the Land Rover – and did it matter if the work was a Canova? Was it his to sell - and did that matter either? Was it bent, stolen? Was it a fake? Not a fake surely?

He gathered his thoughts. First find out what it was. If it was not a Canova it was still a remarkable work. Even a copy would be worth five figures. Even the Duke of Bedford had wanted a copy of *The Three Graces* – admittedly, one done by Canova himself.

He reached for his books. He could find no picture of it anywhere. There was nothing about a missing or lost work. He skimmed through all the photographs he could find, pulling books off shelves until the floor was piled with them. There were lots of pictures, but not of the Girl. As he began to think of her; for Canova there would probably be a classical reference – a nymph or dryad or some such. Jameson was not an idiot. He would have looked for marks and if he had seen anything he would certainly have said something. So there were no marks.

If he followed his instincts he would buy this thing, he knew. His glance was usually enough for him at auction where it did not do to pause over anything; somebody was always alert to any interest shown by somebody with his reputation, his eye. He was rarely caught out and he had learned to trust these snap judgments. Why was he hesitating now? So, the decision formed itself. He would buy it if he could.

106

Now he had made up his mind the next steps came easily. The next morning, Saturday, he went to London; first a call to the British Library, then some discreet conversations with the proprietor of a certain West End gallery. On Monday he would call on Jasper Jameson.

Golightly huddled into the shop doorway against the persistent drizzle. Jameson answered his knock in seconds. Golightly stepped inside.

'Cup of tea, Arthur? With a little something in it?'

Golightly sniffed. Whisky.

'One of us has to keep a clear head.'

'I've just brewed up. Come through.'

They passed through to the back shop, past the chapel chairs stacked untidily along the wall. Golightly looked about the back room, taking in details with his glance. Jameson switched on the overhead light. The fluorescent tube spluttered and fired. Its light was harsh yet hardly enough to reach the corners. They were in what passed for a kitchen, grimy with years of Jameson's neglect. In the middle of the room was the statue, just as before. Jameson had thrown the sheet over it. As he rummaged among the debris on the counter Golightly felt that insistent tingle again. He knew he would buy this lovely thing if he could. He pulled a torch out of his coat, crouched swiftly down and flicked the edge of the sheet. He shone it on the socle base. He scrabbled on the greasy lino to search every part of it. He did not need to. He knew.

'I've looked everywhere for a mark, even on the bottom.' Jameson let out a little giggle. 'Here's your tea. Cheers.'

Golightly thought Jameson's mug looked full. 'Not with tea,' he thought.

'Go easy, Jasper. There is work to be done. Have you spoken to the fellow in the Land Rover?'

'He said he'll be here in an hour.'

'First we need to get things settled between us. You are the finder. I don't think you fancy buying it and that is why you showed me it.'

'It is out of my league, Arthur, I know that. I couldn't make an offer if I wanted to. I'm pretty much hand to mouth these days. You know what it's like. A finder's fee would be fair. I know you well enough to trust—'

'—I'll see you right. There'll be a good drink in it for you.'

Jameson took a pull from his mug.

'Here is what you do—and what you don't do. First you ask him the usual things. Due diligence and all that. Make sure it is his to sell, but don't press him on that. You know, the usual. You have been buying stuff from walk-ins all your life. This is the same thing, but when I join in you shut up. Got that? I will come in at the right moment. I am going to buy it if I can. And lay off that, er, tea.'

On time, the Land Rover pulled up on the yellow lines. Jameson went into his routine of reluctant buyer, not exactly suspicious, just a little bit cautious. Golightly perched in the corner on one of the ugly chapel chairs with his back to the light from the window, unregarded; how he liked it. The man spoke a little too quickly, a sign of nervousness to Golightly. 'He really wants to sell,' he thought.

At last Jameson got to the crux. 'It is a nice piece. Why do you want to sell?'

'Needs must, I'm afraid, old boy. Cash flow problems, that sort of thing. The estate hardly pays the bills these days, what with one thing and another. A harder, malicious tone crept into his voice. 'And frankly I'm growing tired of my wife swooning over it. It is just a bit of rock as far as I'm concerned. I am sick of tripping over it in the library. I want it out of my house.'

Golightly stepped forward.

'Mr. Jameson showed me this over the weekend. He and I do a bit of business from time to time and coincidentally I called into the shop on Friday. He showed me the piece. Let's look at it. Lead on, Jasper!'

They crowded into the little kitchen. Golightly switched on the light. Jameson gave the sheet a tug and it slid to the floor. The statue was bathed in the lurid neon light, just as Golightly intended. Its surfaces had lost their luminous quality. It looked sallow. The ghastly light cast mottled shadows. The thing looked sickly. The sunlit magic of last Friday had evaporated,

'What sort of figure were you hoping for?

'What about ten thousand? I know it seems a lot, but that would clear my overdraft and—'

'—and that is about twice what I was thinking of. How about eight?'

'Nine thousand?'

'Eight and a half. Eight thousand five hundred pounds.'

'It seems a little cheap. It has been in the family for years. My great-grandfather – the fourth earl – brought it home. He spent half his fortune on his Grand tour. Art, he called it.'

Golightly turned to leave. Slowly.

'Cash.'

The seller looked at the statue in the appalling light. The tube above hummed and flickered.

'Eight thousand five hundred? I thought—'

'—Eight seven fifty. That is my last word. It is probably more than it is worth, but I will stretch to it. Golightly stuck out his hand. The man grasped it.

'Oh, thank you! Yes, agreed.'

Golightly stepped briskly into the shop. He pulled out a roll of notes held together with elastic.

'Here. Watch me. He counted aloud. When he got to five thousand he pulled out a second roll. At last he finished. 'Seven hundred. And fifty. Jasper, give the man a bag for this. A nice big one. And one of those horrible chairs. Carry it out for him.'

The man gathered up the money, stepped out of the shop followed by the chapel chair Golightly had sat on. Jameson put it in the back. The man drove off.

'What was that about the chair? It has spoilt the set.'

'He looked like a customer to anybody passing, that's all. I'm off to find my buyer now. My van is right in front of your back yard gate. Let's get it out through your yard. I'll be back later this week with your money. Expect a couple of grand – a bit more if it goes well.'

They struggled it into the van.

'That was nicely done, Arthur. He was grateful in the end. I really thought you were walking away for a moment.'

'An old geezer told me long ago to be ready not to do the deal. But that last two fifty was a nice touch, I'll grant you. If he'd asked for twenty grand I would have offered ten. I never offer a price before I know what the punter is hoping for. You always know what I want, don't you?'

'You always tell me up-front.'

'And you always give me what I ask. Everybody does. Everybody knows I don't like haggling!'

At that he gave a wheezing laugh and drove off.

Golightly dropped the Queen Anne chairs off in the garage at home and drove to London. He did not stop till he reached a row of nondescript lock-ups under railway arches. He was in a blind alley somewhere south of Lambeth. He had been here before. He glanced about in his careful way. Some of the premises had enormous padlocks; some were half open. Nobody was visible in the alley. He worked the bell-push on a little door set into galvanised roller shutters identical to the others apart from the daubed 14 in dull red paint.

A voice asked his business.

'Is Bradley in?'

'He's up West today. Come back on Thursday.'

'I've come a long way. Tell him it's Arthur. Say he's got it.'

'What's Arthur got, then?'

'Just do it. Please.'

A minute passed. Golightly waited. Another minute. Then the shutters rattled up to reveal a bright workshop lit by high tubes and portable floodlights like theatrical lighting.

'Get the van in, then. The boss will be here in an hour or so. He's with a customer at the Great Moulton Street shop. Take it slow. Don't scratch my French polish.'

Golightly reversed slowly into the workshop. The lad got the shutters down almost before the van had cleared the doorway. The two of them lifted the Girl out of the van and through the open door of a steel container. The young man closed the door and returned to his polishing. The familiar smell of meths and white oil filled his nostrils. Golightly looked at the door's complicated arrangement of locks and levers. It looked like a cold store left behind by some long gone butcher. It would serve its turn well. Who would be expecting an antique in such unpromising surroundings?

Georgian brown furniture was stacked against one wall. Chairs were piled on tables. Chests, bureaux, escritoires, a *bonne heure du jour* – the stock in trade of a West End antique dealer – were lined up, all with the rich lustre only a traditional French polisher could achieve. The far wall was a jumble of similar pieces, some in bits with doors ajar, legs awry or missing a drawer, no doubt awaiting the attentions of a cabinet maker.

That would be Bill Bradley, Golightly guessed. He had started out in old Formby's workshop in Birmingham's Jewellery Quarter behind a goldsmith's years ago, he recalled. He was doing well.

He slumped into a leather armchair.

'Nice work, son. Don't mind me. I'll just wait here.' He settled down patiently in one of the Victorian club chairs lining the wall.

Bradley appeared in an hour.

'Arthur! What have you got?'

'I think that it is a Canova. I can't find a piece that matches any catalogued work, but some that are similar. The work is certainly his style and he liked naked ladies. He did commissions and copied his own work for rich patrons. He didn't mind repeating himself if the price was right. I think it could be something like that.'

'He made a copy of the Three Graces, the one in the V&A. The Duke of Bedford, I think it was, commissioned him to make another just the same. He put in some differences, though.'

'Yes, he did – maybe this piece is something like that. You'd better have a look.'

The lad put down his polishing cloth and opened the door. Bradley stepped inside. Golightly remained in the armchair. A light moved about inside the strongroom. He's doing what I did, he thought. Looking for a mark.

At last he emerged, a little out of breath from the exertion, or maybe, Golightly thought, excitement.

'It is a beautiful piece and I will have it of course.'

'I thought you would. You know me. I don't like haggling. I want a hundred grand for it.'

Bradley laughed. 'Nice and cheap if it is a Canova. Too much if it is not. Let me talk to somebody. I agree with your judgment. I can keep it here, out of sight until I'm more confident about it. There are some people I know who would snap it up whether it is the business or not. I'll pay you ten grand now and the ninety grand if it is a Canova – when I have found a buyer.'

'Twenty grand now and I'll trust you with the rest.'

'Fifteen.'

'No. You know me by now. I don't like haggling. Think about it. I'll wait. You will come round to my price. I will trust you on the eighty. You trust me on the twenty.'

Bradley conceded. What was ten thousand when the piece would fly out of his shop for just about any price he asked—and if it was a Canova, well, he hardly dared think.

He took out the cash, just like that, new fifties in their banker's wrappers. Golightly took it, stuffed into the inside pocket in his overcoat, climbed into the van and drove through the opened shutters.

Golightly drove home. He swung open the shed doors behind his ramshackle old cottage just inside Worcestershire's border with Gloucestershire, a little place hardly visible from the lane. He flicked on the light to avoid scraping the van against the Queen Anne chairs. Better get them off tomorrow, he thought. They were good quality, walnut, excellent workmanship, newly upholstered seats in the right taste, fretted splats and the obligatory cabriole legs. It was rare to get so many together. Even though the five grand he would demand tomorrow seemed small beer after today, life goes on.

Two people, a man and a woman, stepped out of a car which had pulled up behind the van.

'Arthur Golightly?' It was the woman who spoke.

They showed their warrants in the shed's light.

'We would like to have a word with you.'

'I've just got back from—'Something stopped him. '—from work.'

'Oh, yes, Sir? Have you had a long journey? Perhaps we could go inside for a moment.'

Golightly said nothing but indicated with his arm for them to go in through the door.

'It isn't locked.'

'That is very trusting for a man in your line, Sir,' said the woman. 'I am Detective Inspector Webster and this is Detective Sergeant Ayling.

Golightly put the kettle on and took down mugs. 'I don't keep anything in the house.'

'Not for us, thank you,' said the sergeant. 'Arthur Golightly, We have reason to believe that you are in possession of stolen goods. You do not have to say anything but it may harm your defence if you do not mention when questioned, something that you later rely on in Court. Anything you do say may be given in evidence.'

The words were lost in a swirl of fear and panic. Golightly's thoughts flashed and tumbled across his mind like broken glass. He sat down, mugs still in his hand. The man in the Land Rover, the Canova Girl he had bought, the trip to London! There was nothing to connect him to the Girl, surely.

'Did you buy a set of chairs from a dealer, Robert Surtees, recently?'

Golightly looked surprised for a moment. He sat silent, his mind in a whirl. Not the Canova? Relief flooded through him. Those bloody chairs! He should have moved them on last weekend as he had planned. He did his best to register the stony nonchalance that served best in negotiations.

'Yes, a set of sixteen walnut Queen Anne chairs including two carvers, in excellent condition. I've still got them. I haven't got round to selling them yet. They are in the garage.'

'We have reason to believe they were taken from a house in Oxfordshire three months ago. How did you come by these chairs, Mr. Golightly?'

'I bought them in good faith. Stolen, you say? I don't buy from crooks. Look, I trade in antiques. They don't usually come with paperwork.' He fished about in his pocket and extricated a silver snuff box he had carried about for months, forgotten until that moment.

'This is two hundred years old. All I know about it is from its hallmark. It is sterling silver, it was made in 1789-90 in London. It has had goodness knows how many owners. It is impossible to know whether it was stolen in the two centuries of its existence. I bought it from somebody I trusted, and that is the best anybody can do in my business. Queen Anne chairs? Yes, I bought them. I know even less about them and nothing about their previous owners. Furniture is not cars. There are no log books.'

The DI pushed a photograph in front of Golightly.

'Do you recognise this man?'

'It's Bob. I've known him for years. I have never heard his surname. I know his bidding number at one or two salerooms.'

'You admit you received these chairs from this man.'

'He is a regular on the circuit. He is known in every auction house in the Midlands. I have dealt with him for years. He is not bent. He's as straight as me.'

'I'll take that as a yes. Arthur Golightly, I am arresting you on suspicion of receiving stolen goods under Section 22 of the Theft Act 1968...'

Golightly heard nothing after that. There were formalities. He was released on bail. The police took the chairs and had a look through the house. There was nothing matching the list on the clip-board. The chairs, it turned out, had come from a great house in Oxfordshire and the owner had friends. Those friends had friends on the bench. His defence that he had bought the chairs in good faith did not convince the jury or the judge. They went down together at Birmingham Crown Court. Golightly got three years. Bob got five.

DI Honour Webster was almost as surprised at the level of sentencing as the two men. She had expected a custodial sentence, but these were first offences for both men.

'Bloody Hell, Bob. Bloody Hell! Where did you get them?'

'From a bloke at Newark Antiques Fair. I bought them straight out of his van. It is not the only time I've bought from him. It never occurred to me that they were bent. I thought he was OK.'

'Bloody Hell, Bob! Bloody Hell!'

Eleven

I've got the deposit here. If you remember, you said that would be all right. Something about the vendor not really trusting banks?'

'Yes, it saves us having to draw cash from our escrow account – which is surprisingly expensive. You would be surprised how often clients stipulate a cash deposit. You have saved yourself a bit of money there. Oh, you need a receipt.'

Tim Stack pulled out a book out of a drawer and meticulously wrote out the amount in longhand, writing slowly and carefully, squinting through his thick heavy framed spectacles.

'Twenty thousand pounds.' He wrote the sum out in words with laboured care. 'Mr. Cheeseman insists on these.' He took the bundles out of the mark's case and laboriously checked. The fifty-pound notes were used, non-consecutive and held in bundles of twenty – a thousand pounds each. There were twenty bundles. Stack counted each bundle deliberately, muttering as he counted. He scrawled his name on the bottom and pushed it across the desk.

'Perfect. If you just sign here.' He pointed to the dotted line. He carefully folded the document and put it into one of a pile of legal envelopes on the desk and solemnly handed the receipt to the mark.

'I'll have the money off to the office straight away. I don't like to carry large sums about. London is full of thieves! As soon as your bank acknowledges the transfer to the vendor's solicitor you'll have the keys. You should be able to move in next week as planned. We hand keys over personally – another thing Mr. Cheeseman likes us to do. It won't be me, I'm afraid. I'm off to Scotland in the morning. The office will get in touch to make the arrangements.'

'Oh, lovely. Fishing?'

'Fell walking. I am hoping to take in a couple of Munros. Let me see you out.'

Stack ushered the man out of the office, turned to lock the door and as he did so removed the name plate. He held the glass outer door open and called a cheery farewell to the receptionist. The mark did not see the puzzled look on her face as she glanced up, too late to get a good view of them. He watched as the mark jumped into his Range Rover and left.

'The ride of choice of crooks everywhere,' Tim thought.

Ben had found the mark. The man had been just a little bit too keen to pay a cash deposit, Tim's litmus test for client integrity, Tim decided. In fact he had offered to pay the full £200,000 in cash if need be. Tim had resisted the temptation out of caution. He was playing the respectable estate agent, nervous even of accepting a deposit in cash. He would have disappeared by the time the mark discovered that the Cheeseman Tucker Estates did not exist, but not to Scotland.

Ten minutes later he was on the platform of the tube station round the corner. The thick spectacles were in a bin. There was nothing to link him to Cheeseman Tucker Estates. It had been easy.

Back in Greenwich he took out the cash. He was home and dry for a while. He could live comfortably on this, the first of his solo hauls. Easy money! He pushed the money to the back of his sock drawer, slipping a bundle into his pocket. A nagging feeling tugged at the back of his mind. He should be celebrating. He missed Jerome at these moments.

He went down the stairs to the back room, the scene of past triumphs, reflecting on the contrast now. The two men in the room ignored him. He ruminated on his present life and how it had changed since the theatre ticket game in Stratford. He felt a little nostalgic for those almost innocent days, his short youth. The London adventure was becoming just his way of life – like a job. This was the first time he had worked without Jerome, taking a deposit for a house he had 'sold' to a mark. Ben had overheard some talk among his old friends on the street and that had been the starting point for the scam.

'He is crooked, Tim. He has a gang of shoplifters working the malls. They give everything to him.'

116

Ben had pointed him out in a crowded shopping mall. Tim had done the rest. He made contact, 'accidentally' bumped into him again and dropped the prospectus for a pretty cottage under his nose. It had been easy, almost too easy.

Tim was lounging in his usual seat in the snug. He was not afraid that he was being pursued by the police. The mark was not the sort to report the loss because of how he came by the money in the first place. There was a good week before the mark would realise he had been tricked, when the promised keys failed to be delivered.

'Am I just another crook now?' he wondered. The thought was unsettling.

This was not what he had had in mind when he and Jerome had set off that day, seemingly so long ago. What adventures they would have! What excitement they felt! This day's work had been easy – and rather sleazy. There was nobody to pay out or explain the intricacies of the scam to; no rabbits out of his hat, no applause, no laughter, none of the elation. No sense of triumph. Tim just felt flat.

Suddenly, he realised, Ben was in the snug, in his corner. The other customers had left. He had not noticed.

'This is a surprise, Ben. How is it nobody sees you coming?'

'You were not really watching. People are not very watchful.'

'I have things on my mind.'

'Me too, Tim. My new boss has been talking to me. He wants me to take on more responsibility. He wants me in the shop every day. I will be manager.'

'Congratulations! That's good, isn't it?'

'Yes. Very good. I am a proper person now, a man, as I could never have been—'

'—before Sharki.'

'I am honest man now, Tim. I know I owe everything to you and Jerome, but—'

'—No, no! Remember, I said you would not be in debt to me. You are free. If I ask you to do jobs for me you can always say no.'

'If I work for Mr. Cole as his manager I will not always be able to take days off doing jobs for you. When I gave up my previous life as a – you know – it was not to become a different kind of – well, thief.'

'We are not thieves, Ben!'

'You weren't. I think now we have become too much like your marks. I wish to be British person. I must be good in the eyes of the Law. I still owe you for rescuing me, whatever you said then or say now. If you really need me I will come, but from now on, as a friend, for the adventure and in a good cause.'

'That sounds pretty good to me, Ben. Friends!' He rose to shake Ben's hand. Ben ignored the hand and flung his arms round Tim. A moment later and he was out through the door. Tim flopped back into his seat. He knew Ben had done something important for both of them. He had redefined their relationship. Now he was Tim's equal in his own mind. That was a huge step for Ben, Tim knew. He had done something else, something wise. A true friend now, Ben had spoken the truth to him and he had crystallised the unease that had been growing in his mind.

'I am drifting. I must make some changes before I become just another grifter, a con artist ripping off gullible, greedy men by manipulating them for nothing more than a simple illicit profit.'

Gloria's face was at the hatch. 'Was that Ben just now?'

Tim told Gloria about Ben's step up.

'No more little errands? He'll want to go straight now, won't he?'

'Yes, he does, but he still feels he owes me. He grew up as Sharki's property. I wonder if he will ever be free of that.'

'Are you all right, Tim? You seem a little out of sorts.'

'I've just had a good payday, so I should be celebrating. It feels – I just feel flat.'

Gloria looked keenly at Tim. 'Do you miss Jerome?'

'Well, yes, of course. But he has other priorities. It was always a bit complicated. His father, you know.'

'Why not just go back to Stratford – for a holiday? Look up Jerome, chat a little.'

Tim remembered their apartment, with its entrance tucked away behind Sheep Street amongst the wheelie bins and litter. It was still his, technically, rent paid.

'Do you know, Gloria, I think I will.'

Jerome had returned to Oxford to complete the degree he had abandoned for a life on the street. Tim considered for a moment. Jerome was in his final year, with his examinations looming. They had seen little of each other in that time. It would be nice to catch up. He could go today, now. He caught Gloria's eye behind the bar.

'I'm taking your advice. I'll be gone for a few days.' He slipped him a couple of month's rent from the money he had kept back. He finished his drink, got up and packed. He saw the bundles of bank notes at the back of the drawer. On an impulse he shoved the money into his hold-all, nineteen grand from that day plus a few bundles of fifty-pound notes – his contingency fund.

He was in Stratford by early evening. The streets were quiet. The shoppers had left and the theatre crowd not yet arrived, their slack time in the old days. If Jerome was around they could catch up over a meal and a bottle of wine. They could go to *Le Bistro*! It would be a change to sit at a table out front instead of balancing their plates on their knees on the kitchen floor. He wondered if the same waitress was there, and if she would remember them. He climbed the steel steps to the apartment. He had a key still but thought it would be polite to knock. The door opened.

'Kate!'

'Tim, how nice! Come in.'

'Thanks'

'Are you here for long? I hope you don't want to chuck me out.'

'No, it was just a sudden impulse. Actually, I was sort of hoping to see Jerome.'

'You know he has gone back to his old college?'

'Yes, of course. I just thought—'

'He visits Mother but he is not coming this weekend. He has exams soon. He will be swotting, I am sure. Do you want to stay here tonight? It will be perfectly all right, so long as you don't mind me being here. Have Jerome's room – well your room, really. I hope you like the changes I've made. I have made the big bedroom mine and moved your stuff into Jerome's. Is it OK?'

'Yes, of course. I want to get away from London for a couple of days. As a matter of fact I want a bit of a chat with Jerome.'

'Are you in trouble?' Kate sounded thrilled. 'Are you in hiding? Is somebody after you?'

'No, it's just money.'

'You're broke?'

'No, I've got loads of the stuff. It can wait till Jerome's exams are over. I'm just feeling a bit down.'

'Is Maggie with you? Why didn't you bring her with you? She's from here, isn't she? Oh, no, are you two not still together? Oh, dear! Have I put my foot in it?'

'It is nothing like that.'

'What have you been up to? Any thrilling tales from big bad London? How is Ben? Is he still around?'

'One thing at a time, Kate. I'll tell you all over supper.'

'As you are in funds you can buy me a nice dinner in Sheep Street, one of those nice restaurants.'

'Let's go to *Le Bistro*. It would be nice to eat there and not be crouching behind the dish-washer. A good chat with you will cheer me up.'

The staff at *Le Bistro* were pleased to see Tim. The waitress recognised him at once. She called to the chef. There was hand-shaking and a little exchange about how many dishes Tim would have to wash to pay for him and his girl-friend to eat in the restaurant.

'How is Jez?' the waitress asked. 'Are you still—did you go to London, like you said?'

'Yes, we did. And we don't call him Jez any more – it's Jerome. This is his sister.'

'And definitely *not* his girlfriend.'

'Whoops.' The waitress and Kate exchanged little smiles.

They were led to a table in the window. It was early and still quiet.

'It was you I saw talking to Jez—Jerome?' the waitress asked Kate.

'Yes, I used to keep an eye on him.'

'Me too. He looked so vulnerable. I used to sneak little bits of food out when I could. I'm glad he's all right.'

'Thank you. I didn't know. Jerome never spoke about that – begging, I suppose. He was very peculiar in those days.'

Just then a party arrived.

'I'll bring the menu.' She bustled off.

Over the meal, Kate asked about Ben.

'Ben, now. How is he?'

'He is fine. I saw him today, as it happens. I was sitting in the snug, thinking - feeling sorry for myself, really. There he was, sitting calm as you like in the corner.'

'Is he still with you, over the pub?'

'He moved out last October. He stays south of the river. He says Sharki will never find him. He is much more confident these days. He has grown and filled out. Sharki should be afraid of *him* these days. Since your mother took an interest in his paperwork he has become British – or at least he has permanent residency. There is nothing for him in Albania. And he is keeping strictly within the law. No more you-know-what for him. He's got a job. It's all regular and above board, in a shop. The proprietor has taken to him. It's a general dealer place in Woolwich. The owner is getting on and is happy to give Ben responsibility. Of course, he has absolutely no idea of Ben's special talents. Ben works hard. Mr. Cole, has asked him to manage the place now. Ben sees himself as a real man now.'

'Well! Good for Ben. I'll tell Mother. She will be pleased. She really took to him, you know. Somebody in her Bridge crowd knew about naturalisation and stuff and that got her started on getting him his papers. What about Maggie? Are you two properly together? You make a lovely couple.'

'She worries about – well – what I do for a living. I tell her it is not forever. I know she thinks I should get a proper job. Maybe I will, just not yet.'

'What about that dressmaking business she talked about? Is she any further on with it?'

'It's money. She does well in the Portobello Road, but proper premises cost a fortune. She puts a bit by when she can, and she has had a bit from the jobs she's done for me. When she scrapes a decent deposit together she will take the plunge. She is very wary of my money, of course.'

'Well, are you surprised?'

'I could easily give her my money, but she wouldn't – hang on!'

'What?'

'She wouldn't take it from me, but maybe she would if it came from Jerome – or you.'

'As an investment?'

'Yes.'

'Great Aunt Harriet!'

Tim looked round the restaurant, expecting to see someone approaching their table. There was nobody but seated diners and the waitress.

'Who?'

Kate laughed. 'I'll explain. Jerome and I used to get Christmas cards from Aunt Harriet. There was always a brand new five-pound note tucked into it. When Jerome was on the street I would find him. I would give him little things, food and little treats. Sometimes I gave him money as well. "From Great Aunt Harriet," I said. I could persuade Maggie, I suppose, if I said it was an inheritance or something.'

'From your aunt? Is she still alive? You could hardly kill her off, even pretending, could you?'

'The thing was, she didn't exist. There was no Great Aunt Harriet. We knew the money was from Mother really. Father was beastly about Jerome's presents. Mother gave him the money and of course she had to give some to me too. So when I gave him money from Great Aunt Harriet he knew it was from Mother. It wasn't, of course, it was from me.'

'Kate, you conned him!'

'I did, didn't I? I should work for you! It was just a little lie. And there was good reason. Jerome needed taking care of. Maybe he knew the truth. One day maybe I will ask him. But it is different with Maggie. I don't want to lie to her. Maybe it is not such a good idea.'

'OK. Maybe you could keep it for me. The money, I mean. Hide it or something.'

'Where is it?'

'In my hold-all in the flat. I was thinking I would keep it here in Stratford, for safety.'

'I could keep an eye on it, I suppose. How much is it?'

'Just a bit over twenty grand.'

'I think Ben and Maggie are right about you. It is time for a change. London was just the sort of adventure Jerome and you were looking for. Maybe it is over. I think you have been lucky. You should quit while you're ahead.'

'What would I do? Tim nine-to-five, in a suit? It makes me shudder. It may come to that, one day. I *am* thinking about it.'

122

'Oh, Tim, you and thinking about it. You haven't changed! Maybe it is time you did. Think about that.'

Tim thought about it that night. He was still thinking about it the next morning as he strolled along Wood Street. He peered into Howard's window, as he so often had when he was penniless, attracted to the silver and the sparkling gems under the clever little lights. He continued towards the market place. He could find a seat in a coffee shop window and watch Stratford as it filled with shoppers and the tourists.

Suddenly he was at Jerome's old doorway.

'Any spare change?'

He looked down. He almost cried out. A man, not much more than a boy sat there. His legs were in a greasy sleeping bag on a pile of cardboard with a scruffy looking dog on a string. He was holding out his dirty hand. For a split second he had seen Jerome – Jez – squatting there.

'Have you had any breakfast? I'll get you a sandwich and a can.'

Five minutes later Tim returned and handed the boy a Marks and Spenser paper bag. Under the sandwich was a twenty pound note.

Next day Tim decided to go to Oxford.

Jerome was in fine form. Despite his examinations he insisted on an hour to chat together. They met over a pie and pint in a little room at the Eagle and Child. They talked inconsequentially for a few minutes. Tim mentioned the boy in the doorway. Jerome pulled a face.

'Oh. Yes, that would have given you a fright. Something is wrong, Tim. I can see there is something on your mind. What has brought you here? Don't say "I've been thinking." I know you.'

'It's true, I have. It isn't another job. I haven't come to ask you do anything.'

'Any other time and I would be a bit disappointed. Once my finals are over I'll be completely at your pleasure. I nearly said "command". It is really nice to see you any time, of course.'

'I have just separated a criminal from £20,000. I should feel good about it, but I don't. Ben saw me the other day to tell me he is straight now and wants to stay that way. He thinks I am no different from the crooks I —'

'—relieve of their ill-gotten gains.'

Tim sat silent.

'You are not yourself. That was when you were supposed to say "college boy", like you said in Stratford when we first talked about going to London. Then I could point out of the window there at an actual college. Anyway, Ben has shown you the error of your ways. What else?'

'Something Kate said last night. She said we – I – should quit before my luck ran out. She is right. Ben was right.'

'There was always something other than the money, wasn't there? Dougie got what he deserved. Sharki too. Ben was rescued. Charlie P and that woman had what was coming. Natural justice, remember?'

'You are right. That's it. I have just lost sight of that. You must be a good influence. I could – I should – just stop, walk away. Maggie would like that.'

'I am done with Oxford soon. Maybe then we could get together for something spectacular.'

'Finish on a high and call it a day?'

'A *grand finale*. Something like that, yes. Get it out of our systems. We can sit in the snug and make a plan.'

Twelve

The mark, Krotov, was an Azerbaijani, pockets full of oil money made when the USSR imploded. He was looking for a home 'in your lovely country'. Ben found him.

'Maybe this will be your last job for us, Ben,' Tim said.

'I think this is a dangerous man, Tim. He reminded me of Mergim Sharki, a little.'

'Well, he is from your part of the world.'

'Azerbaijan is not my part of the world. And now I am Londoner. It was something about him that was cruel. Cold like ice. Be careful, Tim.'

'I will. You know I am always careful.'

The man Krotov was looking for a substantial house in England, not too far from London but secluded, discreet. The estate agency had just the place. The senior partner had gone to school with Sir John, the owner of the house. He would arrange for Krotov to be taken there personally by the baronet, who happened to be visiting London. He knew how little time such businessmen as Krotov could spare. The baronet had met Krotov at his hotel and driven him down from London in a mud-spattered Range Rover.

Tim had dressed for the part in tweeds. He waved his arms to encompass the view from the terrace, a magnificent avenue of ancient trees marching to the horizon.

'It has been the seat of the family for centuries. We decided it was time to sell when Lady Sophie found a turd floating in the below-stairs lavatory. We thought of it as a sign that it was time to go. You can't have any land beyond the ha-ha. That was sold off by my grandfather after the war. Death duties ruined us all.'

A few paying visitors wandered about the garden. Tim paid them no attention.

125

They entered the house and passed the kiosk with its tickets and brochures in six languages. A well-dressed, pretty girl was standing at the inner door.

'Good morning, Sally.'

'Good morning, Sir John.'

The pretty girl held the door and the two men passed entered the great hall. She quietly closed the door, walked down the steps to the terrace and slipped round the corner to the visitors' car park. She had been at the house for less than five minutes. None of the staff had seen her, of if they had, had no reason to think that she was anything other than another visitor.

Tim showed the big man round the ancient pile. The real owners were on the French Riviera. Tim was not expecting any trouble from them. The staff and volunteer stewards expected a visit from a surveyor after a reported sighting of mice. That part had been straightforward. The previous week Kate and Ben had set a couple of them loose on their visit. Within minutes they were gone, just before the shrieks from the paying public had alerted staff to the problem.

Tim and Krotov had a free rein to roam where the public were allowed but Tim knew he had to show Krotov the private upper rooms as well. He pointed out ancestors on the wall in a vast room off the central hall.

'Just take a look at those portraits,' he said. 'That one was mistress to Charles II; that one died at Ramillies. Please, have a good look. there will be no room for them when we move into the Dower House. We could throw them in as part of the sale if you are interested. You can let us look at them now and then.'

Krotov gazed about with evident satisfaction.

'Ready-made ancestors!' he remarked. Then he looked more closely.

'Look for the family resemblance!' called Tim as Krotov advanced into the large room.

'To you – or to me?'

Tim laughed at the little joke. Another piece of the bait swallowed. He waved some paperwork at the steward at the foot of the stairs. He spoke quietly so that his words would not carry.

'The mice were reported on the ground floor, but we will give the upper rooms a quick check while we are here.'

They only spent a few minutes on the upper floors. Tim opened a couple of the doors behind rope barriers. Krotov was not very interested in the room that Queen Caroline had slept in. He did not care where the second Baronet had kept his mistresses. He counted the rooms, aloud in a foreign language.

'Don't worry about the details, Mr. Krotov. It will all be in the prospectus when it comes out.'

'Maybe I save you trouble. If I buy there will be no need for others to come. You will not need your prospectus. Let us talk about money.'

Krotov would make a cash deposit of £190,000 with the balance of £1.85m to be made by bank transfer when the money was moved into his British bank. He quite understood that the cash part of the transaction was to be discreet, not for Lady Sophie to know about. He was happy with the arrangement, even pleased.

'I like this English way of trust, Sir John.'

'Jack, please.'

'Er Jack. It is so much better than dealing with those damned Russians. They have no honour.'

Krotov did not notice that the pretty girl at the door was no longer there when they left the house.

And so it was all agreed and the paperwork duly signed off. The family solicitor was sniffy about the end of an era. If he had had his way the deal would never have gone ahead.

Nearly there. Everything in place. The car with the disabled sticker was in the bay nearest the exit. Twenty minutes to the motorway. The papers were signed. Krotov was on his way. The office was all cleared away – not a sign, literally. It had been unscrewed two minutes after the meeting. The exchange would be simple and unhurried. He would hand over the deeds and the mark would put the hold-all by the chair. Straightforward, easy, Tim thought. It would be his last long con, at least for a while. It was time to take a rest. 'Somewhere warm and sunny, with a beach,' he thought.

Tim ran over the plan in his mind, getting into the part. It had been complicated, convincing Krotov that the place was his to sell. The tour of the house, the respectful demeanour of Kate, ever happy to have a part in Tim's dramatic productions, at the front door, Jerome as Tucker, the stuffy family solicitor – all set up. Now a simple exchange, a briefcase full of documents for a case full of cash, and away.

Stack could see Krotov among the tourists making their way to the Birthplace, sauntering toward the terrace of three cottages knocked into one house and celebrated as the place where Shakespeare had been born. He was the one with the wheeled travel-case. Stack slid the briefcase slightly into the sunlight to let the yellow sticker show. This was just psychology; the sticker had been on the case when the documents were put inside. Stack did not know how this was reassuring to marks, just that it was. It was a good place for the hand-over with bollards at either end of Henley Street, making it pedestrian only. The little alleyway that ran past the Andrew Carnegie Library and led to the disabled carpark was just a few steps from the table and seating of the little coffee shop. He would be gone in seconds – just as soon as Krotov was out of sight. Little knots of tourists were taking photos of each other with the Birthplace behind them across the road.

All the mark had to do was sit at the table. He was headed for the office he had sat in before and Stack had to deflect him. That would be easy. He mentally rehearsed. 'It is a beautiful morning, so I thought we could meet out here. Tucker is full of cold, sneezing all over the office.'

He glanced casually about, looking for Krotov. He spotted him about thirty yards away, glancing about, looking for the brass plate. He would have to wave. Krotov spotted him. He trundled his suitcase towards the table and sat down. Then several things happened at once.

Two of the tourists, a man and a woman turned away from the Birthplace and approached the coffee shop. The woman sat at Tim's table while the man remained standing. She looked familiar to Tim. At the same time four men in black pointed automatic weapons at the table. More of them were emerging from a black van which had appeared from the side street. They quickly formed a cordon round them.

'Armed police! Do exactly what I say. Lie down with your hands where I can see them! Now! Lie down now!'

Two of the officers had Krotov handcuffed in a moment. The woman spoke.

'Dadash Voskresentsky, I am arresting you on suspicion of committing offences relating to section 23A and 24 of the Drug Trafficking Offences Act 1986. You do not have to say anything but it may harm your defence if you do not mention when questioned something that you later rely on in Court. Anything you do say may be given in evidence.'

He was hauled to his feet and dragged away into the black van.

'Tim Stack.'

The woman was smartly dressed and looked very business-like. Tim recognised her.

'Honour Bright!'

'It's Detective Inspector Webster now, Tim. Timothy Stack I am arresting you on suspicion of committing offences relating to section 23A of the Drug Trafficking act 1986. You do not have to say anything but it may harm your defence if you do not mention when questioned something that you later rely on in Court. Anything you do say may be given in evidence. You are nicked, Tim.'

'That's what you said when we first met.'

'Come quietly, do. You saw the APU in action just now.'

'APU?'

'Armed police. Guns, Tim. You saw them. Oh, this is Sergeant Cherry. Don't mention blossom. He doesn't like it. Sergeant, the brief-case.'

Tim tried to stay calm. 'Voskresentsky? Never heard of him. Who is he? What are you arresting me for, Detective Inspector?'

'Well, Tim – or are you Sir John these days? You are going to help me with my enquiries regarding the hundred and odd grand we expect to find in Mr. Voskresentsky's bag. We believe he was bringing it to you as part of a money-laundering operation. That money is dirty, Tim. I did not think it was your style. Now tell me what you were doing in Stratford-upon-Avon this morning just as Voskresentsky was queuing up for the guided tour.'

'Having a cup of coffee?'

In the unmarked police car Stack tried to work out what had happened to alert the police. He felt sure he had been as careful as always. Yet Honour Bright knew all about the scam – calling him Sir John made that clear. There might yet be a way out. He and the man he knew as Krotov had not made the exchange, not even acknowledged one another. Stack had not received the money. He had not laid hands on the suitcase. He had not even reached out to it. The papers in the briefcase were evidence of intent but they did not have his signature on them. Honour Bright – he smiled a little even now at the nickname – had jumped in too soon. It was all in the timing, he thought. There might be a glimmer of light there. Maybe Krotov had seen something. They were arrested at the same time but could the police be sure they were connected? Had Krotov led the police to him? Tim did not think so. He was fairly sure Krotov was not the sort to go to the police. Only honest men do that. Yet the cops arrived with him. The unmarked car sped on. Honour Bright had said 'drug trafficking'. That was a worry.

'Voznovitch is it? What has this man got to do with me? He was going through the motions now and the DI Webster was not impressed. 'Never heard of him.'

'I see where you are going with this, Tim. We lifted him a second before the exchange and you think we jumped the gun. Tell us about those deeds to Broadhurst Place in your briefcase, Tim.'

'Not my briefcase, DI Webster. You never saw me actually touch it. You won't find my fingerprints on it or in it. My name does not appear on any of the papers. And this Voznovitch, you say? Never heard of him. So what am I doing here? There is something else, right?'

'Let me tell you something about your mark, Tim. He is not Krotov. There is no Krotov. He is known to us as Dadash Voskresentsky. He is not an Azerbaijani, not Russian. He may be Georgian or Chechen or South bloody Ossetian for all I know. He is not an oil baron or an oligarch or whatever he told you. His business is borders, specifically crossing them. He moves drugs – heroin, cocaine, – and most recently girls for prostitution. It was him we were after, not you. You were a bonus, a bye-catch. You just got caught in the net.'

'You could always chuck me back in the sea.'

'No. Let me explain. As things stand you are a person of interest in a coordinated operation against an organised crime group. We expect to put Voskresentsky behind bars for a long time on drug smuggling and people trafficking offences. You are facing charges as an accomplice in laundering his dirty money, specifically the hundred and ninety thousand pounds we seized today, linked to a fraudulent scheme involving forged papers indicating ownership of a property in Oxfordshire, namely Broadhurst Place. You will be regarded by the police as member of the gang. The Crown Prosecution Service will agree to that.'

'I knew nothing about where the money came from. You know me, Honour. All right, not that well. I'm a grifter. Do you think I'm a drug runner – a trafficker?'

'We have witnesses linking you to Voskresentsky and Broadhurst Place, we have forged documents relating to the transfer of Broadhurst Place to Krotov. We will establish that Voskresentsky and Krotov are the same person. There are actually two ways this can go. You can go down with Voskresentsky as a drug smuggler and pimp—'

'—Or?'

'Or as the grifter who nearly sold a stately home to a Russian oligarch.'

'Let me think.'

'You blundered into an Interpol operation targeting Vostkresentstky that has involved the police of five countries that I know of. You were placed on a watch-list from the first time you made contact with the target. You have hardly been out of the line of sight of the police for the last three weeks. That is how we got to know about Broadhurst and Sir John. There are photos. You are on video. You don't need to think for long.'

'OK, I will cooperate. I'll plead guilty to the con.'

'I thought you might. There's more. We need you as a witness.'

After a night in the custody suite in Leamington Spa Tim found himself opposite DI Webster in the interview room at the police station back in Stratford. The tape was running. A duty solicitor sat at Tim's side.

'Now, your man Krotov or Voskresentsky. We have a witness who saw you speak to him at a restaurant in Oxford. There were three men at the table with him. I've got some photos here. Do you recognise any of them from that meeting?'

The solicitor whispered to Tim.

131

'Now I really am helping with enquiries. I am to be a witness? You want me in court with a Bible in my hand? I would really love to have that drug dealing business scrapped.'

'It's not that hard, Tim. Tell us what you know. You either go into the witness box and go down as the grifter who sold Broadhurst Place or you go down anyway as the British branch of Voskresentsky and Co, purveyors of class A drugs and minors to the Western World.'

'All right, that's clear. Show me your pictures.'

DI Webster opened her folder and fanned out half a dozen photographs. 'Do you recognise any of these men from that meeting in the Smith-Langley Hotel?'

'I was just meeting him there. It was to arrange for him to visit Broadhurst Place.'

'You met him over breakfast. He did not offer you anything. An under-cover officer saw you enter the room. It's all there on file, Tim.'

'Then why do you need me?'

'We did not get everything. We want to know who else was at the meeting. You might be able to tell us.'

'Something went wrong, I am guessing. Such surveillance and you don't know who was there?'

'Interview paused.' Webster stopped the tape. She leaned forward, confidential.

'The Met were covering the meeting. They had a feed from the hotel security cameras. There was a break in the recording. The camera in the hallway outside the meeting room suddenly went dark. It is a mystery. My superintendent is hoping you can fill the gap. If you can he will discuss the charges with the CPS— Crown Prosecution Service. Basically, the more you can tell us the lesser the charges.'

The duty solicitor whispered in Tim's ear again.

'OK, start the tape again.'

'I would like you to look carefully at these photographs. We need to identify one man in particular.'

'Well, there were no introductions so no names.'

He looked carefully, examining the pictures one by one. Voskrosentsky was in all of them. Other men were with him that Tim did not recognise. They had not been at the meeting as far he could tell. Tim held up the last photograph. There were three men, Voskrosentsky and another who had been at the meeting in the hotel. The third was standing away from the other two.

'Yes, him, I am pretty sure. He was sitting opposite Voskrosentsky. I only saw his face for a second or so. He had his back to me most of the time. He spoke to a waitress. He grabbed her. I didn't hear what he said but the waitress was upset and left. He turned to watch her and I saw his full face for a moment. Have you any more photos of him?'

'This man here? Oh, yes!' She stabbed the photograph with her finger. She looked intensely at Stack. He got the impression that the crux of the interview had arrived. He stared at the photograph.

'There was something about the way he seemed to stare. It made me think he had a glass eye."

Webster said nothing. She pushed another photo across the table. The photo was grainy but clear enough.

'Well spotted. He is blind in one eye. Please say which eye.'

'The right.'

'Ooh, I'll put in a good word for you if you say that in court.'

'And this big bloke here. He was not at the table. I got the idea that he was a minder or bodyguard – or something like that?'

'We are looking for him on another charge. He need not concern us now.'

Webster casually put another photo on the table. It showed pictures of the same man with Voskresentsky and some others he did not recognise.

'Yes, that's him.'

'Well done, Tim.'

One edge of the picture had crude scissor marks. Some of it had been cut away, crudely and obviously. Stack noticed but said nothing. At last it was over. Webster gathered up the photographs.

'Some deal,' Stack thought. 'I'm going to prison!'

Voskresentsky and the other two were tried together at the Old Bailey. It made national headlines for a week. Each morning they were brought up from HMP Belmarsh in separate transports with a police escort and motor-cycle outriders for each. It played havoc with the traffic but went down well on News at Ten. Stack was kept handy in a cell in the segregation unit 'for his own protection'. On the Friday morning, the fifth day of the trial, he put on his 'court suit'. Just as he was about to be put on a transport to join the convoy to the Old Bailey he was returned to the block and told that he wasn't going anywhere that day.

That turned out to be wrong. That afternoon he was taken out to an interview room in Belmarsh.

'Honour Bright! A lovely surprise! What's happened?'

You won't be called. The defence has collapsed. They have changed their plea, I'm not sure why. Actually, I have a nasty feeling about it. There were some faces you weren't shown. One of the photos came to me already cut up. I thought you noticed at the time. I don't know who they were. I asked about them of course. My superintendent told me it was above my pay grade. I sort of sensed it was above his too.'

'Influence! Men in high places! Are they going to get off? I hope you can see the irony of my position if they do.'

'I doubt it. They are pleading guilty about now. They will get hefty sentences. At worst they might be extradited after a year or two, if any country will admit to them being their nationals. They are two brothers and a cousin, apparently. They say they are from Uzbekistan, but have passed for Azerbaijanis, Turkish Kurds and Rumanians. All these countries are denying them at the moment. Anyway, it is a win for us.'

'And me? Perhaps you could arrange for something nicer than the block.'

'You won't be called as a witness. You are no longer in danger so have no need to be protected. You'll be out of Segregation by tomorrow or the next day. You'll do time, but nothing beyond the usual. I expect your willing cooperation will count for something with the beak.'

When it came to it Stack got 30 months. It could have been worse.

Thirteen

The first weeks of Tim's life inside were grim. His clothes were taken and replaced with the grey tracksuit bottoms and tee-shirt. He was informed that if he behaved himself for the next fortnight he would be allowed to wear his own clothes. He could have a television in his cell and buy little things from the canteen list from his weekly pay. After this 'induction' as the officer called it, he could apply for prison work.

'There are a few vacancies in two of the workshops – Woodwork and Building Trades. If you get one your pay will be 18 pence per hour. The laundry and the kitchen pay 22 pence, but there is a waiting list for those jobs. You could be out before you get to the front of the queue.' The officer smiled at his little joke. 'Tomorrow you will go to the library and meet various people who will explain more about work and education. One of the chaplains will be there, somebody from Programmes will talk to you about rehabilitation, one of the Education staff – oh and there'll be the BOV. Board of Visitors. Some men find them helpful. They'll explain. They will tell you your rights – stuff like that. While you are there you will get a chance to borrow some books, if you can read. If not, the Education Department can put you on a reading programme.'

'Of course I can read!'

'Good for you, lad. Association is at 12.30, dinner in the mess at 12.45 and the exercise yard is open till 13.30. You'll soon make new friends.' The prison officer swung the cell door shut with a firm click and peered through the flap. He flipped it shut. It made a little slapping noise. Tim heard his boots scrape on the steel gantry as he left.

He looked around. He was in a single cell for now. There was a narrow bed against one wall with a desk and hard chair tucked under it against the opposite wall. A shelf and cupboard were screwed to the wall. Tim sat on the bed. He could easily touch

135

the back of the chair without stretching. The wall opposite the steel door had a barred window, high enough not to see out without standing. A narrow window panel was open a crack. He looked through at an empty yard surrounded by a high chain link fence topped with razor wire.

That first fortnight crept by. The wing was for two sorts of prisoner; those remanded in custody awaiting trial and about the same number, like himself, starting their sentences. He signed up for Maths and English GCSE courses which would give him a chance he had denied himself. 'Why not?' he thought, 'at the least it will pass the time. And maybe it will come in handy.' He put himself down for a vacancy in the arts class. 'It will be like school again. Maybe the art teacher will be pretty, like that teacher at Stratford, the one who had a soft spot for me.'

By the end of the second week Tim was moved to another cell in another wing. He found himself sharing a slightly larger cell with another man. He was a thoughtlessly cheerful fellow who had been in and out of prisons all his life. Prison bore no terrors for him. The man was a consistent loser, a hopelessly incompetent thief who considered prison to be just a hazard of life.

'What's the point of mopin'?' he said. 'It is warm and dry. The food is a bit shite, but it is regular. That's more than can be said for some of the places I've lived in, an' that's a fact!' Tim decided that if this happy-go-lucky man could stay cheerful, so could he.

Jerome visited Tim after a month. Tim was entitled to visits from family and friends – if they were approved – and Jerome was a person of unblemished character. They sat in the Visits Hall, each a little shy and embarrassed at the circumstances. Tim asked about Jerome's progress at Oxford, Kate and his family – and Maggie. Jerome told him he had completed his degree, getting the expected 2.1, explained that this was a respectable grade, good enough to impress employees and even his father, who confessed that he had struggled with his degree and barely achieved it because of his passion for sport and the distractions of undergraduate life.

'I think that was part of our quarrel, Tim. He wanted me to have the success he missed.'

'You are going into the firm?'

'I suppose so. I'm not finished with the wide world yet, though. We can have some good times together yet!'

'In two years and five months? Let me think about it. As a matter of fact I have been thinking. There is lots of time here for that.'

'And it's what you're good at.'

'Could you do me a favour?'

'You know me, Tim. Anything – ahem – legal.'

'I want to give Maggie a bit. You know she has dreams of running her own dress-making business? Maybe you could get her to take money from me – or find out if she would take it from you.'

'I could try.'

'She can be stiff-necked about it. She always thinks I am a thief.'

Jerome indicated with a jerk of his head. 'Being here – in here, Tim. It doesn't help your case. I think you should talk to her.'

'Well, I've been thinking.'

'Here we go again!'

'Maggie probably won't take my money. She would – maybe – take it if she understood it was yours, or better, Kate's. As a business investment.'

'She is not to know that it is your money we are funneling to her? Is that it?'

'Once I am out of here I will tell her the truth. I mentioned it to Kate once.'

'If anybody can make that work you can. I'll get them together. You could help by making the suggestion to Maggie yourself.'

'Would she visit me in here?'

'I'll go to see her. I could do with a trip to London!'

The following month Maggie turned up on a visit. She approached Tim, already sitting in his allotted place. She stared wide-eyed at the bleak surroundings, at the other visitors and prisoners.

'This is awful, Tim. I never in my life expected to be visiting anybody in – in a place like this. I almost didn't come. I got as far as the gate and almost turned back.'

'I'm sorry. I know how you feel about this. You were always bothered about the things I got up to, right from the start. I know I can probably never make things completely right between us.'

'I have missed you, Tim! I still find myself glancing over at the café window half-expecting to see you at our table. Mabel asks about you. I don't know what to say. I told Moshe. He has been kind. He doesn't judge you too harshly.'

'And you?'

'I miss you. Then I am angry. Then I cry. Oh, I don't know! I almost wish I hadn't come today.'

'I miss you too. Look, one day I will explain about how I got caught. I was doing what I do and I bit off more than I could chew. I got stuck in the middle. I just got caught up in a police sting. It wasn't me that they were really after.'

'They caught you, though, didn't they?'

'Can we change the subject? Tell me about yourself How is trade?'

Maggie told Tim about successes she had had, some good quality clothing that came from one of her regulars and best of all, a frock she had made on commission which had pleased the customer.

'She said all her friends were jealous, Tim. I could get more work like that. I know I could.' She was filled with an enthusiasm that smote Tim.

'Maggie, there is something I want to talk about.'

'What is there to talk about, Tim?'

'Money, Maggie. Kate's money. Jerome says that Kate is looking for an investment. Kate has money from an inheritance or something. Some aunt left her a lot of money.'

Maggie stiffened. 'I have scraped together quite a bit myself, you know. I could just about manage on my own in a year or so.'

'It would be an investment. Kate could be a sort of sleeping partner.'

'Is this your idea?'

'Well, shall we say it came up when Jerome visited last month. It would be good for her, too. You've seen how stylish she is. And she has contacts these days. Apparently she is working for a firm with some very high class clients. She could bring in quite a bit of business, get you talked about, that sort of thing.'

'Let me think about it. Oh, Tim, I am beginning to sound like you!' She reached over the table to grasp his hands. For a moment they were the only people in the place, lost in each other. The glaring overhead lights of the Visits Hall seemed to fade. They were cocooned in a soft radiance where all Tim could see was Maggie's lovely face.

'No touching!' called the officer at the high desk. They were in the glare of the prison lights once again.

'Good luck mate!' Tim and his cellmate for six months high-fived briskly and for the last time. The other man was shipping out, on his way to freedom. He wondered about how long he would be on his own, who he might be sharing with next. He knew all about the overcrowding, so he expected company soon enough. He might be lucky and have some respite for a day or two. After eighteen months he thought he knew the ropes. He hoped he could make the best of it and rub along with any new cell-mate if he kept his head.

The hardest thing was coping with other prisoners. He knew that during association a wing was only a couple of minutes from trouble – senseless quarrels between young men pent up with frustration or anger, or some idiot deciding to jump on the netting to make some obscure point – just for devilment or out of sheer boredom. Such times as these brought nobody any good. He knew that he could be dragged into whatever broke out. It was difficult even for Tim to talk his way out of the guilt by association in the reports at the inevitable adjudications which followed.

He would manage – just so long as his next cell-mate was not some piss-head hard man full of attitude or a rattling junkie fresh from court, still coming down after his last big score before settling for his guilty plea. He had had both kinds.

Sometimes the screws put a young tearaway in with a more settled prisoner in the hope that they would settle the boy in. Tim suspected that he was seen as such by screws. Sometimes it worked. He was a grifter after all and dealing with people was part of his stock in trade. What he feared was being associated with the inevitable drug searches, the fights on the landing and worst, the nickings such men could somehow attract to the people round them. When you shared a cell who could be sure who that little wrap of smack belonged to? You could never trust a druggie not to drag you into it. Lying was natural to them. He had completed all the programmes the psychology department required of him. He had only once been drawn in by such a one. It had taken his fixing skills to have the guilty verdict of the adjudication set aside. He was determined that that was how it would be for his parole board.

His new cell mate arrived after two nights of not having to share the loo or endure the stink of a stranger's piss at three in the morning. Generally, there was a ritual to get through, negotiation for the top bunk and for what goes where in the narrow cell – careful little steps which could determine how the next weeks and months would work out.

The man was stocky, bald and hard shaved, wearing his prison blue tee-shirt, track suit bottoms and trainers. His strong frame was hardened by hours – years – spent pushing weights in the gym. He was, maybe, sixty, though it was always tricky to judge age. Men on the inside often looked far beyond their age. There was nothing about him that did not say 'Basic Prisoner'. That was a worry straight away. No old man would be Basic if he was not some sort of head-case.

The man did not trouble with these niceties of introduction. He wasted no time on negotiating which bunk he would occupy or how to share the little space. He unpacked his plastic box of possessions quietly and methodically. He stowed his little stock of clothing neatly in the drawers. Tim observed him. Nothing much to see there, only what looked like prison issue stuff – not a thing bought or sent in. Next, he took out a poster of Glasgow Rangers football team posing with a huge trophy and stuck it carefully on the wall with Blu-Tack by the bottom bunk. He arranged his toiletries in a careful row to one side of the hand basin, avoiding any overlap with Stack's own carelessly dropped stuff. He took out two oranges, two bananas, a little radio and two photos in plastic frames and arranged them in careful symmetry on the bare lower shelf. He hardly glanced at Tim until they were arranged and the empty bunk made up.

Tim watched. The lotion next to the shaving soap was not something a basic prisoner would be allowed. Probably not a head-banger after all.

At last the man spoke to his new cell mate. 'It's all the same to me. I've done nineteen years and I've got one more before my parole. I've been in better places and worse. If it's up to me we'll get on fine. Giovanni Rossi. Call me Jo.' There was a strong lilt of Scottish in his voice - Glaswegian probably.

'Tim Stack.'

Rossi grunted, then was silent. Tim noted that he seemed instantly at home, comfortable, even content. After ten minutes he became almost invisible, as if prison had rubbed him out leaving only a faint outline of a man. Perhaps Rossi would turn out well for him.

Eighteen years had taught Rossi that less is more, property is clutter and clutter gets in the way. He might as well have been a monk and this his monastic cell. The austere rhythm of prison soothed him, anchored him. It did not matter to him where he was because his head was always in the same place. The drab painted brick or smooth concrete walls were all the same to him; the view of nothing much through the narrow panes of the cell window unchanging. He had been in many cells in many prisons. He knew how to wait. Eighteen years of practice; at first as the Cat A prisoner moved from cell to cell, from prison to high security prison, searched and watched, counted out and back in again. He waited. His prison record showed him to be compliant, respectful and a calming influence. Security departments shared his occasional discreetly informative reports about certain troublesome men. The more perceptive of them considered that these nuggets of intelligence might have something to do with Rossi's sensitivities. Rossi liked order; his reports always fingered certain types of disorderly prisoners.

His level of risk to the public was now considered low enough to be accommodated in a Cat B prison; so there he was, sharing a cell with Stack. There was plenty of time. He knew how to wait. Waiting had become Rossi's life.

There were a few men on the wing who remembered him from earlier times, previous stretches in other prisons. He was a man who commanded respect, a man to step aside for. Word spread round the wing and from there round workshops and classroom sessions. Rossi was there. In his day Rossi had been the best, an elite among the elite. He had been a peter-man, a safebreaker who they said could walk through walls. They said that he had picked the Bramah lock, something only he and one other had done. No lock could detain him. Rossi did not deny it. Tim saw the irony but thought better of mentioning it.

Tim and Jo rubbed along. Tim observed Jo subtly, hoping to draw him even a little out of his box. Jo gave little away. It was as if they were strangers on a train conceding to one another with a few politely guarded words the necessary adjustments that avoided familiarity. It is surprising how little actual contact occurs between people in an apparently jostling crowd. Tim and Jo were close but they did not touch. Tim learned that Jo was indeed from Glasgow, one of many descendants of Italian immigrants who settled during the famine years of the late Nineteenth Century. His forebears were involved in the razor wars of the Gorbals. Tim wondered if this was Jo's veiled hint of his own past and filed it in his mind under 'another thing to think about'. Jo did not at first discuss his criminal past despite Tim's subtle invitations. This reticence could not last. There had to be a time when Jo would open up, surely?

Days in prison were never easy but the nights were worse. In the long dark of night the barriers broke down – just a bit. Jo dreamed and sometimes spoke out. Wakeful, Tim heard. Jo's secrets might come bubbling out and even if Tim was interested he did not want to be too informed. There was no upside to knowing Jo's secrets. He should let him know about the problem. It was a delicate matter.

'You shouted out last night.'

'What did I say? Nothing incriminating, I hope? Nothing embarrassing?'

'I couldn't hear exactly, it was sort of garbled — or Scottish. I mention it because, well, I don't want to know things you would rather keep secret. I guess you haven't shared a cell before, coming out of high security. You could have been blurting out all kinds of stuff and nobody would know. The thing is, what to do. You don't know what you are saying and I don't want to know.'

They talked quietly in the dark, at first about inconsequentials. Rossi's solitude was deeply ingrained. It had always been something of a safety mechanism for him long before his prison days. After a month he had become more open than he had ever been about his past and about his disastrous early life in Glasgow tenements with the gangs, how he wanted to be out, his apprenticeship to a locksmith which soon developed into an entirely different sort of training. His gaffer was a master at his trade and Rossi was a willing, gifted pupil.

Tim surprised himself and perhaps Rossi by letting slip a few salient facts about his own past, his unhappy home life with his drunken father and cowed mother. He was a grifter and he admitted to Rossi that while he always knew when he was lying did not always tell the truth even when it did not matter. Rossi laughed, a low grunting guffaw, like a boulder rolling down a hill. Stack had never heard him laugh. Maybe it was the first time in years.

'Oh, aye, I've met grifters who couldn't order their pint of heavy without spinning the barmaid a yarn. It wasn't always helpful.'

After this they spoke often. They acknowledged one another on the landing. They sometimes messed together or played pool before bang-up with other men. It was the most social either had been – for Stack in months – for Rossi, years. In their cell they discussed men on the wing; who was dangerous, who would be ready to grass on others, who was simply 'too thick to pour' in Rossi's words. Stack expressed irritation about a man who had barged in front of him at the server.

'You don't want to make a big issue of it, but it rankles, you know. Little things like that can blow up. People like him are just itching to kick off.'

'I know yon bampot! Have you noticed he's sniffing up all the time?'

'Now you mention it.'

'Plug, I call him.

'Who?'

'From the Bash Street Kids.' Tim did not know. Jo reached across to his shelf and handed Tim a Beano annual. Have a look at this. Next time you see him sniff remember Plug.'

The advice worked. There was a next time with some other man at the pool table. Barge. Sniff. Stack tried not to laugh.

Rossi would dismiss prisoners and officers with a laconic word or give them a nickname which very often punctured the image or reduced the annoyance to a joke. Stack quickly picked up on it and it became a tacit game between them. Soon they had a stock of names for the head-bangers, swaggerers and jack-the-lads – numpties and dunderheids, as Jo called them. They ran out of Bash Street Kids but there were plenty more names in that old Beano.

It was a trick Rossi had picked up during his years in high security. It had become a small part of what kept him sane while others around him cracked and crumbled. Stack found it worked for him too.

The time wore on in the dull way of prison days. There were testosterone fuelled spats among the younger men. That was pretty normal. There were incidents of drug-induced misbehaviour. Neither of the two men let it trouble them; they would never get involved.

The time came when Stack was to prepare for his return to the world. There had been some discussion with his probation officer over how the transition could be managed. Stack himself had little idea; he had never actually worked for wages since his days as a paper lad, not a line of work that would impress the probation officer.

'So, what are you going to do when you get out?' Rossi asked after the tricky encounter. 'It isn't as if you have got a job lined up.'

'I suppose I'll just pick up here I left off—and be very careful. It is all I know.'

'I think you need some careers advice, Tim. You should go to the library.'

'Oh, yes, and get a book out?'

'You could get a book out, but that's not the point of your trip. You need to get to know the librarian, Arthur. He will be on the desk tomorrow. He was in Belmarsh for a while. He had a job lined up.'

'I'm a grifter. What would I be doing stealing antiques?'

'I know, you are not a thief. Nor was he, really. He got caught with stolen goods. He was an antique dealer, what they call a 'runner', strictly confidential trading, no premises or nothing. His big thing was finding stuff that the owner didn't know the value of – sleepers, he called them. He reckoned that he had done some really big deal just before he was sent down.'

'Prison talk! How often have you heard that in here? Every useless little crook will tell you that.'

'Aye, right enough. This was different. It was when he had just been sentenced. It was just after my Cat B adjudication. I looked out for Arthur for a bit when he was taking it hard. He was in a poor way when I met him.'

'I got a bit of help from somebody myself. My first pad-mate really cheered me up. I think they do that sometimes – put men together that way.'

'Aye, maybe. Anyway, I reckon he was telling the truth. He told me he had found something bigger than he could handle on his own. He said it was something huge, an Old Master or something.'

'I don't know where I come in. I'm a grifter. I don't sell valuable things. That's sort of the point.'

'He told me a bit about what he had planned. He was sure there was a big payday for him. I think it is right up your street.'

I'm not a thief, Jo, you know that. I don't steal. People give me money but they get something in return. Usually they go off happy because—'

'—they never know they've been conned! I know.'

'Why would he tell me about it?'

'You are a grifter! It should be child's play for you. Or you could mention my name. Look, Tim. He can't go back to the antiques trade. It is all about reputation and his is shot to pieces. He might never be able to go back to it. I think he sees this as his chance. Make him a promise he thinks you'll keep, and maybe keep it. There'll be something in it for me too, Tim. I won't be inside for ever. I'm coming up to parole myself.' I am going to give you something and I will want something back.'

'If I did not know you better I would say that sounded like a threat, Jo.'

'No, not a threat. More doing me a favour. I have plans for when I am out. I might need a good man to help me. There is nobody on the out that I can trust now.'

'Hm.'

'Go to the library and look up some careers advice. Get close to Arthur. If you don't do it I'll have to find a new man. That will be a pity because I think you are ideal for it. And what's to lose? It is not as if you have anything better to do.'

'At the least, I can get a book out. That probation officer will be pleased, I suppose.'

Fourteen

Arthur Golightly had found prison a real hardship. He discovered that his life among antiques had been precious to him. He had briefly lost himself in prison. He had spent several weeks being watched as a suicide risk. He spent his long days remembering pieces he had found, deals he had made. He did his best to forget the sixteen Queen Anne chairs which had been his downfall and to put thoughts of the man who had sold them to him out of his mind. He thought of the Canova he had left in that meat safe in that Lambeth lock-up. 'It will be long gone by the time I am out of here,' he thought.

Tim easily picked out the old man trusted to run the library while the actual librarian sat in her office drinking herbal tea. By the third visit he was speaking to Arthur like an old friend. When he mentioned Jo Rossi Arthur brightened.

'I heard he is here,' he said. 'I don't think he is the reading type so I don't expect him to come into the library, but he helped me in Belmarsh. He was steady when I wasn't.'

'I know what you mean. Steady is exactly right. He shares with me now. He has a couple of years to do. He is waiting for the word to be sent to an open prison. He said I should look you up. He said we could help each other.'

'I told him something in Belmarsh. Maybe I shouldn't have.'

'He said you had found something big, something you probably couldn't handle on your own.'

'Bloody Hell! He said that?'

'He said I was just the right man for the job. The trouble is, he didn't say what the job was.'

'No, I don't suppose he did. I didn't tell him all that much. He must have guessed. Maybe I said more than I intended.'

'Jo is clever. He picks up on little things. Look, I don't know where I come in. I know nothing about antiques. The nearest I've come was selling an old watch once.'

'Do you know anything about art?'

'As in painting, that sort of thing? Not really'

'Read this book.' Golightly took a book from the shelf in the corner of the room. 'When you have finished it I will tell you some more.' He stamped the book and wrote Tim's name on his clipboard.

The librarian popped her head round her office door. 'Closing time!' she trilled. The two exchanged looks. Tim rolled his eyes. Arthur Golightly thrust the book at Tim and turned took a book from another prisoner.

Tim flicked through the first pages of the library book. It was mostly full-page colour prints of oil paintings. He glanced at the accompanying text. Jo looked on.

'Has Arthur given you homework, then?'

'I'll look at it properly after association when we are banged up for the night. It's got pictures.'

'Aye, right. Like a bairn's book.'

'Not really.' Tim held up the book to reveal a reclining nude. 'He was asking after you.'

'He couldn't really take in what had happened to him. When I told him how much time I still had to do I think he managed to put his wee stretch into perspective.'

'I remember feeling much the same. I should think it is harder for an older man.'

'Oh, aye.'

In the hour between tea and bang-up there was association when prisoners could play pool, exercise in the yard or lounge in the evening air. For many this was the best time of the day. Tim took Arthur's book into the sunshine. By bang-up time he was well into it. He finished it the next day. It was more interesting than he expected, but he still did not know why Golightly had given him it. All the pictures were in museums, it seemed, and utterly out of reach of thieves. And Tim was not a thief.

On his next visit to the library Tim returned the book. Arthur was there as usual and stamped it with a flourish.

'Good read?'

'It was, but I'm not sure why I had to read it. I'm not a thief, you know. And if I was those paintings are in some of the safest

148

places possible. And in any case they are so well known nobody would buy one of them. They would know they were hot.'

'Yes and no. Some people will buy such pieces regardless of their status, just because they can. Did you see the Vermeers?'

'Those domestic scenes with rather plain girls reading a letter and stuff? Yes, very nice.'

'And priceless. Did you read that there are as many fake Vermeers as genuine?'

'Yes. Is this going somewhere?'

'I know where there is what I think is a fake Vermeer, hanging on a wall where nobody is interested in it.'

'You are thinking I could pass it off as genuine.'

'I am thinking you could help sell it to someone, but not as a Vermeer.'

'You've lost me.'

'It is a long story. The screw is looking at us. Go and choose a book.'

Tim chose another art book. It was full of pictures of Dutch masters.

'Good choice.'

'What a collection! I'm a bit surprised that expensive books like this are in the prison library.'

'I ordered them. The boss-lady hardly ever leaves her office. She leaves it to me. Send Jo Rossi and I'll lend him one. You can look at it together.'

Jo visited the library for the first time in all his years inside. Arthur greeted him like a brother. He showed him to the shelves holding the art books Arthur had carefully brought into the prison.

'Just browse for a bit and choose something to take away. It doesn't matter which one, so long as you give yourself a reason to come back.'

'Oh aye, I'll do that.' Then in a quieter voice, 'Why do I think you are cooking something up?'

Golightly glanced over his shoulder. The librarian was visible though the glass panel of her office, gossiping with the officer. 'You'll see', he muttered. She looked in their direction; the screw did the same.

'Oh, good choice, Jo,' he said out loud.

149

A sign went up on notice boards around the prison that the library was starting a Fine Arts study group with special emphasis on Dutch Masters, to meet on Friday afternoons.

'That's our cue,' said Rossi.

'It is an official prison notice.'

'Aye, Tim, it is. He's got that librarian in the palm of his hand. We'll apply, eh?' It was not really a question.

They duly turned up and found that there was no-one else present.

'There were three others wanted to come but I threw their applications in the bin,' said Arthur. 'Let's make a start.' He led them to a large table already spread with the art books. 'I've asked the librarian Mrs Jenkinson if she would like to sit in for these sessions. She likes to get off early on Fridays, so there's not much chance of it. Jo, let me tell you what this is about. I know where there is a Vermeer that is not in a gallery or museum. It is not even secure because the owners don't know what it is. The only trouble is that it is probably a forgery.'

'That explains the lack of security' said Jo, almost to himself. 'What's the point of locking up a fake? You are going to a lot of trouble over this painting, Arthur. What's up? I know you find sleepers. Is that what this is? I've never heard of a fake sleeper.'

'I think I understand, said Tim. 'The fake is valuable too. It reminds me of a job I did once.'

'Let me show you,' said Arthur. 'Here it is.' He opened one of the art books at a marked page. 'Read that.' He pointed to a passage opposite a painting entitled: 'Woman with her Maid'.

Baron Henning Ferdinand Busson von Sonnenberg am der Ruhr was not a self made man. He was what has become known as 'old money'. On his father's side of the family the Baron was heir to self-made men made rich by the railways, steel and coal; on his mother's, he was descended from Electors of the Holy Roman Empire, bankers to Napoleon and before that to the Hapsburgs. His family counted themselves as Austrian though they had lived in Germany, close to their factories, for many years. He could boast of a shared lineage with crowned heads and dukes of the Renaissance. He wielded the

150

subtle, whispering power money and titles gave him. The fate of nations seemed to await the word of such men as the Baron in that time when Europe stood on the brink of war. He wore the responsibility lightly. He moved with the smart set in his youth and was a well-known figure in the salons of European capitals in his maturity. Outside these fashionable circles he was hardly known at all.

What does a man like him do with his days? The Baron was a collector. His education had made an aesthete of him: student days in Berlin, London and Vienna showed him a world beyond the smoky homelands of industrial Germany. He had perhaps inherited some of the good taste of his aristocratic mother and her refined forebears. His preference was for Old Masters; as money was hardly an issue more or less any painting which came to market and appealed to him he simply bought and installed in one of the family apartments or the castles which had come to the family on the death of some princeling. His acquisitions hung alongside works from the Renaissance onwards, many of them commissions from the artists themselves.

Wherever he travelled he enjoyed the solace of fine art. And bought some more. He was a shrewd buyer and bought almost exclusively from men who were known for probity. His own reputation as a connoisseur brought him a little fame in certain circles. Inevitably, he received invitations to exhibitions and gallery events. That is how he met Leo Nardus, a sophisticated criminal. Nobody saw anything odd or suspicious in the name, or if they did, said nothing.

Nardus introduced him to a painting by Vermeer. Vermeer was not fashionable despite the admiration of the artistic elite for the few known paintings by him. Works by the Dutch master hung in the Rijksmuseum but only now were attracting attention.

Nardus thought the painting's owner Theo van Weingarderen, a dillettante and collector, could perhaps be persuaded to sell. Introductions were made, the painting viewed by the baron and one or two of his expert friends and the subject of the sale of the picture was broached. The repeated refusals to part with the painting were countered with increasingly eye-watering offers. Weingarderen could be paid in guilders, marks or pounds sterling – any currency he liked. Henning von Sonnenberg even offered to send a bank messenger with a banker's draft. In the end van Garderen's resistance was broken down. An undisclosed sum was paid and the picture was delivered to the Baron. He had of, course, been the victim of a confidence trick, a fact that would eventually be revealed when the celebrated forger van Meegeren was arrested. But this was after the War, long after the Baron had parted with the work and, indeed, this life.

The painting hung in one of his retreats, a discreet villa on the shore of Lake Garda where the Baron slipped away when the duties of his estates and enterprises allowed. In the way of collectors he eventually lost interest in the painting as he pursued other prizes. He was besotted with the Austrian Secessionists; then it was Impressionism. He drew the line at Expressionism for its raw emotion and was frankly repelled by Cubism.

The 'Vermeer' remained in a private room, unremarked and seldom viewed. Nothing much is known about it after the War. It might have formed part of the settlement when he and his second wife divorced. She ended up as the wife of an Englishman. It may have left the castle in 1939 along with other pieces to be stored in Switzerland. At any rate it is not at the lakeside villa now. Where is it? Nobody knows.

'You think you know where the work is,' said Jo.
'Well, I think it is in a house in Warwickshire.' He stopped. It was the librarian. 'Ah, Mrs Jenkinson, glad you could spare the

152

time. We've just got started. We are beginning at the top and working down.'

She glanced at the open book. 'Rembrandt, is it, Arthur?'

'Well spotted, Mrs. Jenkinson!' said Tim. 'Are you interested in the Dutch Masters? Perhaps you could join us. None of us are experts.'

'Another time. I'll be off, Arthur. An officer will keep an eye on the library this afternoon. I have asked him not to disturb you.' She swept out, leaving the scent of Lily of the Valley in the library air.

'I think we've got the place to ourselves for a bit,' said Arthur. They heard a noise like a rusty hinge. Arthur Golightly was laughing.

Over the next three Friday afternoons they hatched a plan.

Fifteen

Gloria laid a tray of champagne glasses onto the largest table in the back room and poured out the first of the bottles of his finest bubbly. He spread his arms wide to include the whole room.

'Welcome home, Tim!'

'Welcome home!' called the others.

Jerome and Kate were there of course. Jerome in a suit! Kate dashingly smart in a well-made dress. Ben sat in his corner, watchful. Maggie sat uncertainly at the edge of the group.

'It is lovely to have you back,' continued Gloria. 'You must see my new act. I've got new songs and lovely new uniforms. I put in a prison officer specially for you! I'm working on a routine with handcuffs.' He gave a little giggle as he fussed over the second bottle, at last popping the cork with a flourish. 'I have kept your place upstairs. Jerome has been paying the rent.'

'It is a handy place to have now that I have to make trips to London for the firm,' said Jerome. 'And we couldn't have you homeless, could we, sleeping in doorways?' His eyes met Tim's for an instant.

'That would never do, Jerome.' Tim sat in his old place, taking in the company, hardly daring to believe he was free. He had waited two years and four months for this moment.

'Thank you, said Tim.

'I know it's early days—'

'—it's my first day, you mean, Jerome! You are wondering, aren't you? You are all wondering – am I the same Tim Stack you knew two years and four months ago? You are, aren't you?'

'It's been a long time, Tim. We wouldn't be surprised if the experience had got to you. It can't have been easy. We have been worried, you know,' said Kate.

'I am a sadder and a wiser man. Not all of it was bad. I have learned things. I have met some characters. In some ways I am stronger for it. And I have been thinking,' said Tim.

'Ah, Tim is back all right!' said Kate.

Gloria fetched sandwiches in on a big tray.

'This is an improvement on prison food!'

'That would not be difficult, Gloria. Is that smoked salmon?' Tim reached out. 'Oh, Gloria, this is a taste of paradise! Thank you.'

'The porridge sandwiches went soggy, Tim. I had to make do.' Gloria gave sniggered. 'Welcome back!'

They gathered round the table, old friends enjoying their reunion.

At last Maggie moved to Tim's side. She spoke, quietly enough for only Tim to hear. 'It's good to see you again, Tim. I almost didn't come today. Jerome and Kate said I should. They think—'

'—I'm glad you came, Maggie. I—' Maggie stopped him from speaking with a finger on his mouth. Tim leaned in. The conversation faded. The little back room in the Greenwich pub disappeared.

'I have to look after the shop,' said Maggie. Her head was resting on Tim's shoulder.

'Stay a little bit longer. Tell me about the shop. Is it what you talked about before, er, before?'

'A shop and design studio.'

'Yes. How is it going?'

'I love the place. It is a bit shabby but that's all right. Kate says it has atmosphere. It has a big room upstairs which I have turned into a cutting room. I have taken on a girl – Daisy – part-time from college for the needlework. I do the designs and cutting. She helps make them up. People are starting to come in on recommendation. Kate wears some of my dresses when she meets clients and she tells them where she gets them. I am selling two or three dresses almost every week. It's working, Tim. It's doing well! I really believe in it.'

'Have you given up the stall? I dream – used to dream – of you there with your hair tied back.' Maggie squeezed his arm.

'No, not altogether. I have brought in another dealer and we share the rent. She has a different eye from mine, more voguish and up to the minute but we can sell each other's stock. I daren't give it up entirely yet. It is like insurance. Come and see my place.' There was no mistaking the pride in her voice.

'I will. I'd love to.'

'And now I must get back to it. Here is where to find me.' She slipped him a plain white business card and slipped out of the room.

That left Tim, Jerome, Kate and Ben.

'Like old times,' said Jerome.

'You know I am on parole,' said Tim. 'I have to see my probation officer and she will want to hear about my plans for getting a job. I have decided to enrol at art college.'

'Is this anything to do with what you have been thinking?' asked Jerome.

'I shall enrol. That will please Mrs Craig. Now I can tell her I have got an address as well. My parole is just the two months I got off for good behaviour, so that takes care of that. And yes. There is a plan.'

'Something's coming,' said Jerome. 'I could tell.'

'I made some connections inside. In particular, with an antique dealer. He is getting out in a few weeks. He was hatching a plan before he was had up for receiving stolen goods.'

'We are not thieves,' said Ben. 'Not even me any more. You know I am doing proper work – and doing well. One day I will be running a business for myself.'

'I don't want to risk that. Ben. There will be nothing illegal for you. If you could just find a mark with spare cash to invest—'

'—Maybe, Tim. I am legal now, and that is how it must be in the future.'

'Agreed. Here is an address. I would like to know as much as possible about the owner of this place. Can you buy one of those polaroid cameras? Can you afford a couple of days off? Visit Kate in Warwickshire, maybe? And take a couple of holiday snaps?'

'Mother would love to see you again, Ben.'

'The house is about to close. Please make your way to the exit.' People looking at the shelves of porcelain shuffled towards the door. A family began to organize to leave, children lagging after a long afternoon. A young man and woman stood back to allow them to squeeze past with a baby buggy laden with paraphernalia. With the room empty the woman casually took a photo of her companion who pointed to an oil painting hanging above a fireplace.

'No photography, please!'

'OK.' The woman continued to wave the camera haphazardly. The young man stood at a table before the fireplace with a porcelain figurine and a metallic head of a man, an African. He smiled.

'Sorry, it's the rule. Photography is not allowed.'

'Just one more! To remember our visit?' The young man, hardly more than a boy, grinned cheekily at the attendant. The camera clicked.

'The house is closing. I am glad that you have enjoyed your visit, but—'

They left the room and the house without a fuss. If asked the room attendant would be hard put to describe them. Medium height, ordinary clothes. The young man wore a cap. They had paid at the door, were not seen at the café or the shop. Not that they had done anything very wrong, and the staff were unlikely to be questioned. If anyone had looked at the photographs they would not have seen either of them in frame. The photos had captured a smallish picture of a Dutch interior in sharp focus, on a pier table; below it an ornate porcelain figurine and an African head. The plaque screwed to the wall read: '*A Lady in at her Toilette with Servant* once attributed to Vermeer.' The figurine and head had no plaque.

'Let's get off. If we move now we should get to the Fleece before Arthur. If we are not there when he arrives he might just slide off. He's being so careful.'

Golightly turned up minutes after them. He slipped quietly into the bar.

'Have you got them?'

'Hi, Arthur. Yes, have a look.' Kate held out two polaroid images.

'Hmm. That's the one, all right.

'Now drink up and push off. Be in your car and away before I finish my pint. And, er, thank you.'

'A pleasure.'

Kate and Ben slipped away. They didn't look back as they drove off. If they had they might still not have seen Golightly watching after them from the doorway, nor Tim making his way in from the pub garden.

Arthur shoved the picture under Tim's nose.

'That's it? It looks the part, I can see that. Light streaming in from the left through an unseen window. Tiled floor. Is that a map on the wall behind?'

'Yes. The snap doesn't do justice to the colour, but the palette is close to Vermeer's. I am pretty sure it is a very good copy – or a decent forgery.'

'Or the real thing?'

'I doubt it.'

'It doesn't matter for the deal, does it? Jo shipped out last week. He is at Ball Cross, the open prison. It is really handy for the Old Kent Road. He can be into London and out again in next to no time. He is sending a list of equipment he might need. I haven't found a mark yet but Ben is on to that, I hope.'

'Can he just get in and out with nobody seeing him? It sounds too good to be true.'

'We'd best leave that to him. He will tell us when he is ready. I will let him know when to make his move. I should see this painting properly, Arthur, to be convincing.'

You know it's at Binton Chadlow Hall in Warwickshire. In the morning room, whatever that was for. Easy to find. The house will be closed to the public by now. They hire out part of it as a conference centre. I have some business in London. That Bill Bradley still owes me eighty grand for the Canova.'

Ben found it easy to find the Binton Chadlow owner. He looked him up in Who's Who, found his London address. He got Eddie, the pickpocket from south of the river, to watch him and find out how he spent his days. Ben reported to Tim within the week.

'Peter Alexander Heinrich Witts Witts-Chadlow was at Eton, got a degree at Cambridge and had a spell in the army, retiring with the rank of major. He has tea with his mother in Fortnum and Mason's every Thursday. She always has toasted crumpets. His grandmother was married to Baron von Sonnenberg of Witts-Nurmann. I cannot say his full name without laughing. The titles were abolished after the War. He is just Major the Honourable Peter Chadlow these days. I found another use for the polaroid camera.' Ben put a photo on the table. 'That's him. He is a rich man, Tim.'

'That's the sort we like.'

'No, really rich. Money is nothing to him. He is not your usual sort. You cannot con an honest man, you said. He is honest.'

'I'm not after his money.'

'Now you've got *me* thinking, Tim.'

'Here's something for you. I've put in a grand for expenses. You can pay Eddie out of that.'

Binton Chadlow was in a hollow among ancient woodlands. A discreet sign pointed to the driveway off a minor road with high hedges. Beside it a sign read 'House Closed. Next open day: June 1st'. Tim drove into the estate. At the end of a wooded carriage drive the house sat in a lawned space. It was a mixture of red brickwork and mellow local sandstone. There was a gatehouse with a high arch leading into a courtyard. By the main door directly opposite the arch was a small placard standing on an easel: 'Welcome to Meditation Workshops' with an arrow pointing to the steps.

Inside was a reception desk and a young man in a white suit with a lapel badge. 'Brian' it said. Tim signed the book, took his lapel badge and followed the arrow through the hall into a room. A dozen or so people were already there, sitting on plastic chairs arranged in a semi-circle. The room was dominated by a large white screen and an elaborate projector. 'Mrs. Craig will be pleased when I tell her,' he thought. The session started with an earnest lady, also in white, outlining the day's activities.

'For our first day's activity the whole group will work together on exercises in relaxation techniques you will find useful during the week here. You will build up throughout the day as you progress through stages. Each stage is represented by a different room.'

Tim shuffled out with the others. The group went through Relaxation, Concentration, Mind Calming and whatnot. They at last entered a room lined with cabinets full of porcelain. Brian called it the 'Empty Mind' room. Tim saw the picture at once. He stood before it, taking his time. Close to, he could see why Arthur had got excited. The palette was Vermeer's. He was brought back in a moment to that prison cell, poring over those art books. He saw instantly that the overall composition resembled the interiors by Vermeer he remembered from his studies in that old cell. The light from a window on the left of the canvas fell on the woman's maid rather than on the ostensible subject, the woman in the fine clothes before a mirror. On the back wall was a printed map. The maid was looking out of the painting. She was half-smiling, either at a remark of her mistress or at some secret shared with the artist – or perhaps the viewer.

'Are you ready, Mr. er, Simpson, we are waiting. Could you take your place please?'

Tim turned to the white suited young man. It was Brian from the reception desk. 'Yes, I think so.' He strode off through the house, out of the front door and away.

Back in London Tim went straight to Fortnum and Mason. He glanced about the bright cafe-style room.

'What about that table there?' He pointed at table near the windows with a Reserved sign. The waitress shook her head.

'I'm afraid it is booked for tomorrow as well. It is a very popular spot, Sir.'

'Oh, I expect that is Peter's usual table. I wouldn't want to inconvenience old Chadlow.'

'No, Sir, Major Chadlow always sits in the corner there.'

'Haven't seen him in years. He used to bring his mother here, I remember.'

'Yes, Sir. I expect they'll be here tomorrow as usual. Shall I put you at the next table, Sir?'

'Lovely! Yes, please!'

Tim called on Maggie in her shop. She was upstairs with Daisy, poring over some sketches.

'How would you like to have tea and scones at Fortnum and Mason's tomorrow?'

'It isn't really your style, a place like that, Tim. You are up to something, aren't you?'

'Wouldn't you like to show off one of your lovely afternoon frocks to the idle rich? I bet you will make people look up from their gateaux when you make your entrance. I have booked a

160

table. How about meeting you here at three-thirty? We can stroll down Piccadilly together just in nice time. Daisy can cover.'

'Maybe, Tim. We have lives, you know, even when you are not around.'

'If you can't, you can't. I'll feel a bit funny on my own, but if I must—'

'Oh, all right, I'll manage somehow. You can tell me what you are up to over cream tea.'

Sixteen

Golightly turned his old van into the alleyway. Nothing there seemed to have changed. He rang the bell at number 14. The rasping voice asked his business. 'That will be the French polisher,' Arthur thought.

'Bradley. Is he here?'

'Who wants to see him?'

'Golightly.'

'Hang on a second.'

'Arthur Golightly! What do you want?' It was Bradley.

'You know what I want. Let me in.'

'You'll get nothing from me, Golightly. I don't deal with the likes of you. I'm surprised they have let you out of prison already.'

'I've come for my money, Bill. You know what you owe me.'

'I don't deal with criminals, Arthur. You are getting nothing from me.'

I want what you owe me. We had a deal.'

'What are you going to do about it, Arthur, call the police? Now, get yourself off before I call them myself.'

Arthur stood still. His face distorted in frustration. At last he turned and climbed into the van.

He drove straight to Greenwich.

Tim was surprised to see Arthur sitting in the back room.

'I've been waiting for you,' he grumbled. 'I've just lost my eighty grand. That rogue Bradley laughed in my face. I'm pretty sure he has sold that statue. We had a deal, I told him. I've got money put by, it's not that. I suppose it is just the way it will be for me now.'

'It's not right, though, Arthur. Tell me a bit more about him.'

'He was a cabinet maker in the Jewellery Quarter in Birmingham when I first knew him. He knew next to nothing about the antiques trade then. He did some restoration work for me. He was never satisfied with that and began dealing off his own bat. I sold him pieces he could make a handy profit out of and he opened a workshop in Lambeth. He did well. Now he has a very nice shop in the West End. Very exclusive.'

'He has cheated you. That wasn't very nice. He's greedy, unscrupulous and dishonest. You know, Arthur, I think we have found our mark.'

It was a bright sunny afternoon. Tim and Maggie walked the last ten minutes through Berkeley Square and along Piccadilly. Maggie wore one of her dresses. It was just right for a spring day, a white and subtle green cotton print. Her hair was pulled back and secured with a matching ribbon.

'You look lovely.'

'I should. This is an exclusive dress. It is the only one in the world – so far. Daisy is running up another five, each a different print.'

'I wasn't talking about the dress, Maggie. But the dress too. It looks wonderful on you.'

'Lead me to my cream tea, young man, I'm famished. Look at us, though, two Stratford kids going out to tea in Mayfair! Who'd have thought it?'

The waitress Tim had spoken to the day before showed them to their table. The table next to them was occupied by a middle-aged man and an elderly lady. They paid no attention to the couple at the next table. This was a moment that Tim knew well even though it had been a while since the last time. He felt the old nervous excitement. This was what he did best.

'Excuse me,' he said. 'It is Major Chadlow, isn't it?'

'Have we met?'

'Well, sir, it was at Caterham, I think. I was with my father, so I suppose we haven't actually met. I think he pointed you out as his company officer when he was a sergeant in the Coldstream Guards. Just before his Cyprus posting. Simpson, sir. He would love to know I bumped into you.'

'Cyprus, you say? That was a long time ago. What a mess that turned into.'

'My father always says they should have let them get on with it.'

163

'Hmm, I dare say he was right. Please pass on my regards to, er, Simpson.' He turned to the waitress to give his order.

Tim and Maggie's date was rather strained from then on. Maggie resisted Tim's efforts at conversation. In the end she stood up.

'I have to get back to the shop, she said stiffly. 'Daisy can't do the till yet and I must be sure the place is properly locked up.'

'I know. London. It's full of thieves.'

'Not funny any more, Tim.'

Maggie turned to leave.

'Excuse me.' It was the elderly lady. 'That dress you are wearing – it is lovely. Forgive me for asking, but where did you find it?' She turned to her son. 'Peter, your niece would look divine in that, don't you agree?' She continued without waiting for an answer. 'She is just your size, I would say, and something of your colouring.'

'Thank you. It's a little place just off the Portobello Road. It hasn't been open long.'

'I must tell her. What is it called?'

'Just Maggie's. I haven't thought of a proper name for it.'

'It's yours?'

'Well, yes, I—'

'It is your own design? I'll suggest she pays you a visit. How can she find you?' Maggie delved into her little handbag and extracted her card.

'Thank you.' She swept out of the room with her son following.

'Wow! That sounds like a sale, Maggie.'

Maggie abruptly sat down again. 'Now you can tell me what that was all about, Tim Stack. Simpson? Sergeant in the Grenadiers? Blooming Cyprus! You are up to something. This was supposed to be a nice afternoon tea, not something you are "thinking about".'

'I just want to borrow something from him for a bit. Very good, that about 'Just Maggie's'. You should get it up over the window.'

'Won't you tell me anything? I worry about you, you know. If you end up in prison again don't expect me to visit. It was horrible. I won't do it again.'

'I will explain, Maggie. This is not the place – or the time.'

'I helped over that business with the watch. That was for Ben. What is this for, Tim?'

'It is for Arthur. And for Jo Rossi. We shared a cell for a time.'

'For criminals?'

'Ben was a criminal, Maggie. Remember?'

'Ben wanted to escape. What do these men want?'

'It is a long story – two long stories. They are not mine to tell. Maybe they will tell you themselves some day.'

'You'll have to do better than that.'

Maggie got to her feet again and marched out of the café.

Tim watched her go, sat for a while, then paid the bill.

'Must do better,' he thought.

Eddie provided Tim with a second, much better, chance. Major Chadlow stood chatting to an old comrade from his days in the Guards on the steps of the Army and Navy Club. It had been a convivial evening. Dick swayed a little as the fresh air hit him.

'Shouldn't have had that second bottle, Peter.'

'I'll get you into a taxi.' He waved his arm. 'You won't forget the fund-raiser at Binton Chadlow, will you? I am expecting you to be especially generous, old boy.'

'Ply me with drink, Peter. Always works.'

'Half the regiment will be there. It will be good to see them again. Seriously, Dick, it is a good cause.'

'A good lunch!'

'Thursday next.' He helped Dick into the taxi.

Eddie stood still, his back pressed to the stonework. He watched the major turn into St James Street. Eddie slipped away. He had something to tell Tim.

Tim decided he should rejoin the meditation group.

The major came into the room. He was showing his guests round the hall and paying scant attention to the sessions they blundered into. Tim was sitting cross-legged on the floor. When he saw Chadlow he immediately jumped to his feet.

'Ouch!' he yelped. 'Cramp, Brian. I must just stretch my legs.'

'What a surprise! Simpson, isn't it?' The major looked amused.

'Excuse me, may we get on please?' Brian called. The major looked even more amused.

'I think I need to drop out for a minute,' said Tim. He followed the party out of the room.

'I didn't expect you to be part of the Meditation lot, Major,' he said. 'Are you on the course too, sir?'

'No, no, Simpson, this is my house.'

'Blimey! I mean – er – I had no idea. Fancy meeting you again! My dad will be tickled pink when I tell him. Do you mind if I ask you something, sir?'

Chadlow glanced at his watch. 'I am holding a meeting myself with these gentlemen. If you are quick about it, then. Walk with us and fire away.'

'It is that painting over the door in the Empty Mind Room – that is what they called it on the course – it is at the end of this corridor, there. After Vermeer, it says on the plaque.'

'Ah, the morning room, yes.'

'You've got a Vermeer hidden away, Peter?' one of the group asked. 'You don't need any of our money. Sell it, old boy!'

'Afraid not, Dick. It's just some amateur copy. Grandmama had it from some Austrian count she was married to for a while. She liked it. I had forgotten it. What about it, Simpson?'

'I am doing a college course on art history. I saw it and just wondered if – if it could be valuable. It looks the part, as my tutor might say.'

'Maybe I should look at it again. I'll see what it says in the stock book. Will you still be here at –' he glanced at his watch again – '4.30, or thereabouts? We'll be done by then, gentlemen?'

'Yes, of course, Peter, we won't have a penny left.'

'I think I am going to give the cross-legged relaxation a miss. Perhaps I could have another look at the painting?' said Tim.

'Help yourself.' He nodded towards the door at the end of the corridor. The party went off up the stairs and was gone.

Tim spent some time staring at the painting. He was beginning to like it. At last Chadlow returned, carrying a ledger.

'Let's see, Simpson. Here it is. "Woman at her Toilette with Servant; oil painting; artist unknown, once thought to be Vermeer. Bought by Baron Henning Ferdinand Busson von Sonnenberg am der Ruhr. Given in settlement of termination of marriage." That's it, all right. It's not a Vermeer. I am certain that the baron would not have simply given away a real Vermeer.'

'Not knowingly. I have been staring at it all afternoon,' said Tim. 'I would love a closer look. Actually, I would like to do some tests on the paint.'

'Not here, not in the house. No flammable liquids, no smelly chemicals allowed in the house. Can't have that, sorry. Insurance. Fire risk. There are one or two valuable items upstairs. We have to be extremely careful.'

'Perhaps I could bring my tutor. I could maybe persuade him that this work could be part of my dissertation.'

'On Vermeer?'

'No, on painting materials. It is my special study.'

'Well, why not? Who is he? Anybody I should have heard of?'

'I shouldn't think so. Golightly.'

'Doesn't ring a bell.'

'He is interested in painting materials and their development. He says quite a few well-known works by Great Masters now hanging in galleries are not genuine. He reckons the galleries are not keen on people like him getting too close.'

'Could he settle your mind that this 'Vermeer' is no such thing, do you suppose?'

'I think he would be interested. His colleagues at the Courtauld Institute probably could.'

'Fetch him next week if he can be bothered with the thing.'

Golightly stared up at the painting as if he had never seen it before. He glanced round the room, then back at the painting. 'Huh.'

'Not Vermeer, then?' asked Chadlow. His amusement at the idea was showing.

'No, I don't think so. We could do tests.'

'Not here. I have explained to young Simpson here that we cannot allow tests here.'

'At the Courtauld. It would need an electron microscope. You couldn't get one through the door here.'

'A what? Would it not destroy the work?'

'Not at all. That's the beauty of it. No chemicals necessary. It could be done in a day once it is set up.'

'Why not? Simpson, will it help your dissertation?'

'Well, Professor, what do you think?'

'It could be, er, interesting, yes. There was a forger of Vermeers around the turn of the Century. Even Vermeer forgeries have a certain value in their own right.'

'It could be a draw when the house re-opens to the public, I suppose. Get on with it, Simpson. We will both get something out of the thing. Still don't see what grandmama saw in it.'

The day was overcast. A chill wind blew off the Thames Estuary across the open ground of the bird sanctuary. It was a reunion. Tim, Arthur and Jo sat in a birdwatchers' hide. Tim handed round sandwiches and cans he had bought on the way.

'Are you sure this is all right, Jo? Are you really allowed to be here?'

'Oh, aye! It's my job now. I maintain the hides, tidy up after the twitchers. They've even given me a key.'

'There is a certain irony there, Jo. Have they forgotten who you are?'

'Maybe it's the governor's little joke. I've got to be back for tea or it'll be back to proper locks and keys for me.'

'OK, we'll be quick. I've found a mark. Arthur knows him. He swindled you out of eighty grand, right Arthur?'

Arthur said nothing.

'I'm setting him up with someone to buy a Vermeer. You have to pinch it from his workshop. Could you be away from here for a couple of hours without them noticing? At night?'

'You want me to break out of an open prison? I could walk out. But they would certainly notice. I need an overnighter – resettlement, they call it. Och, it'll be a doddle. I've made the list of tools, specialist stuff. I've put a list of suppliers who won't ask too many questions if you act like a locksmith. One or two of them should still be around – I hope. Anyway, be sure to get the ones I have underlined. The rest might be useful but I should be able to manage without them. Here.' He handed Tim a scrap of paper covered in tiny writing in pencil.

'Right. It is all in the timing from now on,' said Tim.

Seventeen

A Bentley rolled to a stop in the middle of the road, ignoring the traffic building up behind. The driver, in his peaked cap, opened the door for a youngish, stylish fellow, returned to the front seat and set off unhurriedly. The man stepped into the antique shop without glancing at the window display. A young lady approached from the pretty *bonne heure du jour* which served as her desk.

'Good morning, Sir. Can I help you?'

'I doubt it, Darling. I want to see Bradley. Is he here?'

'I believe he is with a customer at the moment. Can I help?'

'Have you any spare Canovas lying around?' He stared hard at her.

The young lady's polite professional expression disappeared in a moment.

'I'll fetch Mr. Bradley.' She almost ran through the door at the rear of the gallery. There was some hushed speech and Bradley came out.

'Bradley! I thought that would fetch you running. I'll get to the point. You found a marble figure for a friend of mine. "Possibly a Canova," you said. My friend paid you very well for it.'

'It was a fair price. I'm not sure what you are suggesting—'

'I'm not questioning the price, Bradley. Nor its quality. My friend is delighted with the piece. He thinks he would like another one.'

'I'm afraid the art world does not work quite like that.' Bradley smiled indulgently at the young man's naivety. I doubt if another Canova will come onto the market in my lifetime.'

'No, but rare antiques and old masterpieces go missing sometimes. Then mysteriously turn up again. Our friend would like to obtain another work of art. He reckons you are just the man to find him one. He will be paying cash. Are you following me?'

Bradley swallowed. 'Well, pieces like that come to my attention only rarely. I cannot simply order one up.'

'Let me make myself clear. Our friend has a cash problem. He's got lots of it which for reasons you will understand he cannot put into the bank – the same problem that you helped him to solve before. Now are you following me?'

'I am beginning to. This purchase, supposing I could find something to suit him, would be entirely a cash transaction?'

'Naturally. You are following.'

'That would be acceptable, sir. The same terms as before.'

'He will pay cash for a work of art that has little or no provenance if he is sure that it is what you say it is.'

'Yes, I understand perfectly. Discretion is required.'

'What have you got?'

'Look around, sir. Felicity will show you our stock.'

'The sort of thing we are talking about won't be on display. What have you got in the back?'

'I have just acquired a very fine piece by a rather neglected Nineteenth Century French sculptor. He is still reasonably priced but I think he is becoming more recognised—'

'—Stop messing about! He's looking for a museum piece, a Grand Master. Something that should be in a gallery. A rarity. He likes to impress. Understand now?' He glanced out of the window. The Bentley was drawing in to the kerb. The traffic in Bond Street was piling up behind it.

'I'll come back in a day or two, maybe tomorrow. Try to have something for me.' He walked out of the shop and into the waiting car and in a moment was gone.

Felicity came through from the back room, her eyes round with fright.

'He sounded quite threatening, Mr. Bradley. What does he know about the Canova? You never explained where it came from, or why you were so discreet about selling it. All that closing the shop when a certain client was due. You were acting rather oddly, I thought at the time. I wondered why I never actually saw the buyer.'

'Some customers like to be discreet, Felicity.'

'Was that marble figure, really an unknown Canova? Was it stolen?'

'I bought it in good faith. I am not a crook. However, it turns out that the fellow I bought from was. Now it appears that the customer with the preference for anonymity is a criminal as well.'

'I did not like that man's tone. He is a criminal too, isn't he? Are you in danger, Mr. Bradley? And what about me? He was staring at me.'

Bradley forced a smile. 'Well, all I need to do is find some piece – a Grand Master, he said.'

'Sotheby's are holding a Grand Master sale in two months here in London. The catalogue is on my desk. It came in just yesterday.'

'Do you understand that I sold the Canova, or whatever it was, below market price?'

'For cash?'

'Of course. That's not unusual in the antique business. You know that, Felicity. If I buy at market price I will be ruined. In any case I can't wait two months.'

'What will you do?'

'What can I do? I don't know.'

Felicity did not know either.

The painting was propped against the wall in the lobby at Binton Chadlow. Tim and Golightly stared at it. Golightly pulled it forward and examined its back.

'It has never been out of that frame,' he said. 'The frame is late Nineteenth or early Twentieth Century. I'll get that examined too. Is that label one that your family would have used?'

'It is von Sonnenberg's. He was a collector. He had everything catalogued. I think there is a number. That small label is ours. It corresponds to the stock book entry. And there is the insurance company sticker.'

'I'm afraid it will have to come out of the frame, Major Chadlow. It will all be properly preserved, I assure you.'

'Yes, yes, I'm sure. It is all a bit of fuss over very little. Of course, if it will help your, er—'

'—My dissertation. Yes, I think so.'

'There will be nothing quite like it in his year,' said Arthur. 'Simpson did well to spot it on your wall. Even if it comes to nothing it is one of the most interesting undergraduate projects for some time. It will be back on your wall in two days, three at most. Everything is in place. You will hardly miss it.'

'Ha! I won't miss it at all. As I said, I don't know what Grandmama saw in in it in the first place.'

They heaved the picture into Golightly's van.

They were outside the Lambeth lockup inside three hours. Golightly rang the bell at number 14. The speaker crackled. It was the French polisher' voice.

'It's Golightly. I want Bradley.'

'He's not here.'

'Get him here. I've got something for him.'

'He said he wasn't doing business with a jail-bird. He told you.'

'He'll change his mind when he sees what I've got. Get him here.'

'He's at the shop.'

'He'll make an exception for this. Get him here. This won't wait. Tell him I've got something he'll want. I'll wait.'

'I'm finishing off, then I'm going home. Mr. Bradley doesn't pay overtime.'

'Call him at the shop.'

'All right. But once this job is finished I'm off.' Arthur waited. After a couple of minutes, the loudspeaker crackled again.

'He's on his way. He says to let you in. He'll be half an hour at the most. He didn't sound pleased.' The mechanism rattled as the doorway rolled up. Tim reversed the van in through the gap. Tim stayed well down in the cab. There was no need for Bradley to know Arthur was not on his own.

'Mind that bureau! Five minutes and I'm off. Mr. Bradley says to lower the door. You can raise it when he arrives. He doesn't like it wide open.' He fussed over the bureau under the harsh workshop lights until he was satisfied. He stepped back.

'That's me done. I can't get it better than that.' Then he was gone.

'All clear. You can come out now, Jo. Jo slipped quietly out of the rear of the van. He peered round. The old meat safe was

172

standing open and vacant. He examined the jumble of furniture in various stages of restoration. He looked more alive than Tim had ever seen him. There was a glint in his eye and a half-smile. He was wearing the latex gloves he had put on Tim's list. He pressed the red knob of the shutter mechanism and the roller came down.

'Let's have a bit of privacy,' he said. 'Don't touch a thing. It will make it easier to clear up when we leave.'

'Look at the lock on that safe door. Do you think you can open it?'

'That clapped out old piece of junk? I would say so. I was the best. Still am, I reckon.' He looked round the workshop, up at the railway arch that formed the roof of the lockup. He felt round the back of the ancient meat safe. There was a narrow gap.

'Arthur, let's get the picture out.'

'We'll stand it over there, where the office light will be on it. Those tubes rob it of its colour.' Arthur looked about the space.

'You weren't expecting to see your statue again, were you? It's long gone, Arthur.'

'No, I suppose not He's sold it!'

'Right. I'll just squeeze in behind here. Make sure there is no sign of me when I'm in place.' Tim nodded. Jo squeezed into the space.

They had to wait twenty minutes.

The shutters rattled. Tim climbed into the cab of the van and crouched out of sight.

The shutters rolled up. Bradley strode in.

'What could you possibly have that would interest me, Golightly? I have already told you I don't do business with the likes of you.'

'And yet, here you are.'

'Here I am. This had better be good. Is it stolen, like that Canova?'

'The Canova Girl was not stolen. Maybe we can still do business, Bill. This is what I've got.' Arthur waved his arm at the painting. 'Look at it before you say anything else. Come and look.' Bradley brushed past Arthur.

'What have you got? Has it fallen off the back of a lorry? How do I know it is yours to sell?'

173

'It isn't mine. I'm just the middle man. Take a look. Use my torch. The light in here is awful.' Bradley glanced contemptuously at the painting.

'Is this some daub you want to foist off onto me, Arthur?'

Arthur could not keep the anger from his voice. 'I've never foisted you off with anything. All I have ever brought to you has been good stuff. You have done very well out of me over the years. I haven't forgotten the time when you hadn't two brass farthings to rub together. So come off your high horse. Look at it. Properly.'

Reluctantly, Bradley looked at the painting. He took the torch from Arthur and began to examine the painting, carefully, inch by inch. He angled the torch this way and that. He stepped back to take in the entire picture. He knelt before it in his Saville row suit, ignoring the grimy floor.'

'Arthur, what have you got?'

'Well, I think it is a fake. It looks like a Vermeer but it is not in the Catalogue Raisonné. I reckon it is one of van Meegeren's forgeries.' Arthur paused, looking hard at Bradley. He waited for it to sink in. Tim, in the footwell of the cab, held his breath.

Bradley did not reply at once. He looked at Arthur. He looked again at the painting. 'I know the story. He sold fakes through intermediaries. There was a dealer with an odd name.' Tim breathed again. Bradley was taking the bait.

'Leo Nardus. You couldn't make it up. People fell for it, though. There are van Meegeren fakes in galleries, kept away from the public out of embarrassment.'

'So they say. Is that what this is? Who are you acting for?'

'As if I would tell you that! I don't want you going behind my back. Here is the deal. I sell you this as a van Meegeren forgery of a Vermeer. I want to be paid up front. You pay me in full, in cash tonight.'

'I will need some verification. You can't expect me to simply pay you for this – this pig in a poke, Arthur. There are tests I could get done.'

'If you take it to anybody in the art world the story will be out in no time. There is a test you can easily do yourself.'

'The Formula 409 test, I know.'

'Look at this cloth. Shine the torch on it. See that yellow streak? That means Bakelite. He used Bakelite resin in the pigments and baked the paintings to harden them off.'

Bradley shone the torch. He sniffed at the cloth. The faint whiff of the cleaning agent known as Formula 409 still clung to it.

'I did the test this afternoon. It's Bakelite. That means van Meegeren.'

'How much are you asking?'

'Well, first there is the matter of the eighty grand you owe me for the Canova. It was real, wasn't it? Or you convinced somebody it was. Cash was it? Somebody with a lot of funny money lying around? I'm right, aren't I?' Bradley did not reply.

'I'll take that as a yes. No new Canova appeared out of nowhere. I kept a close eye out for news. A previously unknown Canova on the market would make the headlines. Nothing. So, here is the deal. Two hundred thousand pounds for the van Meegeren plus my eighty thousand. Tonight. In cash.'

'What? It cannot be worth that much.'

'I think it is worth that and a bit more. You know me, Bill. I always leave room for a decent profit. I'm famous for it. Anyway, I reckon you'll declare it to be a lost Vermeer. Maybe your cash buyer would like to hang it alongside his Canova.'

Bradley gave Arthur a sharp look. Arthur stared, unblinking. Tim was sure now. Bradley appeared to think for a moment. 'Maybe I could find a buyer. I can't find that sort of money right now. It will take time to get it together – even if I agree—'

'—You'll agree.'

Bradley hesitated.

'Think about it, Bill. You know you can find a buyer who'll ask no questions. You've as good as admitted that already. You've got a buyer in mind right now, haven't you?'

'It's too much. I can go to one fifty.'

'You know me. I don't haggle. That's the price. Take it or leave it. Which is it?' Arthur paused for a second. 'All right, I'll put it back in the van.'

'No, no, wait! I can get the money. It's in my safe at home. It will take me a couple of hours to get it.'

'I knew it. You've still got cash from the Canova.'

'I always keep cash.' Bradley swallowed hard and continued. 'You know the antique trade. Lots of deals are cash transactions.'

'I'll wait here. I've been waiting for years. I can wait a couple of hours.'

Bradley turned to leave.

'Just a moment, Bill. You should be careful dealing with a jail-bird like me. I could work a switch on you when you leave. You had better lock it away in that safe there.'

Bradley hoisted the painting into the strongroom and closed the door on it. He locked the safe with a flourish and pocketed the key. He turned and was gone. Arthur lowered the shutter behind him.

'Two hours,' said Jo, as he slipped out from behind the strongroom. Tim, get me the tools. I'll have a little practice on that lock.' He took the tools and set a little timer.

He fiddled with the lock for a while.

'Och! It is pretty straightforward. Give me another minute. It's like riding a bike. You never forget. I'll crack it.' He grunted. He squinted.

'I think the lock is a bit rusted. Maybe a dab of oil,' he mused. He delved among the tools Tim had brought along. 'I'm looking for a boomslang, Tim. Did you find one?'

Sorry, no. It wasn't one that you underlined on your shopping list.'

'Aye, fair enough. It would have helped. Maybe this hook will do the trick. I'm pretty sure it is a speck of rust or something that has dropped between the wards. This thing should clear it.' He tinkered with the new pick for a while. 'Ach! It is such a little thing! The mechanism is pretty ancient. It's on its last legs. I could force it open but the thing mightn't lock again. The man has to unlock it.'

Jo worked on. Nobody examining the lock would see signs of his picks, any scratches or oily marks around the keyhole.

The little timer tinkled. 'I'll not play about any more for fear I cannot get it shut again. I know I can get the thing open, so we are safe to get the picture out and be on our way once you've done the business. It might be a bit messy, but needs must when the Devil drives.'

'All right, Jo. We'll manage.'

'Aye, Tim. No battle plan survives first contact with the enemy. I've been in worse fixes than this.' Jo looked about to make sure there was nothing left lying about to catch Bradley's attention and stole back into his place.

'Jo's habit of neatness again! Everything in its place.' Tim thought. He was suddenly, just for a moment, in their cramped prison cell again with Jo's little store of belongings in a neat row on the shelf. He remembered his habit of straightening up his bunk as soon as he had risen. Now, all his tools were back in the little container. He wrenched his thoughts back to the present and put the toolbox out of sight in the van.

'We'll wait,' muttered Arthur. 'It's all I ever seem do these days. This is the last time I will set foot here, that is certain.' They settled into an uneasy silence. Somewhere a rat scuttled about behind the furniture.

At last they heard a car pull up in the alley. The shutters rattled. Bradley was outside. Tim slid into the cab and ducked down into the footwell again.

Bradley stepped through the doorway, a suitcase under one arm and a bunch of keys in his hand. He pressed the button to lower the shutter. His face was pasty in the harsh workshop light.

'You've brought the money? All of it?'

'Yes. Count it.'

'You know me. I always count it. Put it down on that bureau.'

Bradley placed the leather case on the bureau and opened it for Arthur to see. Bundles of fifty-pound notes, some with paper bank-wrappers, some held together with elastic bands, arranged in untidy rows. Arthur picked one of the bundles from the bottom of the case, flicked through with his fingers and thumb. He picked out three more from different parts of the case. At last he was satisfied that the bundles were all made up of fifties. He laboriously counted one of the bundles, his lips moving as he worked through it.

'£2,000 per bundle.'

'Yes.' Bradley watched as Arthur's fingers took the corners of the bank-notes.

Then Arthur counted the bundles, out loud.

'...One thirty-eight, one thirty-nine, a hundred and forty. Right. I'll be off.' Arthur made for the van.'

'Not so fast. Arthur. I'll just check that the painting is still there.' He strode to the strongroom and pushed and twisted. The key met with resistance. Bradley twisted harder. The key turned. The door swung open.

'Still there, Bradley?'

'Yes.'

'Use my torch. Have a good look. Make sure. Then get that door up. I am done with this place – and with you as well.'

Bradley muttered under his breath as he got down on his knees again. At last he stood up.

'Satisfied?'

'Yes. Our business is done.' The shutter rolled up. Arthur climbed into the cab. In seconds he had maneuvered out into the alley and driven into the darkness.

Bradley stood before his new acquisition. He wanted to examine it away from the harsh fluorescent tubes of the workshop. He pondered on his plan of action. He could take it to the shop where the lighting was carefully arranged to flatter and enhance the stock and examine it there. The back shop was secure. He lifted it out of the strongroom and propped it up where Golightly had put it. He stepped back. He stepped first to one side then the other, never taking his eyes from the painting. The palette was right. The subject was typical of Vermeer. He had believed Golightly when he said that the work was not catalogued. There was always the possibility of a sleeper, a lost work or an unknown piece. It happened all the time. Golightly had found a few himself and made money for them both. Vermeer was himself unknown – or forgotten – for two hundred years. That had been van Meegeren's big chance and he had certainly produced some fake Vermeers. Which was this?

Golightly's Formula 409 test was pretty reliable. Bradley rummaged fruitlessly among the bottles and tins on the French polisher's bench. He would have to test it in the morning as soon as he could lay his hands on the stuff. Some hardware shop would stock it.

Golightly was right, of course. He could not involve anybody else. Either way, as a genuine Vermeer or as a van Meegeren fake, nobody must know of its discovery. The shop was secure, but the girl Felicity was bound to see it when she opened up. She would certainly ask questions. She was already suspicious of the Canova

178

deal. It would have to remain in the strongroom. Nobody, apart from Golightly and himself knew it was here – or that the thing even existed. It was safer here than anywhere. There was no need to risk its discovery by taking it into the shop. He decided to leave it and do the test in the morning.

In the narrow space behind the strongroom Jo was waiting patiently. 'Twenty years stuck in a box, and here I am stuck in here!' he thought. His knees ached from crouching. His nose itched. He had pins and needles. 'What is he doing?' He strained to catch the slightest noise. He could hear that rat again, scratching about. He heard Bradley grunt as he moved the picture. He heard his shoes on the concrete floor.

At last Bradley returned the painting to the strongroom. Jo heard the door hinges creak and felt the slam of the door. He heard the key turn in the lock. He heard footsteps. The lights flicked off. Then, at last, the shutters rattled down.

He waited five minutes before sliding out from his hiding place. He stretched his aching back and paced about to get his circulation going. At last he heard Tim's soft knock on the shutters. He groped for the switch and pressed. The shutters rolled up. Golightly reversed the van into the workshop.

'He's gone, Jo. Let's get to work. Tim lowered the shutters, found the lights and handed Jo his toolkit. 'Maybe the lock will be smoother now.'

'Aye, maybe that wee bit of an obstruction has cleared. If it hasn't, I'll leave traces.'

'We've got to get the thing away tonight. And you've got to be back before eight o'clock.'

Jo applied himself. 'There! That'll do nicely.' He gave a little tug. The door creaked open. Tim and Arthur took the picture and loaded it in the van. It took seconds.

'What have you touched?' Jo had a rag in his hand.

'Nothing, like you said.'

'Tim, you touched that button to operate the door,' said Arthur.

'No problem.' Jo wiped it. 'Anything else?'

'Better give the table over there a quick wipe,' said Tim. 'Where Arthur counted the money.'

'Aye, right.'

Arthur pulled forward clear of the shutters. Tim jumped into the cab. Jo stowed away his gear, turned off the lights, pressed the door switch and stepped through as the shutters came down.

'Job done.' He peeled off the latex gloves and stowed them away in the toolbox. 'Lose this after you drop me off – at least ten miles from the hostel. It wouldn't do for them to be found. It is just possible that any marks I made could be a match.'

They dropped Jo round the corner from his night's lodging – the bail hostel where he was on Temporary Leave of Absence – with five minutes to spare. Tim pressed a bottle of beer into Jo's hand.

'Let your man smell it on you.'

'Aye, Tim. I'll just have a wee pull now.' He swigged and raised the bottle high.

'Job done!' he said again.

The Bentley rolled to a stop outside Bradley's shop just as Felicity was opening up. The driver in his cap made a show of opening the rear door. The car slid away into the traffic as the man entered the shop.

'Felicity, isn't it? I hope he isn't going to be long. I hate hanging about.'

Felicity's expression was coldly formal. 'I always make coffee for Mr. Bradley. I could make you a cup.'

Felicity bashed about in the back for a while and brought the man a china cup and saucer, setting it down on a little wine table. The man lounged on a gilt settee. He put his feet up. Felicity scowled but said nothing. She sat at her *escritoire* and sorted the post, looking up from time to time. The man stared, unsmiling, at her.

Bradley did not appear.

'He should be here by now.' muttered Felicity, almost to herself. If only this man would go! 'He might be at his workshop,' said Felicity, her voice brightly brittle.

'Hmm!' I can't wait all day.' The man sat for a moment, thinking. He seemed to make his mind up. He got to his feet.

'Who should I say called?'

'He'll remember me from yesterday, won't he, Felicity? Just like you did. The workshop – Lambeth, isn't it?' He got up, strolled to the street door and was gone.

Felicity shuddered. She picked up a pen and a sheet of Bradley's headed paper. She wrote a short note saying that she was never coming back. Then she left the shop, locked the door carefully and posted the key through the letterbox.

Bradley was excited. He could hardly wait to get the picture into the daylight. He had just about convinced himself of the picture's authenticity. He twirled the plastic bag with the American all-purpose cleaning spray with its red and blue logo, the rag and a spatula to scrape off a little bit of paint to test. He could hardly contain himself. The shutter rolled up noisily. He switched on the lights.

The strongroom door was wide open. Bradley rushed forward. He looked around in disbelief as if hoping to see the painting propped up somewhere. He knew he had locked it in the strongroom. He walked in. It was totally empty.

'Bradley, old chap! Are looking for something? You look as white as a sheet.'

'What are you doing here?'

'Our friend says to say thank you for the painting. It looks just tickety boo.'

'What? How—'

'I've been watching you. I knew you would find something for me. It was just a matter of time.'

'You took it!'

'Ah, now you understand at last. Our friend likes a bargain. So I got him one.'

'You owe me for that picture. It is a Vermeer, priceless on the open market.'

'It wasn't on the open market, though, Bradley. And it was never going to be.'

'But – but – I've paid for it. It took all I had. I'm cleared out. Can't we come to a reasonable understanding? I could let you have it at cost – three hundred thousand pounds. It's priceless.'

'So you said. But you haven't got it. How could you sell it?'

'I'll call the police. I'll have you arrested, you thief!'

'Careful. I dislike being called names. I get really annoyed, in fact. Anyway, you cannot prove a thing. What painting? Have you any evidence that you ever had a Vermeer? Have you got a receipt? Who did you buy it from? Someone reputable? Is there evidence of a break-in? And do you know anything about who might have stolen it? I doubt it. So go ahead, call the cops. See what happens.'

He spun on his heel. Outside, the Bentley drew up. The driver in the peaked cap was out in a moment with the rear door open. The car drew away as quickly as it had appeared. Bradley stood open-mouthed in his workshop.

The van pulled up in the Binton Chadlow courtyard. The major was waiting.

'Well, is it what you expected, Simpson?'

Tim's face was glum. 'Well, sir, the test was a disappointment, I'm afraid. The work is late Nineteenth Century or early Twentieth, not of course a Vermeer. The pigments tell us that. Nor is it a van Meegeren. Any faker of old pictures has to get over the problem of aging the paint surface. Van Meegeren used Bakelite resin instead of linseed oil. He then baked the whole lot at 200 degrees. It sounds crazy, I know. I think I might give it a try for my dissertation—'

'—Yes, yes. Well, you are more disappointed than me, Simpson. Write up an interesting little story for me to stick up on the wall. Don't suppose anybody will be very interested, but we'll give it a mention in the guide's notes. People like a story. I'll have another plaque made up.'

Tim opened the back of the van. 'We'll take it in for you, Major.'

'Yes, please. The room does look a little forlorn without it. The stepladder is still there, I think.'

They got the picture back.

'While we are here we might as well put the table back.' Arthur looked round the room for the pier table and its contents. He picked up the porcelain figurine and turned it to look at the base.

'Meissen,' he said. 'The crossed swords, there, look. And that little asterisk between the hilts – mid Eighteenth Century, I would say. The pretty colours were a sensation at the time.' He was almost talking to himself. He put the figurine down and picked up the bronze head.

'What do you know about this, Major Chadlow?'

182

'It came with the painting. Apparently, Grandmama took a fancy to it, can't think why. I suppose her maid just popped it in with everything else when she left the baron. I don't suppose the old boy missed it.'

'He was a collector?'

'Yes, he was a magpie – anything shiny. Do you like it?'

Arthur nodded. 'It looks out of place next to the Meissen. It's African.'

'Why don't you take it? Think of it as a payment for the work you have done.'

'It could be valuable, you know.'

'Doubt it. If there isn't a number on the bottom it isn't in the stock book. Absolutely everything of value is in that book. Please, take it.'

'Are you sure? Shouldn't there be paperwork? Insurance, that sort of thing.'

'Well, only if it was listed in the stockbook. But it isn't. This is my house, Golightly, and I can do as I please – so long as we don't shout it from the rooftop, anyway! Here, take the thing. It is out of place in this room – always thought so. I never understood why the old girl took it in the first place.'

The major nodded towards the painting now back in place. 'Good luck with the dissertation, Simpson. Now I must get on. There's another of those wretched relaxation courses starting today. Will you be joining it, do you think, Simpson?'

'Not likely! I've had my fill. Brian can manage without me.'

'Goodbye, then. See yourselves out.' Without waiting for a reply Major the Honourable Peter Alexander Heinrich Witts Witts-Chadlow strode out of the room.

'And goodbye to you too,' muttered Arthur as he picked up the bronze head.

Tim waited until they had driven up the avenue as far as the gate lodge before he spoke.

'I expected you to make some offer for that bronze head, Arthur. Are you losing your touch? You said it could be valuable. Is it valuable?'

'It has come out of an English stately home. Before that it was in the possession of an Austrian baron with a passion for collecting. What do you think?'

'I'm guessing, but yes, very. Are you going to sell it?'

'I'm just the middle man these days.'

Eighteen

Tim, Jerome, Arthur, Maggie and Kate sat in the snug in Greenwich. Gloria set a tray of glasses on the table. Arthur had a plastic shopping bag beside him on the seat.

'I am a bit miffed that I didn't get a part this time,' Gloria said. 'I am sure you could have found me something.'

'Sorry,' said Tim. 'Maybe next time.'

'Just waiting for Jo.'

'Isn't he still—'

'—inside?' said Tim. 'In a way, he is. He will get his parole soon. He has been inside for a long time. The idea is for him to get settled, have contacts, get a regular job, that sort of thing. He has weekends in a bail hostel not very far from here. Ben has gone to fetch him in the Bentley.'

'He's wearing the cap,' remarked Jerome. 'He looks the part.'

'I hope Jo appreciates the ride.'

'He'll take it in his stride,' said Tim. 'He is a stoic. Nothing seems to upset his equilibrium. Maybe it was his strength of mind that got him through twenty years inside. Not many have that. He got me through it. I learned a lot from him.'

'I am looking forward to meeting him,' said Kate. 'I don't think I have met a real a proper heavy duty criminal.'

Maggie said nothing. She was still hurt from the unhappy experience at Fortnum and Mason's cafeteria, wondering why she was sitting in the Greenwich pub. 'Maybe next time,' she thought. 'Will there always be a next time?'

Ben appeared and held the door open for Jo to enter.

'Here he is, the hero of the hour!' said Jerome.

'Oh, aye,' said Jo. 'I'm that, all right. I have just heard that my parole hearing has been scheduled for next month.'

Tim chattered, making introductions, acting the host.

'Pleased to meet you, Mr. Rossi. Does that mean you will be free?' asked Kate.

'It should, aye. I have behaved myself, got through my time. I'll know when they tell me.'

'Arthur, your parole is up soon. When you are a free man, what will you do?'

'I've got a plan.' He glanced at his plastic bag. 'What about you?'

'Yes, Tim, what about you?' It was Maggie.

'Well, my probation officer is satisfied. She thinks being at college is just the thing. She thinks I am in need of qualifications.'

'Little does she know!' said Jerome. 'Tim is quite the best con man I have ever met.'

'You don't know any others,' said Kate.

'Yes, I do. Half of father's customers are pretty slippery, and the other half are outright crooks. They won't pay on time, or they won't deliver on time. Tim can get money out of anybody. There's a job for somebody like him in the firm.'

Tim went on. 'Next, our last little job has worked out fine. Here are your wages.' He handed Arthur a large packet. 'Your eighty grand, payment of a debt, plus interest and a sum for compensation for all the trouble you were put to.'

Arthur took the packet and looked inside. He felt with his fingers. His lips moved as he counted bundles under his breath. The company was quiet. At last Arthur sat back, put the packet into his coat pocket.

'I never haggle,' he said. His creaking laughter filled the snug.

'Jo, what about you? This wouldn't have happened but for you. I cannot give you your pay now.'

'No, they would not be very impressed back at Ball Cross. Keep it safe for me.'

'What will you do when you are properly on the outside, Jo?' asked Kate.

'I'm not very employable as a locksmith these days. I've got a bit of a plan. I've got some money put by. I had friends, shall we say, who owe me a favour or two. And I know where the bodies are buried.'

Kate stared open-mouthed in horror.

'In a manner of speaking, lassie', Jo continued. 'No actual dead bodies that I know of. I know enough about certain people who are now living off the fat of the land – that land being the Costa del Sol. I think I might be visiting them fairly soon. When I'm out they'll know about it.'

Jo's voice was level. Only Tim noticed the edge in his tone. For the first time Tim thought Jo's confidence was a bit shaken. 'After so many years in prison it is not surprising,' he thought. He made a mental note to watch out for Jo when he was finally released on parole. He owed Jo so much from those days in the shared cell that could never be fully repaid.

'Jerome, this is for you.'

'A fee for services rendered, I suppose. It was really very little trouble, and scaring that Bradley was a pleasure. Felicity, not so much.'

'Felicity?' Kate asked.

'The young lady assistant in Bradley's place. She seemed to be quite a respectable type. I think my presence in the shop unnerved her. I just wanted her to say something to Bradley if I missed him in the Lambeth place. I needn't have as it happened.'

The snug door swung open. A large man in a flowing white robe appeared. He inspected the company, his eyes examining them imperiously.

'Mr. Ogochukwu!' said Arthur, the only one unsurprised by his appearance. 'Come in.'

'Mr. Golightly.' The man swept into the room. 'I did not expect to find you in company.'

'These are friends. They helped me obtain the thing you are interested in. This is Mr. Ogochukwu, from the Nigerian Embassy. He has the task of finding and recovering looted artifacts for his government.' Arthur drew out the bronze head from the bag at his side. He set it down in the middle of the table.

'And this is one of them!'

'Oh, that is lovely, Arthur!' cried Maggie, her face suddenly animated.

'Let me see,' said Mr. Ogochukwu. He took the head carefully in his hands. He looked at it proudly, reverently. He turned it. He held it high. The light gleamed on its metallic cheekbones, casting shadows across the face as he turned it around. His hands caressed its surfaces, tracing the planes of the piece, feeling the sharp edges of the stylised hair.

The group were silent as they watched. All eyes were fixed on the head. In the light of the snug it seemed to gleam as if new polished. Tim, who had seen the thing before without registering any feelings about it saw it properly for the first time in Ogochukwu's hands. Time seemed to stretch out. Arthur sat still. He knew the feeling when a treasure is first revealed. He thought of the first sight he had of the Canova when the light from the skylight in Jasper's back room fell on it. He saw, again, why he sought out ancient beauty. He knew how he was going to spend the rest of his days. Jo sat quiet and suddenly very still.

In the end it was Ogochukwu who broke the spell. 'Yes, there can be no doubt,' he said at last. 'I will inform the Ambassador immediately. He will wish to examine it for himself – and to thank you on behalf of my country. He takes a great interest in the work I am doing.' He turned to the others. 'Mr. Golightly has done us a great service. My country will reward him.'

'What is it?' asked Maggie. She was more animated than she had been since she arrived. 'It is stunning. It is so powerful! May I?'

'Certainly,' said the Nigerian. 'Take it for a moment. You will be the last English person to touch it. It is going home.' She held it, turned it round in her hands the way he had.

'I love it,' she said.

Mr. Oguchukwu took it gently from Maggie's hands and wrapped it carefully in a broad strip of cloth he took from a leather satchel among the folds of his robe.

'Please come to the Embassy tomorrow morning at 10 o'clock, Mr. Golightly. Ask for me. I will take you to the Ambassador. He will wish to express his gratitude to you.' He turned and was gone.

'Reward, Arthur? I hadn't expected that.'

'You have heard me say it before. I'm just the middle man these days.'

'So, what was – is – it? You didn't mention the bronze when we were hatching our plan in the prison library,' said Tim.

Jo spoke. 'No, you didn't, Arthur.' His voice was still level, calm.

'It is from the Royal Palace of the Kingdom of Benin. It is part of a load of metal wares stolen – looted – by some British soldiers during a punitive raid. Many pieces were sold to collectors. The so-called experts refused to believe the Benin craftsmen were capable of such fine work. The Kingdom is now part of Nigeria and the government is trying to get everything back.'

'When did you know about it, Arthur?' asked Jerome. 'Did you just spot it when you went to rehang the Vermeer, or did you know all along?'

'I guessed long ago, when I first saw the painting in Binton Chadlow. There it was.'

'You recognised it – just like that?' asked Kate. 'I'm impressed. I wouldn't have noticed it at all if you hadn't made a point of it when Ben and I went to Binton Chadlow with the polaroid. Actually I think you said we should "take a snap of the crockery!" Your very words!'

'Yes, I knew it almost as soon as I saw it that it was a special thing. I am an antique dealer – and always will be.'

'You are a cunning rascal!' said Ben from his corner. He had learned to read and took pride in using expressions he encountered. Kate looked proudly, affectionately, at her protégé. She caught Ben's eye. He returned the look with the adoration he felt for her from the first day in this very room. She was to him like the older sister he would never have.

'I was the best. Finding sleepers is what I do. It is what I will always do. I had only seen a picture of a Benin bronze but it was enough.' He went on, warming to his subject. 'Benin metal wares are not like anything else. That is why they were fetching good prices for those thieving Tommies in the first place.'

'The picture was a sideshow, really,' Jo said, his voice still quiet and unruffled. Tim waited. This, he felt was some kind of ending, though to what he wasn't sure.

'I was always after the bronze.'

Jo stood up. 'Aye, Arthur, you had us both there,' he said in that level tone. His face was stone. Jerome sensed his power. Here was a man of force. He caught Kate's eye. She saw his concern. Jo stepped across to Arthur, as light on his feet as a boxer. His looming menace filled the room, suddenly chilly as if a frost had descended.

'Just as well that picture did so well, there, eh?' he said at last. 'You are the second man to have taken a lend of me in twenty years. The first one put me inside. You – you are, as Ben here has said, a cunning rascal! Shake my hand.'

189

Jerome sighed with relief. Kate shuddered. The moment had passed.

'A side-show for Arthur,' said Tim. He seemed to be the only one unaffected. 'It was a good payday for us all. So, what's next for you, Jo?'

'It's back to prison for me, at least till my parole hearing. After that, I think I'll take that little holiday on the Costa del Sol. Long term, back to Glasgow, maybe. I still have a few connections there. And I can afford a season ticket at Ibrox Park.'

'Arthur, what about you?' asked Tim.

'To the Ambassador in the morning, as you heard, for my reward. Then I'm going to search for some more Bronzes. I think Mr. Oguchukwu will arrange for me to have a retainer.'

'I hope it will be generous, Arthur' said Tim.

'You know me, I never haggle.' Arthur's creaking laughter filled the snug.

'You said something in the van when we left Binton Chadlow. Remember, I asked you if the bronze was valuable. You said "it was in the possession of an Austrian baron with a passion for collecting. What do you think?" Remember that, Arthur?'

'Yes. Has the penny dropped at last, Tim?'

'I think so. Why is the painting there?'

'We know why,' said Maggie. 'The baron's wife brought it away as part of a divorce settlement or something, because she liked it.'

'Yes, we know that. The question is why was it in the baron's collection in the first place? A pretty imitation of a Vermeer might have fooled many people, but the baron was no fool.'

'Not an imitation, Tim. A copy. Major Chadlow let it slip. He said it was "just some amateur copy". He knew all along.'

'Aye, Arthur, that'll be right. When did you think of that?' Jo was still calm. Tim caught that edge again.

'Well, at first I thought it was a genuine Vermeer – or at least a van Meegeren copy. For the same reason – the baron would not knowingly buy a fake – or a copy. Then I thought of something, a reason for the painting's existence.'

'Now you mention it, he said the same thing when I was on that ridiculous mindfulness course' said Tim. 'The baron himself had the copy made. He kept the original for himself. So there really is a Vermeer somewhere?'

'I think so. Maybe in the same place the Benin bronze and that Meissen piece came from. I looked the baron up in the prison library in a book that Mrs. Jenkinson signed the order for. I've got a list.'

'And you are going travelling for that Mr. Oguchukwu!' cried Jerome.

'You'll be visiting some big houses on your searches for the bronzes, no doubt.' said Jo. 'Chances are, the picture will be in a secure room. We should keep in touch.'

Tim thought Jo's voice was smooth again. He would keep the faith with Jo. He owed a lot to Jo's self-control and quiet stoicism when prison had oppressed him. It was Jo who had made the last adventure happen. In a way Jo had got the least out of it. He had long ago worked out that Jo's prison term was in part because of the treachery of others, men who had somehow evaded arrest. He was sure these were the men that Jo was planning to meet again in Spain. He had seen Jo's power just now, the force he wielded. If it came to it, Tim knew who he would look to if he needed help.

The rest of them had gone. Tim and Maggie sat opposite one another. Maggie sat upright on the edge of the bench, frowning. Tim lounged back on the bench across the room, thinking how pretty she looked.

'What about you, Tim? What are you going to do now?'

'I don't know. I don't want to go to prison again. I learned a lot about how to cope on the inside. Jo taught me. But—'

'—there is only one way to keep out, and you know it. Here you are again, sharing out the loot from your last job, and you are still on parole. You are living dangerously, Tim, you must realise that. I cannot live with that, thinking all the time that you could just be arrested, for goodness knows what next.'

'I am not a thief, Maggie. I sell things people want. The people I get money from are the thieves, not me.'

'You cannot con an honest man, I know. But you stole the picture. You tricked that man into lending it to you. You sold it and stole it back again from—'

'—and returned it to its rightful owner. I helped to put it back on the wall myself. That wasn't theft, was it?'

191

'You always make out that you somehow were doing something good.'

'Look, I know some of the things I have done have not come up to the highest standards of honesty. But remember the Sharki affair? Didn't he deserve what he got? And isn't Ben safe now? Look how well he is doing. Would he be managing a shop now? Would he be reading books – in English?'

'You always do that!'

'What? Do what?'

'Make it all seem as if you were Robin Hood with your Merry Men, righting wrongs and rescuing—'

'—Fair maidens? Only one, Maggie. We got your money back. You were glad then. And look at you now! Sitting there as beautiful as you are, a career woman with prospects and a growing reputation for original design in a competitive field.'

'Tim, Tim! Something has to change. I know you won't change. I don't want you to be a different person. I just want—' She put her hands to her face. She turned away. Her shoulders shook with the sobs that burst from her. Tim crossed the room. He sat at her side, hardly daring to touch her. She edged away, just a little. The sobbing stopped. Maggie took her hanky to mop up the tears. Tim took it from her and gently touched her face.

Maggie turned to him. She buried herself against his shoulder.

'There's only the one.'

'One?'

'Fair maid. You.'

'You said "beautiful as you are". Is that how you think of me? What do you think of me? What are we going to do, you and me?'

'I've told you, Maggie.'

'You are thinking about it, I know.' She sighed. She drew away from Tim, smoothed her skirt, straightened her back and composed her face. 'Well, that makes two of us. I don't know what you have in mind but I know what I am going to do.' She kissed him.

'What does that mean?'

She stood up and crossed the little space towards the door.

'It is something for you to think about.'

Just then Gloria brought another tray of drinks.

192

'You are not going already, Maggie? I've poured this for you. Please just try it. It's my new cocktail. You can help me think of a name for it. I'm thinking of 'Slow Burn' because the kick comes at the end.'

Gloria's frame and the tray he held filled the doorway. He did not move away. He held out the tray to Maggie. She took one of the three glasses. She stepped back so that Gloria could put the other two glasses down. Instead of leaving Gloria sat down in the snug.

'Cheers!' He raised his glass and took a sip. 'There's something not quite right. Tim, what do you think?'

Tim sipped. 'It's fine, Gloria.'

'No, Tim, it is not. Now, both of you, listen to your Auntie Gloria. I know you, Tim, better than you think. All that stuff – let me think, I'll think about it – that stuff. This is a moment for a decision. Maggie, you were leaving just now, weren't you? And thinking of never coming back.'

'How did you know?' Maggie sat down opposite Tim.

'Call it a woman's intuition, Maggie! Or call it observation, whatever you like. I've been running this pub for years. You see everything from behind the bar in this place. I know a couple meant for each other when I see one. And that's what you two are.'

'I wish Tim could see that!'

'Tim, what do you say? And please something better than "I'll think about it". I'll give you a clue. I stopped Maggie from walking out just now because if she had – and she still might – it could be the last time.' He turned to Maggie. 'It is true, isn't it?'

'Yes. Tim thinks he can string me along with his charm, his pretty words, his lies—'

'—I have never lied to you, Maggie. I admit I don't always tell you everything, but I haven't told you any lies.'

Maggie sat opposite Tim. Her eyes filled with tears.

'Tim, I don't know what I am to you. That day last week when we went to Fortnum and Mason's for tea, it seemed so special. I was charmed. You were so sweet, walking down Piccadilly. Then it turned out I was merely a convenience, an accessory. You were doing one of your – you were up to your tricks again. I was just being useful – a useful idiot, in fact. And the worst thing is that I knew you were up to something when you first asked me to go there with you. I said so at the time.'

'Well, I was just killing two birds with one stone—'

'—Not the best choice of words there, Tim', said Gloria. 'Try putting it slightly differently. More along the lines of – "Sorry, Maggie, that was stupidly thoughtless of me."'

Tim sat, awkward and dumbfounded. Gloria was right and he knew it. He made as if to speak. Nothing came out. The silence in the snug stretched out. Gloria fixed him with a look Tim had never seen before, of patient weariness. He had been watching people's absurdities from his place behind the bar for years.

At last Tim spoke.

'Gloria is right. I am sorry.'

'I want to be in your life, Tim, I do. But not like this. If I am just an afterthought, just – just a prop in one of your plays, then, no. I would rather you were out of my life.'

'I know I was wrong not to tell you from the beginning about wanting to meet the major.'

'Yes, you were. Did you even think how it would make me feel? You didn't even give me the chance to say whether I would be part of it.'

'I thought you would refuse.'

'I might have. Well, maybe I would have gone along with it – for you, Tim. You and your "thinking about it." You didn't think of me then, did you?' Maggie's face crumpled. The tears ran down. This time she let them flow.

'Maggie, there was never a day I didn't think about you. Prison would have been intolerable—'

'—How do you think it was for me? I hated seeing you in that place. I hated it so much.' She covered her face in her hands.

'Well, I got through it. Here I am. Here you are.'

'I am confused, Tim. I don't know what I want. I haven't a clue what you want. I know how I feel. How do you feel?'

'Well, you are talking, at least. I think I'll call my cocktail 'Truth Drug'. Now, please don't leave straight away, Maggie. At least finish the drink. I'll not be far away. Speak to me before you go.' He stood up to leave.

Tim waited till the door had closed behind him. 'Gloria, eh?' he said.

'Yes, Gloria. Our Aunt Gloria! He seems to have got another bit part in one of your plays.'

'He was right about what I said just now. It *was* a date. I loved walking through Mayfair with you. It was stupid not to make it clear from the start that I was working on something. I shouldn't have kept you in the dark. I thought you wouldn't come if I told you.'

'Oh, Tim, I would go anywhere if I thought you wanted me there just for us.'

'I was wrong, Maggie. It was wrong to involve you. It was wrong to use you as cover.'

'Yes.'

'I see that. When we did the Mainbocher trick Jerome and I kept Ben in the dark about Jerome's part. I suppose it was something similar with you. You would look more natural in the café if you didn't know everything. I will never do it again, I promise.'

'You might not get a chance, Tim. Gloria was right. I was going just now, and never coming back.'

Tim picked up the cocktail and sipped it. 'Actually it is quite nice. Try a bit more.'

'You are changing the subject.' She took a sip. 'Actually it is very nice.' She raised her glass in the direction of the little hatch.

'Yes. How about another cocktail? Up West. Somewhere not too far from Fortnum and Mason's?'

'No, let's stay here and have another one of these. "Truth Drug" Gloria said. 'We need to talk.'

'Coming up!' Gloria stuck his head through the hatch.

'You've been listening,' said Maggie.

'You see everything behind the bar in this place.' Gloria's expression was angelic. 'And you hear everything too.'

'We could do with some truth – some straight talking,' Maggie went on. 'And if you don't mind, Gloria, we could do with some privacy.'

Gloria slid the hatch down. In a moment he appeared at the snug door with his tray and two more cocktails.

'That was quick. You had those ready, didn't you?' Gloria smiled angelically.

'Let us talk about you, Tim. I don't know where I stand with you. It has been nearly three years – three years of never

195

knowing what you will be up to next. Not knowing what you are up to half the time. I cannot just keep coming when you call. And that is what I do, isn't it?'

'That is not how I see it, Maggie. I always want to be with you, it's just that it doesn't seem to work out all the time. You had the stall and a full and busy life. Neither of us are exactly nine till five types. Now you have your shop. It is what you wanted – what you always wanted.'

'Yes, and it is thanks to you that I have.'

'Me? I got some money back for you after you were swindled. You had a proper payout when we saved Ben from the—'

'—I know all that, Tim. That money came in useful but I would have opened my shop eventually without it. It was the money Kate put into the shop that got it started. Without that I would still be banging away at the stall, rain or shine. But I know how Kate got her "investment" as you called it. Tim, it was your money. I always knew. At first I wouldn't take it. Kate was straight with me from the start. She told me straight away what you had cooked up with Jerome.'

'And you went along with it? Knowing where it came from?'

'Yes, in the end. Kate is very persuasive when she has a mind.'

'My original idea was just to get Kate to give it to you from me. She has looked after my money since – well, for a long time. I had suggested that I could help you before I got sent down. Kate told me the story of the aunt.'

'I know, she told me too. That was how she persuaded me to accept your money.'

'After you visited that time and you were so upset and I thought I would never see you again I asked Jerome to speak to Kate.'

'You wanted a hold over me through the shop! I am not one of your marks to be steered along the path you have chosen for me. Well, let me tell you now I will buy Kate – you – out as soon as I can. You cannot buy me.'

'Maggie, Maggie, that was never it. It was for you. I wanted to make something right for you after I messed up so badly. It was awful to see how you were when you left that day, so sad, so alone. I couldn't protect you. I couldn't make it better for you.'

'No.'

'Then I thought I could.'

196

'I am not bound to you by it, Tim. I have said I will pay it back, every last penny.'

'I am not interested in the money. I certainly don't want it back. I want us to be together.'

'Well, that is news to me. You have never said that.'

'No, but it is the truth. I have just realised it myself.'

'Is it, though, Tim? You are a rogue – a plausible, smooth-talking rogue. Can I believe you?'

'Believe me now, Maggie. I mean it.'

'I want to believe you. I want to be together, properly together, not just for a week or two and then you disappearing, up to God knows what.'

'I am not sure I can be somebody else. Jerome has gone into the family business, I know, but there is still a little mischievous spirit in him. Why else did he help out this week with the antique dealer? Jerome and I are alike – adventure, living off our wits, daring to aim for the prize. And yet, I am still the lad from Stratford, smitten by a lass from the town with auburn hair and those eyes of yours. And you daring to aim for the prize, too.'

'Me?'

'You are making your shop a success. Soon you will have the rich and famous queuing at your door. It's what you dreamed of.'

'I would have got it without you.'

'I know.'

'I want to be with you. But there needs to be an understanding. I cannot – I won't – be left wondering again, never knowing if I will ever see you again – or if I do, whether it will be in a room with bars on the windows.'

'I want to be with you. I will do what it takes to keep you. Jerome would bring me into the firm if I asked.'

Maggie snorted. I was neither laughter nor crying, or maybe both at once.

'How long could you keep that up? You are still that lad from Stratford, but you are also something else. I am not sure which of the two I love. No wonder I'm confused!'

'Love? You said love. Nobody has said that before.'

'What else, you idiot?' Maggie stood up, took a step. Tim took two steps. They met in the middle of the little room. Tim wrapped his arms round her. They kissed. Tears rolled down Maggie's cheeks. They soaked into Tim's collar.

The hatch clattered open and Gloria's face appeared.

'That's settled, then. You didn't even finish your drinks!'

The couple drew apart. They sat, together, side by side, their bodies touching. They took their cocktail glasses and sipped.

'Truth Drug, Gloria! Good name for it.'

'What is the truth, Tim?' Maggie took him gently and turned him so that they were face to face. 'I fell in love with the sweet-faced, wide-eyed lad in Mabel's café. I didn't know who you really were then. You are still a bit of a mystery even now.'

'Gloria has shown me that I should tell you the truth – always. And I will, from now on.'

Maggie snuggled in at Tim's side again. 'Just promise one thing now, Tim. Keep me on the inside. I will not ask you to promise anything else.'

'We are a good fit, Maggie.'

'I am a seamstress. I make things that fit people. I should make something that fits you.'

'One day, maybe, I will settle for the suit and the nine-to-five routine. Whatever happens, I will always come home to you.'

'I will settle for that for now, Tim. One day, maybe, I will make you a suit.'

'What Jerome and I started is not over yet. You saw it first when I promised Gloria a part next time.'

Gloria's face appeared at the hatch.

'Next time can I be a chauffeuse, Tim? I've got the cap!'

Epilogue

Major Peter Alexander Heinrich Witts Witts-Chadlow sat, sipping a glass of wine from the estate's own vineyard. This was a very private room, high in the old stone tower of the castle. The tower was part of the original castle, still dominating later embellishments. A substantial oak door guarded the winding staircase to the leads. The room itself was entered through a small, unobtrusive, arched doorway in an alcove. It would be easy to climb the winding, narrow stairs and pass it without noticing. It had been built by one of the baron's illustrious ancestors with money given to him as a reward for certain obscure and undisclosed favours to the first Emperor Maximillian. Few people were invited to this place close to the Northern end of Lake Garda. Even fewer were allowed into the old tower. None came into this room.

A little window overlooked a garden and the forest beyond. In the distance fields belonging to the estate caught the last of the sunset turning the fields to gold, glinting on the limpid water of the lake beyond. A few small pieces of furniture sat on the stone slabs. The major gazed at a picture. A maid was looking out of the picture towards him, as if sharing a secret with the viewer. Sunlight from a window fell on fair hair tied back with a blue scarf. The maid was holding a looking glass for her mistress, but it was the maid's face that caught the light. Behind the two was a painted wall bearing a map of the world.

He raised his glass. 'To Baroness Louisa von Sonnenberg. What a girl!'

The major had never heard the preposterous name of Leo Nardus. He did not know anything of van Meegeren or Weingarderen. It never occurred to him to doubt the painting. His grandmother had so cleverly hidden it from the Fascists during the War in the house on Lake Garda; first it had been the Italian Army, then Germans and briefly Mussolini himself on his attempted escape to Switzerland. The house passed to the major's father and then to him. He sat back and poured another glass.

He recalled Lady Louisa's voice as she explained to him how she came by it. She was not taken in by the baron's substitution and told him so. He had agreed to the gift of the picture; as a man of honour and impeccable reputation he was bound by his promise. Her gossipy friends would sooner or later learn the truth and spread the story of his perfidy from the Riviera to the salons of Belgravia.

The baron relented. He had lost interest in the painting after its authority was beginning to be doubted. He had heard stories of a forger who had fooled the experts. He had the thing despatched to Lake Garda with a curt note in his own hand apologising for his conduct and a request that all communications between them should come to an end.

The following year War was declared. By its end the titles and fortune of Baron Henning Ferdinand Busson von Sonnenberg am der Ruhr had been swept away forever.

Printed in Great Britain
by Amazon